DIPT

N

OUT OF CONTROL

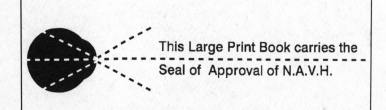

This Large Print Book carries the
Seal of Approval of N.A.V.H.

THE KINCAID BRIDES, BOOK 1

Out of Control

Mary Connealy

THORNDIKE PRESS

A part of Gale, Cengage Learning

GALE
CENGAGE Learning®

Detroit • New York • San Francisco • New Haven, Conn • Waterville, Maine • London

LIBRARY OF CONGRESS CATALOGING-IN-PUBLICATION DATA

Connealy, Mary.
  Out of control / by Mary Connealy. — Large print ed.
    p. cm. — (The Kincaid brides; bk. 1) (Thorndike Press large
  print Christian historical fiction)
  ISBN-13: 978-1-4104-4262-8
  ISBN-10: 1-4104-4262-4
  1. Caving—Fiction. 2. Large type books. I. Title.
  PS3603.O544O97 2011b
  813'.6—dc23
                                                    2011035410

Published in 2012 by arrangement with Bethany House Publishers, a division of Baker Publishing Group.

Printed in Mexico
1 2 3 4 5 6 7 16 15 14 13 12

A NOTE FROM THE AUTHOR

Years ago, on one of my first real adult vacations, my husband and I went to Carlsbad Caverns. That place captured my imagination like few places on this earth ever have. It just transported me to the early days of the cavern. I could imagine the first people who found it, explored it. It is endless and staggeringly beautiful and vividly dangerous.

That vacation sparked a story long before I was writing stories, and it's always stayed with me. I'm thrilled to be writing it now. I used Carlsbad for inspiration, but I fictionalized the cavern, moved it, and changed many things, just because I didn't think it was fair to project a fictionalized history onto Carlsbad when the real history is so well-known.

So, because it truly was the inspiration for this book, I've decided to dedicate *Out of Control* to Carlsbad Caverns and the beauty of the place. And while I'm at it, I'll also dedicate it to my husband, Ivan, who was my companion on that long-ago vacation. My very own romantic hero.

A special dedication to Natasha Kern. Teaming up with Natasha was the best decision of my professional life.

And I'd like to dedicate this book to the person who has probably bought more of my books than anyone else on the planet (except for maybe my mother) — Larry Craig, Mr. Book Look.

CHAPTER 1

Colorado Territory
June 23, 1866
Last time. This is it. Never again.

Rafe Kincaid pulled his chestnut thoroughbred to a halt in full darkness, still a short distance away from the entrance of the cavern.

He rubbed the ugly, jagged scar that ran from the corner of his eye to his hairline just above his ear. He was glad he had it. A lifelong reminder of that awful day thirteen years ago and this treacherous cavern. He'd grown up fast.

A breeze coming down across the mountains cooled the air and made the tree branches bob and dance. Like most summer nights in the Colorado Rockies, a fire would feel good.

Rafe smelled grass. Over the crest of this rugged, heavily wooded mountain, his cattle dozed in the moonlight, spread out over a lush meadow.

But tonight he wasn't looking for cattle. Instead he was looking to make his peace.

Right in front of him was the cave entrance, nothing but a hole in the ground. It looked like a mouth gaped open with a corner turned down in a scowl. Mouth was a good word for it because this place had almost swallowed his family whole.

Then he saw the rope.

A rope coiled beside the entrance to the cave.

Narrowing his eyes, he swung down and hitched his chestnut to a scrub pine. It'd been over a decade since Rafe had fought his battle with that cavern. And he'd faced the cave many times since because he refused to let it defeat him. But he'd never seen evidence anyone else had been in it. Not since Seth had run off.

He took two more steps and heard Seth scream.

Cold control sleeted in his veins as he drew his gun, leveled it. He tensed at the metallic crack as he cocked it.

There was nothing to aim at.

Seth hadn't screamed. Seth wasn't down there.

Another scream split the air.

But someone else was. He holstered his

gun and rushed for the cave.

"Please, someone help me!"

It was Seth. No, *not* Seth.

"Someone help me!" The voice broke. Sobbing echoed off the cavern walls.

Not a little boy. He stuck his head over the cavern entrance.

"A woman?" Rafe spoke aloud. Trying to believe his own ears. The words echoed into the depths.

There was no response, only sobs. But it was *not* his imagination. There really was someone down there.

The crying rose and fell, echoed off the walls until it sounded like ten women crying, all ghostly, terrified.

"Who's down there?" His voice bounced back to him.

Only more tears. The sun was gone. Dank, cool air rose up from the pit.

He could see nothing. After those first words, there were no more. But she might be out of her mind with fear.

Something Rafe could understand.

Rafe looked at the rope but didn't care to trust his weight to it. His eyes went to a flat boulder only feet away. Would it still be there? After all this time?

Rafe muscled the boulder aside, stone scratching on stone, and uncovered a depression in the rocks to reveal . . . "My ladder."

He pulled it out, the metal clinking. It was chain, badly rusted after lying in the ground for years. Long ago Rafe had switched it for the hand-woven hemp rope he, Ethan, and Seth had trusted with their lives.

Then trust had died and Rafe had anchored the ladder to this boulder.

The sobbing had a haunting quality, but this was no ghost — Rafe didn't believe in them — although for a few uncertain seconds, he'd been tempted to consider the possibility.

"I'm coming down."

The sobs stopped. Then he heard them again, softer, muffled, as if she was trying to squelch the sound.

"I'll get you out," he called, his voice echoing. Had someone abandoned her down there?

"Can you tell me your name?"

No response.

He gave his chain ladder a quick inspection and wasn't too happy with its condition.

"I'm Rafe Kincaid. I ranch near here."

Rafe had known the cavern very well by the time he'd given up his exploring. Not as well as Seth. No one knew this cavern like

Rafe's little brother. Seth had run wild down there. Once, in a particularly wild mood, Seth had told Rafe he'd lost his soul down there and had to find it.

Seth had always been a little loco.

Ethan had never gone down after the accident. Instead, he'd covered his fear with good humor and a smile, then left the ranch the day he was old enough and never came back. Ethan was the reason Rafe was out here right now.

"I'm lowering the ladder — that's the sound you hear." He doubted the wisdom of trying to rescue her on his own. Leaving her to go for help would be the smart thing to do. But by the time he got back she might be a slobbering, drooling madwoman.

She might already be.

Dropping the ladder, he smelled the cold, stale air and stared into the darkness, knowing his eyes couldn't penetrate it. There was no way to climb out without the ladder. There was another twenty-foot descent after the ladder ended at the ledge, but it wasn't as smooth as the upper stretch, so Rafe could climb down.

"Are you hurt?" Rafe began talking as he tested the ladder. It felt sturdy. He swallowed hard, said a quick prayer, and swung over the edge. It was like climbing down the throat of a monster.

"I'm coming to help you."

He heard a stifled sob.

"Are you where you can see me?" One step at a time he descended the clinking ladder.

"Can you hear that noise? I've got a chain ladder." His voice pushed against the darkness, but it was a solid thing, too deep to penetrate.

"I mean you no harm." A thousand questions raced through Rafe's mind. He suspected she wouldn't answer any of them.

"We'll get you out of here, and I'll help you get . . . get home." Where in the world could home be? There weren't any women in the area. There hadn't been any since the gold had run out. Well, a few Indians. But her little bit of talking told him she wasn't one.

As he descended, Rafe felt the darkness of the cave press on him like a slowly closing fist, crushing him by inches. He quit talking so he could breathe. After what seemed like forever, he reached the ledge. Stepping off the ladder, he turned, listening. Her breathing was audible. She was close to the left side tunnel, as if she was poised to run down it, away from him.

"Please, don't be afraid. I won't harm you."

In the silence, it occurred to Rafe that maybe *he* should be afraid. What if she got past him in the dark? What if she scaled the rock cliff, climbed the ladder, and pulled it up behind her?

Chills stood the hair on the back of his neck on end as he thought of being stuck down in the cavern, forever. That day when Seth had fallen. No one knew where they were. No one would have thought of coming to the cave to search.

Just like now.

Listening with every bit of savvy he'd learned from living in this hard land, he climbed down the last twenty feet of rock.

"If someone hurt you, it wasn't me. But I can get you out. I *will* get you out." Seth had begged Rafe not to leave him. And Rafe knew Seth hadn't really believed his brothers would abandon him, but it had been the fear talking. So it was most likely her fear too keeping her silent. "I won't leave you."

Then the obvious occurred to Rafe. "How bad can I be? I gotta be better than this cavern. Do you really want me to go away?"

"No!" Something raced at him. A black figure in a black pit. For an irrational second he thought it was something monstrous swooping toward him. A shudder shook him until the ice in his veins nearly cracked.

Then something — someone — slammed into him. He staggered back against the cavern wall. Hands clawed at him. He caught at whomever or whatever it was. Solid. Not a ghost. Human, not a monster. He tried to make sense out of what he couldn't see.

"Help me." Definitely a woman.

"I'll get you out."

"Don't leave me, please." Her voice broke. Her arms clamped around him as if she were hanging on to save her life.

In her mind, she probably was.

He wrapped his arms around her. In the dark he couldn't see anything. She seemed young. She'd come at him fast. But someone older, running for her life, might move real fast, too.

"I'll get you out. I promise." He talked to her as if she were a spooked mustang. "Let's climb up to my ladder and get out of here."

"A ladder? A ladder." The words dissolved into wrenching sobs.

Rafe wondered if she'd be able to climb. She'd have to. He tried to imagine carrying her and climbing the ladder at the same time.

Could the chain take the double weight?

14

He didn't want to test it.

"Here, come this way. We can climb part-way."

"There's nothing to climb." Frantic arms anchored her to him.

"I've got a ladder on the ledge."

"Ladder. A ladder. Yes." She didn't let go, so he lifted her, just so her feet dangled, and turned her toward the wall — not that easy with her hanging from his neck.

Prying one hand loose, he said, "Grab right here." He felt around till he found a grip, then rested her hand on the rock wall and was relieved when she took hold. "We'll go up. One step at a time."

"All the way up?"

A terrible pity for her rang inside of him like a perfect bell toll. He'd been where she was. He'd been right up to the edge of pure loco with fear. "Yes, all the way. I've got a ladder. First we have to climb this one stretch of rock, then we'll use the ladder."

"A ladder. Ladder." Each step was pain-fully slow. Rafe cajoled and encouraged and occasionally begged. She moved forward, her hands so shaky Rafe didn't trust her to hang on, so he climbed along with her. When they reached the ledge, he kept his arm firmly around her waist. The chain was only a few feet away, and when Rafe heard

15

its metallic jingle, it gave him renewed determination.

"Can you do it?"

"Do what?"

He had to calm her down somehow. She'd
never hang on the way she was shaking. He
turned her until she faced him.

"Listen to me."

"Get out of here. I have to get . . . get . . .
out. Let me out."

She was babbling.

It occurred to him that the right thing to
do was slap her. That'd clear her thinking.
Give her a bit of fight, too. It had worked
with Ethan years ago. Sort of.

It'd been more of a punch honestly.

And now that Rafe thought of it, it hadn't
worked well at all. And . . . she was too soft
to slap, and sure as certain too soft to
punch. He just couldn't do it. "You've got
to get ahold of yourself." Pulling her close,
he added, "My name is Rafe. Can you say
that?"

She'd said ladder enough times.

"Let me out."

"No!" He gripped her shoulders. "You say
my name or we're not going. You need to
calm down. We're going to be fine, but not
if you shake so hard you fall off this ladder."

"Ladder."

"I'm Rafe." He shook her hard. "Say it. Prove to me you've got the guts to hang on and climb out of this pit."

"R-Rafe." A long, slow breath lifted her shoulders. "Rafe. I'm sorry . . . Rafe. I'm so scared. It's so dark. I couldn't get out. My . . . my Rafe. I couldn't find my Rafe . . . uh . . . rope. Rope. I need to get out and I . . . I—"

"Stop." Slapping her just wouldn't do.

So he kissed her.

She froze in his arms. He braced himself to be on the receiving end of a slap. He almost hoped her head cleared enough to be insulted.

Suddenly, her terror flipped over into something . . . else. She flung her arms around his neck and nearly lifted herself off her feet in an effort to hold him closer.

Rafe wrapped his arms around her waist and deepened the kiss.

The darkness receded, the whole world was bright and warm. Being far from the outside world just seemed like a blessed chance to be alone with a beautiful woman.

Beautiful?

That thought cleared his head. "Uh . . . you're not fifty or sixty years old, are you?"

"What?" She sounded dazed. Which was

sort of like calm.

"I'm just thinking I haven't really . . . um . . . seen you yet. I mean you seem . . . young. You *feel* really young." *And beautiful.* She felt very young and beautiful. "But if we get out of here and you're . . . uh . . . old and —" *ugly* — "sixty years old or something . . . well, it's going to be awkward."

Her arms were gone from his neck. He should have kept his mouth shut and continued with the kissing. But the notion of getting her up to the moonlight and finding out she was a sixty-year-old woman, maybe with a mustache and a face like the downhill side of a climbing mountain goat . . . not someone he'd choose to kiss . . . in the light . . . Well, that was in his head now, and he couldn't get it out. Yep, awkward, sure enough. And yet, she'd felt very young and beautiful. Very.

"Get your hands off of me."

He loosened his grip but didn't let go all the way because she had a ways to fall — about twenty feet straight down. Then he'd have to climb back down there and start this all over again.

She slapped him.

Which stung, and not just his cheek. After all, he'd considered doing the same thing to

18

her — for medicinal reasons. Life and death, really. But he'd refrained. She should have given him the same benefit of the doubt.

"I think I'm ready to climb now." She sounded much calmer. Deadly calm.

Rafe remembered a long time ago — how long had he been kissing her, anyway? — when getting out of the cavern was his main concern. Now he wasn't in such a big hurry. But he didn't want to get slapped again, either.

"Great. You've calmed down. Let's go." As if getting himself slapped had been his plan all along.

He herded her toward the ladder. He'd dealt with enough kicking, snorting cattle and horses to have the knack.

He heard the chain rattle, so he figured she was obeying him. He was really looking forward to some light — even the dim light of the moon would be a big improvement.

And he was hoping for the best.

"This is a ladder?" She sounded confused. Young and beautiful and confused.

"Here." Rafe took her hands and closed them around the chains, hoping she didn't attack. "Feel how it's two long chains with short ones between? It sags, so it all seems to hang down, but get your hands on the edges and your foot on the chain hooking

19

the sides together, it's a ladder rung."

"Where are the rungs?"

He crouched and, going by touch, found the chain and guided her foot — a very young foot as far as Rafe could judge — to the lowest step, which dangled about two feet above the ledge. She groped with her other foot for the next step up without his guidance. She was thinking clearly. The kiss had done the trick, whether she wanted to admit it or not.

And he guessed he had a hand-shaped red mark on his face to prove it.

He touched her foot on the second rung to make sure she'd found it. The way she trembled and fumbled for the rung, he knew he had to help her take each step. He didn't dare let her climb all the way alone. Considering the age of this ladder, he should. But he saw her falling — very vividly, considering he couldn't see her. He stayed below her so they weren't both on a rung at the same time, but the sides of the ladder were bearing double weight.

Rafe had no choice, so he followed her, guiding each foot. Rung by rung they climbed up.

As they climbed, he didn't look up, partly because there was a little bit of moonlight now, and he was afraid he'd see right up her skirt, but also — and this was actually the bigger part — because he was afraid he wouldn't be able to help but enjoy the view.

Her movements changed. He heard her fingers fumbling for a grip on stone. Judging by the light and his increased ability to see — staring straight forward — he knew she'd reached the top. He kept going, proud of himself for the way his eyes stayed fastened on the ladder. Ashamed of himself for having a fight on his hands to manage that behavior.

Then he gained the top and rolled off that ladder and out of that scowling cave mouth. "Every time I get out of that pit I feel like I've escaped from a wolf pack nipping at my heels."

Or monsters. Or his worst nightmares.

Finally, lying on his back on the ground, he looked at the woman. The moon was out and he could see her well enough.

Not sixty.

Not even close.

Young and beautiful, for a fact, right down to her feet.

She was a barely grown woman. Her wild and curly hair washed blue in the moonlight. There was a remnant of a braid, but more hair had escaped than remained. Even in the dim light he could see her eyes were

21

so wide with fear that all thoughts of skirts and ladders and wolves vanished in the face of her upset.

She had a black line from her temple, along her ear, and down the length of her long, graceful neck. The line spread into a black circle on her calico blouse that had to be blood. She wore a darker riding skirt. All the color was washed out to shades of blue and black in the moonlight. There was dirt under her fingernails. The woman was a mess.

How had she gotten down there?

He didn't ask because it wasn't really a good time. But he wondered how long he had to wait on that information.

They both scrambled to their feet and faced each other. There was so much gratitude and relief that he saw all the way to her soul and felt as if she saw to his, a very warm look beaming heat on his cold soul.

But mostly he just saw fear, eyes wild with fear. For a second he could see white all the way around.

Once, long ago, his horse had taken an unfortunate fall into a saguaro. His stallion still got a look similar to this lady's when they got too near a cactus.

And that was the only way this woman resembled his horse.

"Thank you." She breathed deeply once, twice; then she threw herself at him, wrapped her arms around his neck, and knocked him over backward. For a terrifying second he thought he was going over the edge into the cavern. But his back landed on solid ground. She cut off his air, and though he was glad for the gratitude, he missed breathing.

Then he felt her woman's weight on him and decided breathing was overrated. He remembered the kiss of just a few minutes ago. Remembered it fondly and slid his arms around her waist . . . just as she started to cry.

That took the fun out of it.

Ma had cried a lot. In fact, looking back, that's almost all he remembered about his ma.

A fair-to-middling cook who cried a lot.

They could have carved it into her tombstone.

He'd been left all these years with the strange feeling that his mother had cried herself to death.

It had terrified him then, and it was worse now.

And being terrified didn't suit him, so he took action. "Let's go."

He stood, helping her up. He glared at

that cave for a second and then, with her still clinging to his neck, dragged the ladder up and left it lying on the ground beside her rope. He'd have to come back and stick it under the rock when he was all done with his rescuing. He sort of dragged her little clinging, crying, young and beautiful self along as he stepped well away from that gaping hole.

Dragging her was slowing him down. He swung her up in his arms and hurried toward his horse.

The fiery chestnut had never been ridden double, so Rafe wasn't sure how things would go. The woman seemed bent on draining all the salt and water from her body through her eyeballs. Rafe adjusted her so he held her in one arm and mounted up, then settled her on his lap. His stallion skittered sideways, but Rafe controlled him and aimed the horse toward the ranch and they set out at a fast walk.

"We'll gallop as soon as the horse adjusts to the double weight."

The only response he got was a sniffle.

"What's your name?"

She cried harder. Rolling his eyes toward heaven, Rafe said, "As soon as I get down the steepest part of this mountain, the trail is level and clear of stones so we can speed up. Then I'll gallop for a while, so hold on tight."

She had the grip of a cranky Apache warrior. Only it felt real nice.

He'd lost her!

He wiped his sweaty palms on his pants. Frustrated to have missed his chance. He slipped back into the black depths of the cavern.

How had she been so quiet for so long? He'd even had his friend climb the rope and pull it up to trap her.

"I shouldn't have played with her, toyed with her." He listened to his voice echo off the walls. As if he were down here with a dozen people, all agreeing with him. "Scaring her was fun."

The others agreed.

"I loved it when she ran."

In the pitch-darkness he'd been able to hear her terror. And he'd known that soon, soon he'd have her and she was the key to the treasure he wanted. Then suddenly he'd lost her. He'd searched for hours, but she never gave herself away. Her silence had been total.

But then he'd heard her screaming and had come fast, but the man had gotten to her first.

"Who was that who rescued her?"

The hoofbeats faded as he fumed.

"But she loves it down here. She'll be back." He shouted that and listened to it echo. "Then I'll have what I want!" His laughter echoed back from the world of friends who surrounded him.

Friends?

No, only one friend. It was time to get him to come out.

CHAPTER 2

Rafe spurred his horse to a ground-eating gallop and enjoyed her arms around him way more than was wise.

He figured a woman only had so much water to spare, so he let her cry and hoped she'd run dry soon. The tears finally slowed, and though afraid he'd set off more tears, Rafe cautiously repeated the most obvious question.

"What's your name?"

Pulling away from him, she looked as nervous as a long-tailed cat in a roomful of rocking chairs. Like maybe it had just occurred to her that she didn't know him at all.

He fetched a kerchief out of his hip pocket in case she had a speck of salt water left.

"What's yours?" It wasn't an answer, but at least she hadn't said *ladder.*

"I'm Rafe Kincaid."

With a gasp she caught his left forearm.

27

"I've heard of the Kincaid Ranch. I'm Julia."

"Julia what?"

Suspicion narrowed her eyes. "I need to get home. My family will be frantic. They don't even know where I went, and I was down there a long time. A long, long time. A long, long, long time." Her voice broke, and she buried her face against his chest again. Her arms went around his waist, and she held on as if she were still dangling over a deep hole.

That hole. That dark, brutally beautiful hole in the ground. He knew so exactly how she felt that he could have cried, too — if he was a weakling who wanted to act like a little girl.

He slid his left arm around her waist, while his right arm supported her quivering back and steered his stallion. He found a talent for doing all of that at once.

Every protective instinct in his body and soul, and that was a considerable amount, roared to life. "We'll get you home. I promise. I'm almost to my place. I'll get you something to eat and make sure you're all right, and then I'll take you home."

The location of which was still unknown because Rafe had never gotten that information from her. He hadn't gotten her last name, either.

Based on the crying, he doubted he'd get it anytime soon.

Her arms tightened. As long as she had a good grip, Rafe kicked his horse into a faster gallop. As they raced across the rugged ground, he savored how alive and precious she felt in his arms.

He'd saved her. He'd found someone in that hole and saved her life.

He closed his eyes and let that knowledge pour over the terrible cold place where his soul should have been. It wasn't enough — saving her didn't penetrate it, but it warmed the edges a bit.

The ice had been there ever since he'd felt the crushing weight of that cavern all those years ago when he'd failed his brothers.

And he'd clung to that cold all these years, glad of it, because while it was there he could never be that terrified and weak and out of control again.

This woman, Julia, so vital, so vulnerable, had arms so warm that, for the first time in nearly a dozen years, he was tempted to let go of his icy control. But what if, after so much time, the cold shattered and all that he'd frozen away — his guilt and fear and shame — was too much for a man to bear.

Worse yet, what if he thawed and found he was empty inside? His soul as black as that cavern.

He galloped for the ranch. Just as the cabin came in sight, Julia sat bolt upright.

"I have to go home." In the darkness he could see her eyes were red from crying. Her lips trembled.

"We're almost home." Rafe kept his horse moving. He needed to think clearly, and for some reason he couldn't seem to do that. A fact he blamed completely on her sitting on his lap.

"No, *my* home." She clutched the front of his shirt and got a chunk of skin. "I haven't been thinking clearly. I was so upset."

"Of course you're upset. I'll get you something to eat, get you cleaned up. And first thing in the morning we'll —"

"No, now. I have to go home now."

Rafe looked at the moon already high in the sky. "We can't go tonight."

"My family will be frantic." Julia bit her bottom lip. Rafe urged his horse forward, hoping he could get her in the house while she was busy nagging at him to do something else. He couldn't ride his horse double the whole twenty miles to Rawhide. Especially if one of the riders was a weeping woman who seemed to solve all her problems by grabbing hold of him. He needed to get her away from him before she spent too much longer in his arms. Not wise to get used to it.

Julia squared her shoulders and held his gaze. "I'm Julia Gilliland. My father, Wendell Gilliland, owns the general store in Rawhide."

He was almost surprised enough to quit galloping in a direction she didn't want to go. But not quite.

"I was just in Rawhide, in the general store. The man who owns it isn't named Gilliland."

"Yes he is. Father has always run a store."

"The owner of the store is Hymie Herne. He's owned it for years."

"There must be two stores."

"Nope, no new stores in town. Except . . ." Rafe paused. "There is a new little saloon. It's a dump. A shack that was abandoned and boarded up. The man who runs it — someone said his name. Uhhh . . . John . . . Gill. That's it." Rafe paused again. *Gill? Gilliland?* "A short skinny man. Bald. He favored his right arm like he'd hurt it recently."

"My father's middle name is John." Her pretty lips curved down into a frown. "He's got a really ugly curved scar on the back of

31

his right hand. But it's an old injury — there was nothing wrong with his arm when he was last home."

"Maybe he got hurt since then." Rafe rubbed his own ugly scar. John Gill had come into the general store while he'd been there, and Hymie had introduced them. He'd noticed John, or Wendell, or whoever the guy was, had a scar — it was hard to miss. "That's him. But he calls himself by a different name."

"Why would he do that?"

Good question.

Rafe had been in town for supplies, and he'd also gotten that letter from Ethan. He'd just given a list to Hymie when John or Wendell had come in, his temper steaming like the stinking cigar he had clamped in his teeth, and shoved past Rafe and demanded to go first. Hymie had told him to hold his horses, and Rafe had thought John might throw a fist. But then the man had flinched and grabbed his arm as if it hurt.

Though it didn't suit Rafe to be pushed around, he told Hymie to go ahead with the new customer, since Rafe had other business in town.

Later, Hymie had told Rafe about the new saloonkeeper in town and pointed out the tumbled-down shack that didn't look to be big enough for a whiskey bottle, let alone customers. Though Hymie said a man could get a poker game there anytime of the day or night.

But nowhere in the talk of John Gill had there been any mention of a daughter. And Julia had said *family*. So was there a mother, and other children? Rawhide wasn't that big. Rafe hadn't seen the slightest sign of any women. And he'd eaten at the diner and talked with several other men. He'd heard about neighboring ranches, cattle prices, who was sick, rumors of gold and silver strikes, who was gone from the area, and who was new to town. What he'd never heard was talk of a woman.

Wendell was an ugly little man with an attitude to match. But this was a hard land so Rafe had some patience with hard men. Rafe's pa had been a man as harsh and wild as these mountains in winter. Rafe was a hard man, too. He prided himself on it.

Throw in the way John or Wendell had cradled his arm to his chest. With all of that, Rafe had still come away with a real poor impression of Wendell "John Gill" Gilliland. And none of that explained the unknown family.

"We'll get you to your pa first thing in the

morning. It's a long rugged ride to Rawhide and we can't make it across that trail in the dark. But first thing —"

"What trail?"

"The trail to town."

"But I don't want to go to town. I want to go home."

Rafe fell silent. "You live in Rawhide."

"No, I don't. In fact, if I hadn't been so upset, I'd have realized where we were riding and I'd have stopped you. I live about half an hour's walk from that cavern."

"No you don't."

Julia's brow furrowed over her puffy eyes. "I know where I live, Rafe."

"But there's nothing up there and your pa owns the saloon in Rawhide."

"The general store."

"Whatever he owns" — absolutely *not* the general store — "it's in Rawhide. Why would he live twenty miles out of town?"

"It's not twenty miles. It's about five. And we live out there because Pa doesn't think it's safe in town. He says Rawhide is a rough place."

"True, it is. But how can he protect you out there? And how'd you get all the way to that cavern if you live fifteen miles away from it?"

"I don't. It's about a half-mile walk,

mostly uphill, but I enjoy rock climbing. And I need to get out of the house while the baby is napping."

"Baby?"

Julia suddenly clutched Rafe's arm. "And once I found the cavern . . ." Her hand trembled on his wrist. Then she leaned closer as if to whisper a secret. "It's so beautiful down there, and . . . and I found fossils."

"Fossils?" Rafe had been down there and he'd seen a lot of pretty rock formations, but . . . "I don't remember any fossils." Of course, he wasn't real clear on what a fossil was.

Rafe thought some more about what she'd said. "A half-mile walk home, you say?" Since Rafe had just taken her on a long ride away from the cavern, that was bad news. Just past the cavern were a cliff and an impassable rushing stream; on this side was all Kincaid property, so that still didn't explain where she lived. "Why didn't you say something? Why'd you have me ride all the way to my place?"

Not that he really minded having a beautiful woman in his arms for miles and miles and miles.

Julia's brows lowered, and even in the starlight Rafe could see fire in her eyes. "I was very upset."

Which was no more than the pure honest truth.

"I'd been down there a long time. I'm not usually given to nerves, but I've never mentioned that cavern to anyone, so I figured they'd have no idea where to look for me."

Rafe had made the same mistake . . . when he was a kid. "You should've had more sense. If your pa" — and the baby, she'd definitely mentioned a baby — "had known where you'd gone, he'd've been able to come fetch you home."

"The baby and Audra take a long nap in the afternoon. I've been taking hikes ever since we moved here. And when I found that cavern, I got a long rope and went down in it."

Now there was an Audra?

"Reckless."

Julia shrugged. "We've been out here since early in the spring. I've had a lot of time to hike. I found that cave opening, dropped a pebble in, and heard it hit bottom. Then I got a rope and lowered a lantern in so I was sure the floor was down there. The lantern lit the cave up enough I could see some stalactites and stalagmites."

"Stag-what? You found a herd of deer

down there?" Rafe shook his head. "Not likely."

"I studied rock formations and fossils back East and this is a real find. I subscribe to a scientific journal and I hope to write a paper on this cavern." Julia leaned closer, looked quickly left and right — which was silly since there was clearly no one else around. "I've been trying to get published in that journal for years. Now I've found such a lovely cave. And the fossils . . ." She gasped and got what could only be described as a look of wonder on her face. "Fish."

"Fish?"

She nodded her head. "We've got to go back. I need to study it more carefully."

"Go back where?"

"To the cavern." She leaned closer, which Rafe found mighty pleasant. "There was someone down there. I got scared."

Everything pleasant fled. "Someone else was down there?"

Julia's face fell into a frown. "I guess that means it wasn't you, right?"

"I never go in that place." *Not anymore.* "I wouldn't have gone today if I didn't need to save you."

"Well, someone was down there." She gingerly touched her temple, coated with dried blood. "I was startled. Well, honestly,

I was terrified. I doused my lantern and ran to hide from him. I must have bumped my head. I can't go down there alone again." Then she perked up and smiled at him. "I know. You could go with me. We'll use your chain ladder."

Then she jerked upright as if he'd stuck her with a pin. "You've got to take me home."

"I did. We're home." Rafe pulled his horse to a halt in the yard of Kincaid Ranch. "Steele!"

Rafe didn't need to yell. Steele was already ambling out of the barn. Rafe tossed his reins to Steele and swung down with Julia still in his arms.

Steele arched his bushy gray brows at the sight of a woman in Rafe's arms, but he didn't say a word. That was one of the things Rafe liked best about his foreman.

"We have to go back to that cavern." Julia continued to boss him around while he held her in his arms. "I need to take measurements, make drawings. I'm not good at drawing, but I'll just have to make do." Julia looked at him. "Can you draw?"

"Nope."

"Pity." She shrugged. "I need to look deeper in the cave. I need to check and see if —"

"We aren't going back to that cavern." That broke off her jabbering.

Steele led the horse off. Julia might be taking charge of her life in some ways, but she was still pretty upset or she'd have noticed he was carrying her around.

"We have to," she insisted.

"We can't." The little woman really should stand on her own two feet if she was going to be so bossy. And yet Rafe had no interest in setting her down.

"Well, fine then. I'll have to go alone." She shuddered and gave him a frightened look.

"You can't go alone. It's not safe."

"Then come with me. I have to go back. I *will* go back." She looked stubborn and bossy and young and beautiful, and Rafe considered doing just about anything she asked of him as he walked along.

Ethan was coming home. Ethan, who hated everything about that cavern. More than hate, he feared it. Swearing off the cavern was the only way to keeping him here. Rafe wanted both his brothers back. Missing them weighed down everything he did.

"Maybe if we made it quick. Just once." Rafe could go down and back up and it'd be over before Ethan returned. He could grab whatever it was she wanted. A fish or a stag or . . . He couldn't figure out what she was after exactly. Rafe hadn't spent time down there in a long while.

It had taken weeks after the accident to know Seth would live. The healing stretched out over long, grueling months. His scars were so ugly, a constant reminder of how Rafe had failed. And the nightmares. Seth's nightmares tortured the family until they all dreaded going to sleep at night. And during the day the wildness in Seth's eyes crossed over from recklessness to madness.

Seth shared his wild blue eyes and his nature with Pa. Once he was physically well, Seth had gone back to the cavern as if the meaning of life were hidden in there. Rafe couldn't move fast enough to keep him out, but he'd followed after him even though he hated it down there.

No one seemed to care about Seth but Rafe.

After Seth's accident, Pa's trapping and mining kept him away from home for weeks and eventually even months at a time.

Ma took to her rocking chair and cried herself to death.

Ethan refused to have any part of that cavern.

Rafe was left alone to protect his reckless little brother. Rafe was haunted by the knowledge that Seth's accident had destroyed his family. If Rafe had just taken better care of Seth, the Kincaid family would not have fallen apart.

And now that Ethan was returning, Rafe was never going to even admit that cavern existed.

But maybe he could go down with Julia one more time. Just to get her fish.

Julia patted him on the chest and smiled. "It has to be more than once. I need to explore."

"It's a dangerous cave. In fact, I'm considering getting some explosives and closing that entrance forever so no one else can get hurt down there."

Julia inhaled so quickly it sounded like a backward scream. "You will not!"

"I should have done it years ago. Then you wouldn't have been in danger." He looked down at the woman he held in his arms. He was sure enough enjoying holding Julia Gilliland. He'd never thought much about women. It was a man's world out here and never seeing one of the critters helped keep his mind off them.

Julia chewed on her bottom lip in silence. She really shouldn't do that. It had to be hard on her. Rafe watched her gnaw away and considered scolding her.

"You might be destroying something that could help us learn more about the Bible," she said.

"What?" Rafe stopped so short he almost dropped her. "How can a big old cave in Colorado teach us about the Bible?"

"Well, I told you there are fish fossils."

"So what? Maybe Indians lived in that cave. They eat fish."

"I don't think so."

"You don't think Indians eat fish? Because I know some Indians. They eat fish."

"No, that's not what I meant. I think those fish might've been left there by God."

"Your head is bleeding. I wonder how hard you hit it, because —"

"I have to go back, and whoever was down there with me, well, you need to catch him and make him go away. Oh, and I didn't see my rope anywhere. I searched and searched, but I lost it. So we'll have to use your ladder."

"Your rope didn't get lost. It got pulled up."

"You said that before. Of course it got lost."

"No, it didn't." Rafe thought of that neatly coiled rope. "Someone deliberately left you in there."

"What?" Her chewed-on lips started to

quiver, and her eyes filled with tears. Julia's voice dropped to a whimper. "I might have died down there."

Rafe hated it, but he suspected that's exactly what they wanted.

"But why would anyone do that?"

Rafe thought of the crushing weight of that cavern in the dark, and he tightened his grip. "I don't know. I was hoping you would."

"It was so dark. I felt like I was being swallowed, eaten alive by a monster." Tears welled again. Salt and water aplenty in this woman.

"I know exactly how you felt." He lifted her until he could look her straight in the eyes.

"But if you come along, it will be safe. Maybe some of your men can stand guard at the entrance so no one can tamper with our ladder. I've got to go back down there."

"That's crazy!" Rafe said. "The darkness hides terrible danger. You could get lost and not find your way back to the entrance. You could fall. You could be killed."

His eyes went to her lips, shining from being gnawed. She needed him to protect her, but what was boiling inside of him was nothing like his protective instincts for his little brothers. And that boiling seemed to be melting the cold.

So weak it was barely a whisper, she said, "I have to go back. My cabin, it's so crowded and the walls start to close in around me sometimes. I have to get out. But just walking around, it's a waste of my life. I feel useless. If I could write about that cavern, find something that would really be special . . ." Her forehead sank until it rested on his chest.

When he read Ethan's letter today, Rafe had taken an oath — to himself and to Ethan, though Ethan hadn't been around to hear it — that he'd leave that cavern alone for good. He couldn't say he'd made his peace with the cave, but he'd learned to live beside it, as if he and it were two warring countries that didn't fire a shot but sat with guns on the border.

And now he held a woman in his arms, who wanted him to give up on common sense so she could look closer at a fish.

Only a coward would refuse to help her and he wasn't one . . . So he'd do it, and do it fast, before Ethan got home.

Squaring his jaw with determination, he picked up speed as he carried Julia around the corner to the ranch house steps.

Ethan stepped out onto the front porch.

CHAPTER 3

Ethan saw Rafe ride in carrying a woman in his arms and smiled for the first time since he'd given in to the goading voice telling him to come home.

Rafe rode around the corner to the barn but was soon back on foot with the woman in his arms. Ethan went outside just as his big brother clomped up the front porch steps.

"For me?" Ethan reached out his arms.

Rafe growled.

Which meant the woman was for Rafe.

Well, Ethan hadn't expected much of a welcome-home gift, so he wasn't surprised.

"So, hello." Ethan had been gone awhile. For all he knew, Rafe might carry this woman around in his arms day and night.

The woman raised her head, and Ethan saw she'd been crying. Ethan immediately liked her a lot less.

"Her name is Julia. Let me get her inside.

Been a tough day for her." Rafe brushed past Ethan and it pinched. But Ethan had expected Rafe to hate him.

The more he hurt, the bigger he smiled, so Ethan smiled big and followed Rafe inside. Rafe set the woman on a chair in the kitchen. She had long red hair, messy, knotted up, wild. Ethan looked a lot closer at her.

"Let me get you something to drink." Rafe kept one hand on the woman's shoulder, as if afraid she'd topple off the chair. "How long has it been since you've eaten?"

She shrugged and blinked her large eyes, a pretty shade of green, at Rafe. She looked battered. Her nails were dirty and bloody. She had a streak of dried blood on the left side of her face running down her neck, pooled into a big stain on her dress.

A real beautiful woman if a man could ignore the filth. And since she was clearly Rafe's woman, Ethan found the ignoring easy. After all, it wasn't his job to clean her up.

Ethan had been gone a long time, but not so long that he wasn't amazed at his brother's attention to a woman. After dealing with Ma and her madness, Rafe hadn't shown any interest in hunting up female companionship — not hard to avoid since

46

there hadn't been a woman for a hundred miles in any direction.

Rafe slowly released the woman's shoulder, as if testing to make sure she wouldn't fall over. When she stayed sitting upright, he turned to Ethan. Ethan braced himself for a punch in the face.

"I've missed you." Rafe grabbed him and hugged him so tight Ethan couldn't breathe. Or maybe he just didn't remember how for a second. His arms went around Rafe, and for one horrifying second, Ethan thought he might cry.

"Welcome home." Rafe held him close for longer than anyone had held Ethan in years. Ever. The Kincaids weren't huggers.

With a few solid slaps on the back, Rafe stepped back. Not a smile anywhere. But intensity. Ethan remembered that. They'd been best friends.

Rafe — the leader, organized and intense, making things safe.

Ethan — keeping things loose, making them fun.

Seth — the daredevil, keeping the excitement level high.

The three of them made a good team.

Until the accident.

Ethan veered his thoughts from that ugliness. Never thinking of that place and never

ever going back was the only way he kept his sanity.

"We've got to go back." Julia sounded as if she hated the idea.

Ethan wondered just what he'd walked in on.

"We need to talk about that." Rafe looked between Julia and Ethan.

"Go back where?" Ethan could only think of one place.

"That cavern." Julia trembled and gripped the seat of the wooden chair as if she had to physically hold tight to keep from taking off running.

Ethan could sympathize. "No!" He locked his jaw. He wasn't going to say it again. One thing he could say. "I should've never come home."

"Ethan." Rafe's hands fisted. He spoke each word with complete control. That was Rafe. "Someone trapped her in the cavern."

"Seth's Cavern?" Ethan always thought of it as Seth's Cavern — when he couldn't stop himself from thinking of it.

Rafe nodded.

"There's nothing down there worth the risk."

"But we've got to find out who did it and why. Anyone who'd trap a woman is pure polecat, and he's on Kincaid land." Rafe went to the sink and poured water into a tin cup, then started slicing a loaf of bread.

"We've got to go back," Julia repeated. "I have to show you what I found."

"We?" Ethan looked at the woman. She was so clearly unhappy about going back, Ethan had to respect it when she said it was necessary. Didn't mean he was going to agree to go along, but he could respect it.

"And then I have to get home. No, home first, then go down." Julia looked a little more steady. Her shoulders squared, her chin lifted. Maybe once she got ahold of her nerves, her mind would start working again. Ethan could only hope.

Then he realized what she'd said about going home. "No one lives out here."

"You do," Julia pointed out the obvious.

"Well, the Kincaids are idiots. Never figured anyone else would be stupid enough to try and own a ranch in the middle of a forest."

"I guess there's one family stupid enough." Julia raised her hand sadly. "And we don't own a ranch; it's just a cabin. Pa owns the general store in Rawhide."

"A saloon, Julia. He owns a saloon — and a poor excuse for even that." Rafe set a plate with a thick slice of bread in front of her.

Julia reached for the bread and noticed

49

her hands. "They're filthy." She jerked them into her lap, even though she eyed the bread with longing.

"We'll wash them." Rafe went to the dry sink and poured water into a basin. He moved the basin to the table. Julia reached for the water hesitantly.

"Let me help." Rafe pulled a chair around the corner of the wooden plank table. It wasn't the one they'd had before, Ethan noticed. This was a beautiful piece of furniture.

He looked away from the crazy woman and saw a lot of new, well-made things in the kitchen. Pa had been dead for three years. Ethan had found that out when he'd talked to Rafe's foreman. Though Pa had been gone a long time, to Ethan it was a fresh grief. There was no chance to settle the trouble with his wild, always-traipsing-off father now. Didn't matter much. Pa would've never shown any concern for Ethan — for any of them.

Most likely Rafe had done all this carpentering since Pa had died. Pa had no patience for foolishness like fine woodwork.

Rafe touched Julia's hands, moving slowly, as if he was afraid of startling her. He guided them into the basin and, with a bar of lye soap in one hand, bathed her fingers gently and thoroughly. He got a rag from the dry sink, dipped it in the water, and touched her temple. When Rafe pulled the rag away, Ethan saw blood.

"You've got a mean bump on your head. And your hands aren't just dirty, you've hurt them." Rafe finished with her head, then wrung out the rag and set it aside. He lifted her hand, dripping, from the water and Ethan could see the scrapes, the torn fingernails. Two nails were bleeding, and there was still dirt under all of them. Like she'd just clawed her way out of a nightmare.

Ethan looked down at his own hands. Scarred from years of hard work. He remembered that his hands had looked much the same as Julia's by the time they'd gotten out of the cavern on the day Seth had nearly died. Both his brothers were left scarred by it, while Ethan had walked away without a scratch.

Ethan had never gone back.

Rafe had never been able to stay away.

Seth had run wild in every direction, including down in that cavern, until worrying about him, trying to control him, made Rafe cold as ice. And Ethan — well, he quit caring about what he'd done to his little brother. He'd quit caring about how it had driven Pa into the mountains and Ma into her rocking chair and Seth out of his mind.

Ethan hadn't cared because he wouldn't have been able to handle it otherwise.

Julia was demanding to return. Which meant Ethan was more of a coward than this distraught woman.

He wished he'd never come home.

Audra Gilliland wished she'd never come west.

Where is she, Lord?

She wished she'd never agreed to live way out here, miles from that wretched, dangerous town.

God, please protect Julia.

She wished she'd never married the stubborn old goat, Wendell Gilliland.

Bring her back home safely. Please, God, please. . . .

More honestly, she wished she'd *ever* been given a choice in *anything.* In her whole miserable life.

Maggie stirred in Audra's arms. It wasn't all bad. Marrying Wendell had gotten her Maggie, and she adored her daughter. It had gotten her Julia, too.

Just thinking Julia's name threatened to send Audra into a panic.

Praying, Audra shifted so Maggie's weight

wasn't so heavy on Audra's stomach. Her children might well not survive in the harsh land her husband had stranded them in, and that was something she regretted bitterly. She laid her hand on her round belly and prayed for her children's lives. And that included at this moment, more than anyone, Julia.

Wendell had been unkind back in Houston, too — *after* the wedding. But they'd lived in a safe place, in a sturdy house. Out in the country a bit, and Wendell didn't come home that often — which Audra soon learned wasn't such a bad thing.

She and Julia had done well together. *Please, God, care for her.*

Wendell slammed the door open. "Where did that girl run off to?"

Maggie jerked awake in Audra's arms.

"You haven't found her?" Audra surged to her feet. "Wendell, what could have happened?"

"Ain't the first time she's gone off." Wendell jerked the cigar he was never without from his lips. He was skinny and wrinkled. He had a short supply of hair and a long supply of grudges. Before the wedding, Audra had seen him as wiry. His wrinkles she'd thought of as laugh lines, though he'd never laughed. He was only a bit taller than her, even though she was on the short side for a woman.

But her pa was a large man, a bully, so she'd liked the idea of a smaller man. That seemed safer. Pa had come to owe money to Wendell for a reason she'd never heard. She'd seen the man her father insisted she marry as powerful. Only a powerful man could cow her father. And yet Wendell had been of small stature, so he didn't frighten her. Her father's home wasn't a happy place, so she hadn't protested much. After nearly three years of marriage, Audra could no longer remember why she'd been so stupid as to believe a man who had power over her tyrant of a father would be loving with her.

"But she never goes off for this long." Julia often went outside for a long walk while Audra and Maggie took an afternoon nap. But she was always home for supper. In fact, she always *made* supper. Audra had to move quickly to be allowed to do any work in this household. This time, Audra had awakened to an empty house. Julia hadn't come home all day. Audra had hunted to the extent she could while carrying a baby. Her fear had turned to terror as dusk had turned to dark. Then Wendell came home, as he always did late Saturday nights. He'd listened to Audra's worry, complained about his arm being sore and how tired he was from the long week, as if Julia had gone off strictly to cause him more work. He had at least searched. Audra had heard him yelling for the last few hours.

"Something's happened." Audra stood and walked the floor with Maggie, too nervous to sit still.

"She's tryin' to scare me is all." Wendell was a cocky banty rooster of a man, and was just as likely to peck and claw and flap.

Since Audra liked her stepdaughter a lot more than she liked her husband, his words were no comfort. Wendell only came home after the store closed on Saturday night and stayed until Monday morning. All part of his plan to keep the men away from his women by keeping them hidden.

"There's no reason she'd be trying to *scare* you, Wendell. You weren't even home when she left." Audra preferred to keep the peace, even if she had to twist herself into a knot doing it. Julia was much more courageous when it came to facing Wendell's wrath.

"She fusses all the time about one thing or another." Wendell puffed on his inch-long stub of a cigar using his left hand. It was so awkward, Audra had noticed it as soon as he came home. Now he cradled his right arm close to his stomach. Had he sprained his wrist? She'd been too worried about Julia to even ask.

"She doesn't like this cabin and she doesn't like living way out west." He took one last draw on his cigar and tossed it to the floor. Stomping on it viciously. She had to get that ugly cigar butt tossed out before Maggie could eat it. He fumbled for his metal tube he always kept in his shirt pocket that held another cigar. He had recently taken to carrying two, as if he was afraid to be without something to smoke.

Jerking it out of his pocket, he stared at it so intently, Audra saw his eyes lose focus.

"Only because she's worried about the children. The baby will be here soon, and the cabin isn't tight. We need a better place to live before snow falls. It's too cold at night, even in the summer." They lived in an old shack Wendell had found. As far as Audra knew, Wendell had no carpentry skills. He'd have needed to hire someone to help him build a house or repair this one, and that would mess up his plans to keep his womenfolk a secret.

"It's good enough." Wendell jammed the cigar tube back in his shirt pocket and reached for Audra in an aborted gesture with his right hand. He flinched and cradled the arm against his body. "I can't find her. What do you want me to do?"

"She wouldn't stay away this long." Audra wished Wendell wouldn't shout. Maggie had been nursing quietly, on the verge of sleeping. Now the child's eyes were wide open and frightened, feeding frantically while Audra paced. With another baby on the way, Audra knew her milk supply was nearly used up and they had no cow. Could a woman nurse two babies at once? Audra had no idea. It might be necessary.

Julia had squabbled with Wendell before he'd ridden to town on Monday. She'd demanded they leave or make the house more comfortable. It got cold at night, and the roof leaked. It had snowed one night, and they'd awakened to a layer of the white stuff on the floor.

Instead of saying he'd fix things, he'd boasted about how the men in town were too stupid to notice that he was gone from Saturday night to Monday morning. He'd told Julia she'd be at the mercy of violent men if he brought anyone out to do repairs, and he was too busy and tired after a long week to spend his Sabbath fussing with the house.

"She does this every time she's upset."

Wendell stormed around the cabin. It didn't take long. They had three small rooms for four people. The two back rooms were shanties added to this small front room. They slept on bedrolls on the floor.

It was true Julia went for long walks when her father was in a belligerent mood. "She's never been gone overnight."

"Maybe she finally took off. If she did, then good riddance to her." Wendell poured himself a glass of water with his left hand and drank deeply. He'd been tidy and civilized when she'd met him, well dressed and clean-shaven except for a tidy mustache. Only on their way west had he begun to ignore bathing. His face was bristly with his beard. His pants were threadbare and his white shirt was sweat-stained and dingy, even though Julia and Audra washed his clothes every weekend.

Spilled water was the closest the man ever came to a bath.

"Took off?" Audra ran her hand over her stomach and wanted to weep for the new baby on the way. She'd felt contractions a few times while she'd tried to patch holes in the house to slow the wind. After the second time, Julia would barely let her move and did most of the work herself. Wendell wouldn't help at all. Audra knew she was risking her baby's life by doing heavy chores. She didn't want to deliver her baby in this tiny cabin in this remote mountain hideaway.

Enduring Wendell's touch was her wifely duty. And it had made her a mother at a very young age — with one on the way — after only three years of marriage. He left her alone when she was ungainly from being with child, which was one of the brightest spots in her rather dim marriage. Audra and Julia were always relieved to see him head for town for the week.

"She can't *take off.* Where would she go? Rawhide is the only town for miles, and you'd have passed her on the trail if she'd gone that way. Wendell, something's happened. You've got to keep searching for her."

"Stop yammerin' at me, woman." Throwing the tin cup aside, he turned on her, clenching his fist, which turned the ugly scar on his hand bright red. "I'll keep looking, but I don't need a woman nagging at me." Wendell stormed out and slammed the door.

Maggie jumped at the loud bang and started crying.

Tears burned Audra's eyes, but they didn't fall. She just didn't care enough anymore to be truly hurt by her husband.

She sat in the straight-backed chair, one of their few pieces of furniture. They'd left Houston with an hour's notice, bringing little more than the clothes on their backs and two wooden crates of belongings Julia had thrown together. Julia said her father always decided to move on like this, and she'd learned what to grab quickly — although Audra wished she'd have left some of the heavy books behind and added more clothes. Julia had built this chair, a ramshackle piece of work, but it stayed on its legs, and Audra was grateful for it.

Audra thought of Julia and found tears after all. Audra loved her baby with a mother's heart, but she didn't love Julia as a daughter. Julia was nearly Audra's age and they were sisters, friends, family. Julia was so strong and hardworking that in many ways Audra felt like the daughter and Julia the mother.

And Julia was fiercely loyal. She wouldn't have left Audra to cope alone. Not willingly. Where had she gone? What had happened to her?

A tear rolled down Audra's face and a dam broke. It wasn't possible that Julia had taken off. She was a sensible girl. Yes, she went for long walks. Julia loved nature and talked with enthusiasm of fossils and rivers and rocks. She read her books on the subject over and over and wrote papers that she often got Wendell to mail off for her, trying to get scholarly magazines to publish them. It was one of the few kindnesses Wendell showed his daughter.

But she'd never *leave.* Audra knew that with unshakable certainty. Something had happened to her friend.

Hugging Maggie close, she let her tears fall. It was right to cry when your best friend, your sister, got swallowed up by a merciless land.

CHAPTER 4

"Finish eating. You can get some rest, and then we'll get you back to Rawhide first thing in the morning." Rafe wasn't listening to her. He was too busy giving orders.

Julia decided it was time he found out she wasn't going to obey. "No. I can't go to Rawhide. Absolutely not. I have to go home . . . *now*." She clenched her fist, fought down her temper. Stay calm. Reason with him. Make him understand.

"If I'm out all night, Audra will be crazy with worry." Julia's voice broke, and she jammed her fingers into her hair and pulled it, hoping the pain would distract herself from the panic and stupid crying. She breathed through the tears that were cutting off her voice until she got control of herself. All she and her family had been through since they left Houston in the spring, and Julia had held up well, mainly because Audra needed her to be strong.

Rafe just stared at her. Honestly, that long, quiet look helped get her tears under control better than if he'd been nice.

Which he wasn't. *Yippee.*

It was obvious he was waiting to issue some new order.

"What?" She might as well let him go ahead.

"We've been talking in circles, Julia. First it's your pa, then there's a baby. You live in Rawhide, you have to go home, you can't go to Rawhide. The town where you say your pa has a store is twenty miles from here, yet you say you live a half mile from the cavern. None of these things match up, Jules. And who in the world is Audra? Is she the baby?"

Julia glared at Rafe. She had explained her situation very carefully, several times. She inhaled slowly. "Can you sit down, please, and listen to me for a few minutes. I will say this one more time and try to make it clear."

Rafe's eyes flickered to Ethan, who stood in the doorway off to Julia's right. Rafe was on her left, so she couldn't quite see what passed between them.

Probably confusion. The Kincaid brothers seemed to be easily confused.

"We live outside of town. A long way. Our

63

cabin is about a half mile from the cavern."

"No, it's not."

Rafe didn't sit, and Julia really wished he would so they could pretend like they were having a normal conversation, which might help keep her from screaming when she thought of how worried Audra must be by now. And this was Saturday night. Father would be home. That should have been a good thing; it was better than if Audra was alone. But Father had a knack for making everything worse.

Julia gritted her teeth. "Yes, it is. It's a very steep trail, and I discovered the cavern while hiking. I've walked that trail many times. I know how far I walked."

"There's a fast-moving creek right over the crest of that mountain. There's no way across. You have to go around, so it's a lot longer than half a mile."

"I have a way across."

Rafe frowned and exchanged another look with Ethan. He stepped toward her and took her head in his hands to have a closer look at her temple. "Do you think you were unconscious long? A head injury might explain why you're a bit addled."

She shoved his hands away and snapped, "Just be quiet and listen." She fought her way back to calm. "My father didn't want us living in town. He said it was dangerous. So he found a place outside of town and he only comes home on Saturday nights when the general store is closed."

"The general store is owned by a man I know well. Your father owns a saloon."

Julia threw her hands wide. "Whatever he owns, we live a half mile from that cavern."

"Your pa leaves you alone out there?" Rafe scowled.

"Yes, with Audra, my stepmother. I've got a baby sister named Maggie and there's a baby on the way. In the afternoons, when Maggie sleeps, Audra lays down for a while. The floorboards creak and the door scrapes when I open it, so I can either sit motionless for two or three hours every afternoon or I can go out for a walk. I've had an interest in geological history for most of my life. So when I found the cavern, of course I explored. And I found a fossil."

"And a fossil is . . . ?" Rafe arched a brow and waited.

"Bones. I found old fish bones."

"You found fish bones. Someone probably left the scraps from their meal behind." Rafe sounded as if he were talking to a five-year-old. Or maybe he had the mental age of five; she wasn't sure.

"Not *scraps*. These are *fossils*."

Rafe's expression was the very height of skepticism.

Julia forged on. "I went for a walk today, as usual, but I . . ." She rubbed her head. "That man scared me. I doused my light because it gave away where I was. I ran. I must have hit my head and been unconscious for a while, but since I was unconscious, I'm really not all that sure how long I lay there. All I know is when I woke up it was pitch-dark. I tried to find my way to the entrance, and I did find the ledge; it had to be the right spot. I climbed it, but I couldn't find my rope, and with no sunlight there was no way to see if I was in the right place." She remembered something else. "I left my lantern down there. I need to get my lantern back."

"You're lucky you didn't splash kerosene and set yourself on fire," Ethan said from behind her.

She really wished Ethan would move closer to Rafe so she could keep an eye on both of them. "Well, yes, now that you mention it, I am very lucky." Julia rolled her eyes at the man's imagination. "Of course I'm lucky any number of other things didn't happen. I was quiet for a long time because I was afraid of that man. But finally I couldn't stand being trapped any longer and

I called out for help, and . . . and you . . . you were there. You answered. You saved me." Her voice broke, and she launched herself into Rafe's arms again. "Please, Rafe. Poor Audra. I've got to get home."

"It's full dark." His arms came around her waist, and the strength of them was so wonderful she got ahold of her upset. "It'll be all night getting you home."

"No, I can tell you don't believe me." She pulled back far enough to look him in the eyes and spoke softly, persuasively, using small words with few syllables. "But I'll show you the way." She tried to sound coaxing. Maybe if she offered him a cookie. "I *do* have a trail. How else could I have gotten there? You don't think I hiked twenty miles, do you?"

"So, you've found some treacherous mountain trail that fords that deep, fast-moving water and you want to go home that way in the dark?"

"Yes!" Julia smiled and gave him a quick encouraging pat on the shoulder. He'd finally started to act like a reasonable, intelligent man.

"No."

She'd fallen into the hands of a complete idiot. She let go of the idiot and sat back down. "I can't stay out overnight. My father might kill himself searching for me."

Julia doubted that very much, but she thought it might appeal to Rafe's heroic nature. He really was heroic. A hero didn't have to be a genius after all.

"We'll go at first light."

He really was bossy, too.

"I know your family will be frantic." Rafe picked up one of her hands, and Julia noticed for the first time that she had several bleeding fingernails. Then she forgot about her nails as his touch reminded her of his kiss, though she was sure now that he'd only kissed her to turn her attention from her hysterics.

It had certainly worked. And then he'd asked her if she was sixty years old, in a voice that sounded slightly sickened. And she'd slapped him.

If she had it to do over again, she'd slap him twice. Of course she hadn't been able to see him, either. What if *he'd* been sixty? She controlled a shudder of disgust.

Standing, she gave him one more chance. "Please, will you help me? Help me get back to my father. Now — tonight. I know it's a lot to ask. We can talk about going back down into that cavern later."

"You're not going down there." Ethan's voice turned Julia, so she finally got a better look at Rafe's brother.

She'd been crying when she'd seen him before. As a rule she never cried. But she'd had an extremely trying day.

Ethan looked like Rafe in general ways. He was an inch or two above six feet, and so was Rafe. They both had broad shoulders and narrow hips. Rafe had close-cropped dark hair. Ethan's was lighter brown and too long, the ends bleached by the sun. His eyes were different, bright blue where Rafe's were the color of the blue sky seen through a cold fog.

Ethan straightened from where he slouched in the doorway, and she tried to judge his reasons for being so adamant against that cavern. Fear or stubbornness — or maybe wisdom.

"I can see you won't come along." Julia turned back to Rafe. "For now, I need to get home. Please. The way I walked isn't so steep. We can handle it in the dark. I know the path very well."

"How do you get across the creek?"

"There are rocks."

"I know that creek, and I've never seen any rocks."

"Maybe there was a landslide. I don't know. But they seem solid and they stick up above the water and that's how I walk

69

across. I see no reason we can't make it."

Since Ethan wasn't willing, she didn't even bother to look at him. "Please, Rafe."

His eyes held steady. Cool eyes. Strong. Almost cruel. Finally he looked over at Ethan. "I'm going to help her get home, and I'll help her find what she wants in that cave."

"No, Rafe." Ethan's voice had enough upset in it to earn him a look from Julia. His hands were fisted, his voice flashed with anger, but in his eyes she saw fear.

"When you left," Rafe said, "I quit going down. I saw what it had cost me. I've never been back."

"You were out there today or you wouldn't have found her."

Julia gasped to think of what would have become of her if Rafe hadn't heard her cries. She'd been afraid to call out for help because the man in the dark might come. Then she'd been seized by a terrible fear and screamed for help regardless of the danger. She was near madness by the time Rafe arrived.

Rafe moved up beside her, rested a strong hand on the small of her back, and turned to Ethan. "When I got your wire saying you were coming, I rode out there."

"Why!" Ethan took a step forward, his jaw

70

a tight line of anger.

"I just needed to go one last time."

Silence reigned in the kitchen. No one moved. Finally Rafe added, "It was the last time. And I didn't plan to go down. I just . . . I . . . Well, sometimes I go out there. That cavern, I go there and I remember that it cost me my whole family."

"That cavern is dangerous. She doesn't understand what she's asking."

"I've been down there a dozen times," Julia protested.

"Then, you're a fool!" Ethan's blue eyes snapped with fire. The air crackled with tension.

"For tonight, let's just get her home. We can talk about the cavern later." Rafe's words sounded as if they came from deep inside, from a place full of grief and love.

Ethan looked away. "Sure, fine. Go help her. Go down in the cave if you want." Ethan shoved his hands in his back pockets and went back to slouching in the doorway. "I'll stay. Awhile."

Rafe was silent. He studied his brother as if trying to decipher what Ethan meant by *awhile.*

"Let's get you home." Rafe turned to look at her for a change.

So grateful her knees wobbled, Julia did

71

her best not to lean all her weight against him. She was far too used to standing alone. "Thank you."

Rafe looked at his brother. "Do you want to ride to Julia's cabin with us? I don't like taking off and leaving you alone when you're just back."

Ethan hesitated for so long, Julia thought he'd refuse. "I'll ride along," he said.

Audra clutched Maggie to her chest as she waited for Wendell. "Please, God, please help him find her. Protect her."

Her arms trembled as they held her daughter. The little girl whimpered, and Audra realized she was holding too tight.

"Shhh, baby girl. Shhh, Maggie."

She heard footsteps and listened to the foul, sinful words pouring from her husband's mouth. She was a woman of faith. How had she ended up married to such a man?

A stupid question.

Her father had arranged it. He'd as good as sold her to Wendell to pay off debts. She looked down at her daughter and wondered if her father owed more money. Audra had a little sister, Carolyn. Would her father sell Carolyn to some brute? There was a baby brother, Isaac. He might not be such a com-

72

modity as a girl, but he might already be learning to behave in the image of her father.

Thinking of the fate of her little sister and brother back in Houston almost started her to squeezing Maggie again.

From the words Wendell muttered between the cussing, she knew Julia wasn't with him. He shouldn't have come back without her. Furious with her husband for being angry and cursing the Lord when anyone with a lick of sense would be asking for God's help, Audra straightened her usually limp backbone until it was rigid.

She'd been a dutiful wife, as the Bible laid down. But there came a time when obeying a man so steeped in sin was a sin unto itself.

Well, no more. No more would she stand idly while her husband was evil and her children were in danger and her dearest friend, Julia, was missing.

Her days of letting *any* man control her life were over.

Her father and Wendell had done a poor job of it. She was taking charge.

"Things are going to change in this household." She spoke the words as a vow to God. The changes would start as soon as her husband stepped back inside that door.

She'd always believed a woman must go

along with things. But that was before she'd met Julia and seen how brave and smart a woman could be.

Julia was stronger, smarter, and more independent than any woman Audra had ever known.

Audra was changing right now to be like Julia.

CHAPTER 5

Julia Gilliland was a half-wit, and no amount of Christian charity would change that one speck.

Since the woman was too weak-headed to know what was good for her, Rafe kept his mouth shut as she mounted the horse he gave her to ride and kicked it into a trot, in the exact opposite direction of the cavern.

Julia rode for about a dozen yards before Rafe caught up, grabbed her reins, and said, "Wrong way."

"Are you sure?"

No, he was just guessing. "Weren't you mostly crying your head off the whole ride home? What makes you think you know how to get to the cavern from here?"

"I normally have an excellent sense of direction." She arched a brow at him but let him redirect her horse. "And I almost never cry."

"You've been crying pretty much nonstop

since I met you." The moon was so full and bright it blotted out the stars. He saw clearly how puffy her eyes were.

She sat up straight. "These are not normal circumstances."

"I sure hope not."

"As a rule I have very steady nerves."

"I'm going to have to take your word on that, because I've seen no proof of it. For now, just follow me." He turned her horse and headed straight for that cave on a trail that twisted into the heavy forest and was swallowed up in darkness. He expected Ethan to go stubborn and turn back for home. But he tagged along, bringing up the rear.

"The trail I climb is straight west of the cavern."

Rafe knew there was no trail, but dealing with a half-wit was teaching him to just be quiet and let her figure it out for herself. Especially since, somehow, she had reached the cavern. So she might well be right. The fewer words he spoke, the fewer he'd have to eat.

She rode her horse astride with no complaints. Sidesaddle was more correct for women, Rafe had heard. But the Kincaids didn't own a sidesaddle, or a woman. He had to admit that, for the last five minutes, she'd been steady as a rock.

Then she kicked her horse and got ahead of him, staying on the wider trail when they needed to veer off to the south.

"You don't know where you're going," Rafe called after her. "So just calm down and let me get us as far as the cavern — then you can take charge."

He shuddered at the very thought.

Wendell slammed his way back into the cabin. "I can't find her anywhere. A night outdoors'll teach her a lesson. Why'd she go off like that?"

Audra had just made a vow of turning over a new leaf. Now, faced with the same old Wendell, her selfish, cranky husband, she wasn't sure how a woman took control of her life.

"We know something happened to her. She wouldn't stay out overnight."

"She's always going off. And she never has a decent word to say to me when I'm home. I'll betcha she's just hiding to be spiteful. She wants to go back East." Wendell drew deep on his cigar and stank up the cabin when he exhaled. It little mattered; he stank up the cabin just by walking inside.

"You've brought us to a place that isn't safe." Audra had heard Wendell say those

77

very words many times. "Why else are we hidden here so far from town? She worries about the baby. She wants us to be close to a doctor after that episode with my labor pangs. She wants a life that isn't so hard."

"She's lazy is what she is." Wendell jabbed his fat, black cigar at her. Left-handed. "Don't hurt her to do some heavy work."

"That girl works from before sunrise until after dark every day. She's the hardest working person I know. And she won't let me help because of the baby. Her concern is for others, not for herself. We have to leave here, Wendell."

"This is your home now. If Julia'd had any sense, she wouldn't've wandered off. I can't find her in the dark. If she's hiding to worry me, she'll come home on her own. If she fell off one of these steep trails, I'll find her in the morning. Now get to bed. You look like a wrung-out dishrag when you're tired."

"Which is all the time." Audra heard her voice rising. She didn't intend to have a shouting match with her husband. She'd heard him yelling plenty and knew she couldn't best him. But she could be honest. She could speak up instead of letting herself be cowed into silence. There was strength in that. "She won't let me do the heavy chores, chopping wood, tending the garden.

I don't want to lose this child. We need you, Wendell. You've got to move us into town. This life is too hard for two women alone with a baby and another on the way."

"You're staying out here."

"Town can't be any more dangerous than this place. Julia being missing proves that." Audra glanced down and saw that little Maggie had fallen asleep while Audra stood bickering. She ducked into the bedroom and laid the baby down on the pallet Maggie shared with Julia. Audra closed the door quietly and stepped away from it, hoping the baby would sleep through this first sign of her mother having a backbone. It might be noisy.

"We aren't living out here anymore, Wendell."

"Shut up." He slashed his cigar at her. He was still favoring his right hand. "I'm the head of this house, and I say we're staying, and that's final."

"No, I will *not* shut up, and what you say is *not* final." Her words froze him in his tracks.

Fear made her heart pump fast.

"What did you just say to me?" Wendell turned to look at her, his eyes blazing. He hadn't ever hit her, but then she'd never challenged him before.

His rage had been awakened by his annoyance at Julia, but he was fine with taking his temper out on his wife. Then Audra looked closer. He didn't look right. His eyes almost . . . almost . . . glittered. His skin had a dry, flushed look to it. He seemed ever so slightly . . . mad. Audra wondered if he would come at her with his fists, but she wasn't backing down no matter what he did.

"I'm leaving here as soon as we get Julia back." She could have waited. Picked a moment when he was calm. But he was never truly calm, so she forged on. "We're moving to town. If that doesn't suit you, we'll go back to Houston."

"You're not going anywhere." He threw his cigar on the floor and stomped as if he wished it were her neck. Then he stepped right up to her face.

"Yes, I am." She smelled his fetid breath. She noticed a rotten egg smell that was worse even than usual. "I'm going even if I have to walk the whole way carrying a baby. I am *done* with this place, and we'll be coming to town to take a stagecoach, so there'll be no more keeping us a secret."

"There's no stagecoach in Rawhide." He sneered the words, calling her stupid.

"Then I'll get a ride on a freight wagon." She felt strong as her temper rose.

"No wife of mine is gonna talk to me that way." Wendell caught her arm and jerked her forward so she slammed into his chest. He made a soft grunt, as if the collision had hurt, and for a second his hold on her arm shifted, almost as if he was using her for balance. Then he was steady again, and she wondered if she'd imagined it.

Even though they were close in size, she didn't fool herself that she was stronger. A man's strength would best her if it came to a fight. But she had twice the brainpower Wendell had, so she used that.

"You've got *one* wife, and she *is* going to talk to you this way. We should *never* have come to a place so dangerous we couldn't live in town with you. You should have found a better place to settle."

She saw his eyes narrow and his teeth bare. But she didn't back down even though everything in her wanted to. It had finally come. Life and death. Audra was choosing life, and that meant leaving this place.

"If Julia was here, I'd go away with her right now in the night." She yanked her arm free and was surprised Wendell's grip broke. Well, she could only hope her mild little effort to not be pushed around bothered him a bit. "And if she dies, I'll leave on my own. And I will raise your children to know that their father is a *fool.*"

Wendell shoved her with his left hand. She stumbled back and slammed into the wall. Her head hit so hard her knees gave out. As she began to sink, Wendell reached out his right hand, checked himself, and with his left caught her braid and held her on her feet, nearly tearing her hair out. He dragged her forward until their noses almost met. His eyes were blazing, and so close to him she felt heat coming off him in waves. He was feverish.

"You'll mind me, woman." He shook her by the hair so hard her teeth knocked together.

The pain cleared her head of worry for the old coot. "I will *not* mind you if it means I have to watch my children die." She rested her hand on her stomach. The one she still carried was at more risk than Maggie, but neither was safe.

"You're the one that'd be killing them if you're so stupid as to leave me."

"No." Audra grew more determined with every word. "That would be on *your* head if you let me go alone."

"You try and leave, and I'll stop you." He twisted her braid until she cried out with pain.

But the pain just made her angry. "You

82

can't stop me because you're never here. I'll leave as soon as you do. I'll follow you to town; then your secret will be out. Everyone will know you have a wife, two daughters, and a baby on the way. You have to let go sometime, and when you do I am leaving. Now you take your filthy hands off of me."

He released her hair and shoved her against the wall again. "I told you to shut your mouth."

She shoved him back and bumped his right arm. He flinched as if the slight blow hurt terribly, though she suspected any hurt he felt was to his pride.

Wendell's eyes narrowed, but he didn't raise a fist. He'd been cruel with words and yet he'd never hit her. Right now, judging from the strange, almost glazed fury in his eyes, she was very much afraid he was capable of it. "We can't go back. Don't you know why we came out here?"

"You talked about heading west to California or Oregon. You said we'd start another general store."

His voice cackled with cruel laughter, a sound she'd never heard from him before. His eyes seemed unfocused, as if he looked through her to the past. "You really think I paid for that house in Houston and your clothes and food with money earned from a pitiful store?"

Audra frowned. She had no idea what his income source had to do with anything. "Of course I believe it. How else did we live?"

"Gambling." He spoke the word with grim satisfaction, and his eyes took on the glazed look of a fanatic.

"What?"

"Why do you think your pa married you off to me?" Wendell had never spoken of gambling. But now his manner was wild, as if he'd forgotten to keep things to himself.

"I knew he owed you money."

"He owed me for a gambling debt he couldn't pay. A big one." Wendell rubbed his unshaven chin as he eyed her. "I shouldn't have taken you in trade. I'd've been better off with the money — 'cept your pa didn't have any, and a man has weak moments. You were a pretty little thing. Innocent. It appealed to me to have you in my hands." His hungry gaze made her sick.

"And I knew Julia had one foot out the door," he added. "She was fixing to leave first chance she got, and I needed someone for cover."

"Cover?" That made no sense. None of it did. "What did you gamble on? You ran a store. Isn't most gambling done in a saloon? With card games?"

"I didn't have a store in Houston. I had the best little gambling house in town. And a man don't need a card game to gamble."

"What then?"

"Horse races, cockfights, boxing mills, a throw of the dice." That cruel laugh escaped again. "Honey, a man gambles on anything and everything, and the back of my saloon was the best place in town to put money down on a race or fight."

"Saloon?" Audra shook her head. "My father lost money to you gambling?"

"He did. And I sent men to hunt him down and take what was due. He didn't have it so they dragged him in. He was on his knees begging me to forgive the debt. He offered his pretty daughter as payment for his sins." Wendell leaned closer. The stench of him was unbearable. "Every time I come to you in the night, it's like you're working that off. You might as well work abovestairs in a cathouse. Your pa as good as put an innocent out on the street corner to earn money."

Audra had to fight to keep food in her belly at the ugly things her husband was saying. However Wendell wanted to twist it, she was his wife and she'd done nothing wrong by giving him husbandly prerogatives. "Then why are we out here if you're such an important man back in Houston?"

The laughter cackled with a desperate edge. "I got my hands on the richest haul of my life. And I saw my chance, so I took it and ran for the West."

"Richest haul? You mean money? We have no money. No great pile of it anyway."

"Sure we do. And I hightailed it out of town with my wife and family for cover. Men hunting me were looking for someone traveling alone. Didn't you wonder why I came home one night and said we were heading west before first light?"

"You know I wondered. I asked you many times why you decided to move."

"I've moved on a lot of times in my life. Ask Julia how many towns we've lived in."

Audra knew Julia and her father had wandered. That was part of the reason Audra hadn't bothered to fuss about the sudden trip. Julia acted like it was something she'd done many times before and had just begun packing without acting upset.

"The kind of man I owe will find me if he has to hunt the rest of his life. Men like him have been the reason for every move I've made. I put enough down to buy a building in Rawhide and opened up a new gambling business under a new name. The rest of the money I've hidden where you'll never find it." He laughed and reached for a cigar as if to celebrate his genius with a smoke. "I stuffed it in a deep, deep hole."

His story made her dizzy. His talk of her father made her ill. She didn't have time for dismay. Maybe she could appeal to his greed. "What good is your money if you can't spend it?"

"I plan on living out here for a few years, then getting back to a bigger town somewhere." He shoved the metal cylinder that held his cigar back in his pocket.

Audra was relieved she wouldn't have that vile smoke in her face.

"I picked a new name. In town I'm John Gill. But there ain't enough money or people out here to run a good game. When we head out next time, I'll set up somewhere under another name and start the gambling up again, and you'll live in the country again and you can call yourself by any name you want because nobody will know you exist."

Audra couldn't handle any of what he was saying, but she latched on to his complaints about the town not being big enough. "Let's go now. We'll find Julia and get out of here before anyone dies." If only Julia was still alive. Lost, maybe hurt, but alive. "Please, Wendell."

She sounded like she was begging, and

that wasn't her intention. She wasn't going to ask for his permission. She was leaving with or without him. But with him they had a lot better chance of making it. She gave him one more chance.

"Think of the children. We can't raise them out here. There are too many risks." When she said those words, she suddenly focused on what her husband had done all those years for a living. "Is that it? Is risking your daughter's life just one more gamble to you?" Audra looked squarely into the face of evil and stood strong. "I'm leaving."

"No, you're not." He sank a crushing hand onto her wrist.

She shoved hard. Wendell stumbled back. His skin went from flushed red to a sickly shade of gray, and he seemed to shrink right before her eyes, until he was more a slinking rat than a vicious wolf.

He had only the power over her that she chose to give. And she would no longer give any. "I'm leaving this place as soon as I can find Julia, and I hope you *don't* come with me, because I'm ashamed to have you for my husband."

Then she watched in horror as Wendell slowly sagged to his knees, then tipped and sprawled backward on the floor.

CHAPTER 6

Julia fell off her horse. She grabbed at the saddle horn just as strong arms came around her.

Her heavy eyelids popped open to see Ethan lifting her out of the saddle. His face was cast dark blue in the starlight. The moon had set. Dawn must be approaching. But for now it was the darkest hour of the night.

"What happened?"

He smiled at her. "You fell asleep."

She looked at his handsome face, took in his charming smile. He was an easier man than Rafe. So why did she regret that Ethan held her?

And then he was. Holding her. Rafe.

Rafe dragged her out of Ethan's arms. Looking between them, Julia saw Ethan resist letting her go. Rafe tugged harder. Ethan smiled as if his only objective was to torment his older brother.

Then Rafe had her. "You lead her horse if you need something to do so all-fired bad." He spurred his horse forward. He'd been leading, which came as no surprise to Julia. She suspected the man took charge of every situation.

"I can ride." She rubbed at her burning eyes and was coherent enough to notice she was sprawled across Rafe's lap. She pushed at her skirts and found her legs decently covered. She only hoped the darkness had concealed any immodest situation when Rafe and Ethan had been playing tug-of-war with her.

"Just rest. You've had a hard day."

"I'll say." Julia tried to sit straighter. "But you've got to be exhausted, too. I don't want to add to your burden."

A humorless laugh escaped Rafe's lips. "Too late."

"Will we be at the cavern soon?"

Rafe grunted but didn't say anything.

He shifted his arms and tipped her toward him until her head rested on his chest.

Looking up at his square jaw and straight nose, his skin cast in the blue of moonlight, his determination shining out of fog-shrouded eyes, she had no doubt he could ride all night with no sleep. And carrying a weak woman didn't even slow him down.

Clearly, burdens were to be borne with no shirking if you were Rafe Kincaid.

But the way he'd taken her away from Ethan was too possessive, and she'd liked it too much. Which reminded her of something she didn't like.

"What do you mean the rope was moved? Who would have done such a thing?"

"I intend to find out. Whoever harmed you did it on Kincaid land, and that makes it my business. I'm not apt to forget it."

Julia didn't like the determination in his voice. Rafe sounded a bit too much like her stubborn pa. But he looked better and smelled much nicer.

They rode on.

Julia decided to stay awake so she could enjoy the feeling of his strong arms.

She dozed off almost instantly. It suited him that she felt safe enough to sleep in his arms.

She stirred just as the cavern came into sight. Her eyes blinked open. It was dark enough that their color didn't really show, but he remembered. They were grass green. Spring green, like reborn life. Her fiery red hair glinted in the starlight and seemed to dance in the mountain breeze. It surrounded her face with a riot of curls.

She was pure color and life and vitality

and heat. All things Rafe found he craved.

He'd never considered much of a future with a woman. There weren't any women around to consider such a thing with. But now he had one in his arms, and the thought of keeping her appealed to him something fierce. The thought of a lifetime of protecting her pressed on the cold place at his core and warmed him a bit. And Rafe, who refused to fear anything, felt a frisson of fear. He didn't want what was frozen inside to thaw and be let free.

The temptation to have her warmth in his life was staggering.

He spoke to stop himself from kissing her. "The cavern's just ahead."

She gave him a groggy smile, then nestled closer into his arms and rubbed her cheek on his chest. A man might well risk anything to wake up to such a smile. Then she gathered her strength and began looking around.

"We have to leave the horses here." Pointing at a grassy slope, she said, "Picket them and we'll walk."

Rafe did what the bossy bit of goods ordered.

He swung off his horse, and when it came time to set her down, he realized just how comfortable he'd gotten holding her in his arms. When his feet hit the ground he released her legs. Maybe she could have stood on her own, but just in case, he kept his arm around her. He stood with his tall stallion between them and Ethan. Their eyes met. He moved a bit closer — and he was mighty close already, so that was saying something.

He felt as if he searched for something in her eyes. He had no idea what.

The moment stretched, and then Ethan led away the horses that had given Rafe a sense of privacy. Ethan's horse was already staked out to eat grass. How long had Rafe stood there searching in Julia's eyes?

Shaking her head to clear it, she saw the first whisper of the approaching dawn. "I've been gone all night. Audra will be frantic. Come, we have to hurry."

She darted toward the nearby crest. She heard Rafe and Ethan moving and glanced back to make sure they were following. It occurred to her they didn't need to go home with her. She could obviously walk home. And yet the dark and the strain of yesterday and the fear that would have Audra in its grip, and Rafe's certainty that her rope had been moved deliberately so she couldn't get out of the cavern kept her silent.

She stepped to the top of the knoll and stopped so suddenly Rafe bumped into her. She pointed to the west. "Look at that."

The rising sun was shining on the snow-capped mountaintop miles away. Rolling, rugged mountains cloaked in darkness in such a way that distance meant nothing. That mountain shined white, cast with the pink and orange of dawn.

"So beautiful." Her words were mere breaths that joined with the brisk morning breeze. "Like that cavern is beautiful. The heights and the depths. All created by a God who loves us."

She was finally able to tear her eyes away from the sight of that snowy peak washed in color. Below her was a steep descent to rushing water and the rocky span she needed to cross. Looking at Rafe, she said, "I hope you're used to a rugged trail."

Rafe shrugged. "I reckon if you can do it, I can."

Ethan snickered.

Men.

Julia sniffed and started down the slope. Let them keep up.

Of course they were very strong men. And one of them had saved her life. And now they were both protecting her while they saw her home.

Men had their good points.

Something she never thought about much, considering her father's cranky nature.

The descent took them out of the line of vision of that distant white mountain. And they went from a glimpse of dawn to the dark of night in a few steps. "It's like being swallowed up by darkness."

"There's nothing here that could be called a trail. Are you sure we're going the right way?"

Julia's eyes narrowed, she knew it, but she kept her back to Rafe so she could be as irritated as she chose. "That boulder there, the one that looks like a five-hundred-pound duck . . . ?"

"A duck?" Rafe muttered from behind.

"I see a loaf of bread," Ethan said. "But then, I'm pretty hungry. I'd eat duck too if we had any."

"We go to the right side." Julia ignored both of them. "Then we'll need to do some climbing to get down the next stretch."

"And you found this place on your afternoon walk?" Ethan didn't call her a liar. That really wasn't what she thought his point was. More likely he meant she was stupid. On that, he might be right.

"Yes."

"We have to climb down a cliff?" Rafe

sounded just the littlest bit impatient. "And climb back up it once we've gotten you all settled and safe at home?"

Maybe slightly *more* than the littlest bit impatient.

"Well, I told you we couldn't bring our horses. Why did you think that was?"

"Just keep moving." Rafe was very close behind her as they rounded her duck rock.

"Be careful here." The mountain sheered off in a fall almost straight down to a level maybe thirty feet below. But the broken rocks revealed layers in the earth, and Julia had no trouble using those layers for handholds and toeholds. It was almost a stairway.

Julia turned and Rafe was only inches away. He said, "We should use ropes. Tie ourselves together. Then when you fall I can save you."

That was nice.

Disrespectful, definitely doubtful, slightly sneering even, and she was very tempted to punch him in the nose. But his underestimation of her was rooted in his wanting to keep her alive, so there were heroic overtones to his sneering.

And that was nice.

She turned and began picking her way down, hanging on to the rock face. "It's not the least bit death defying. I'm sure you'll be fine."

She heard Rafe grumbling, but she decided it was wise not to ask him to repeat himself.

"So, you found fossils down in the cavern? Bones?" Rafe asked.

And that cheered her right up. "Yes, bones. The bones of a fish. I know quite a bit about fossils. I discovered my first one in Illinois when I was twelve. I've studied them extensively."

"I thought you said you were from Houston."

"My father likes to travel around. It's been fine." She thought of how completely *not* fine it was. "I've developed an interest in geological studies and the search for fossils. And I am hoping to get an article published through the American Philosophical Society."

"A society? About fossils?" Rafe asked.

"The *Proceedings* is their quarterly journal."

Rafe grunted.

She reached a level spot, and when Rafe came down next to her, she leaned close and whispered, "I believe my findings might make me eligible for the Magellanic Premium." Julia felt the excitement shining out of her.

"You don't have a brain in your head, do you?" Rafe sounded sad but resigned, the idiot.

Julia resumed climbing to keep from going for his throat. "I've tried to get articles published before. I found the tusk of a mastodon when we lived in Kentucky."

"You moved from Illinois to Kentucky?"

"I told you I've lived all over." Julia's fingers hurt. She hadn't given much thought to how she'd come to have blood under her fingernails, though she remembered a bit of clawing as she tried to find her way out of the cavern in the pitch-darkness. But now that she was clinging to the rocks, she realized she'd broken off several nails below the quick. She decided talking to Rafe and Ethan, however lacking they were in intelligence, was better than paying attention to pain she couldn't do anything about.

"What's a mastodon?" Ethan was still with them. For some reason, Julia kept waiting for him to go home. He just seemed like the type.

"It's sort of like a wooly mammoth."

"A wooly mammoth?" Ethan sounded very doubtful. "I've seen most the animals in these parts. I guess buffalo are sort of wooly. And grizzlies."

"It's a prehistoric elephant."

"Elephant?" Rafe was joining his brother in being a doubter. "I've heard of elephants. But never in America."

"There aren't any." Surely he'd heard the word *prehistoric*. She'd said it quite clearly.

"There aren't any, but you found one?"

Ethan really should just go on home.

"They're not elephants, but they're similar. And they're extinct. There aren't any in America *anymore*." Julia really couldn't think of any smaller words to use with the Kincaid brothers. So she decided to move on from her talk of American elephants. That wasn't what she was so excited about anyway. "I'd be glad to let you see the papers I've written. My work is quite extensive. If I can get an article published about the cavern, maybe they'll show some interest in my other work. I keep copies of everything and bring my work when we move. And paper, plenty of paper and pencils."

Another grunt from above. She might as well have been accompanied home by pigs.

She reached a less treacherous stretch of the trail and dusted off her hands. She set out walking before the doubting Thomas brothers were down. The sky had taken on the gray light of dawn. And she'd be able to make good time now.

"So you've gone from elephants to fish," Ethan said. "Has all the big stuff been found?"

That thought gave her pause. What if all the fossils had been found? How many could there be anyway? What would she do then? There were always rock formations of course, but she didn't find them nearly as interesting as fossils. Worried, she became all the more determined to study those in the cave. Why would there be fish in a cave at the top of a mountain? There would be only one reason.

Indians eat fish. Hah!

And why would Indians have a meal in a cave they had to climb down into like that? Rafe would change his tune when he saw it.

She glanced back at the menfolk and realized she could see them pretty well now. Still no sun down in this gully, but it was more shadows than nighttime.

Rafe smiled at her and she stumbled. He grabbed her arm and kept her from falling. Rescued again. She sighed silently and went back to watching where she was going.

They came up to a ledge and she pointed down. "See, we can cross on that."

Rafe came up on her right. She saw him look down and study the stone path about eight feet below that spanned the rushing waters. "We can cross on that? Uh . . . do you just jump down to that first rock?"

"I'll show you." She sat down on the ledge and rolled so she lay on her belly, her feet dangling. She found the slender gouge in the smooth stone for her toes and, with no trouble at all, lowered herself to the first slab of granite in the bubbling creek. The stone was flat and it stuck up high enough that the top never got wet. A few of the stones were just barely above water level and they'd been submerged a few times when there'd been rain, but today it was as easy as walking on a sidewalk.

Julia scurried across and found the narrow cut that she could walk up. She didn't even look back; getting home seemed most important now. Not to mention that looking at Rafe had an unsettling effect on her knees.

She climbed, using her hands to steady herself, but able to walk rather than needing to scale a cliff like they had on the other side of the creek. She came out onto a clear view of her home about a quarter of a mile down the mountainside.

She stopped to let Rafe catch up and smiled. "There it is." She thought it rather mature of her not to say *I told you so.*

Rafe scowled. "That creek will flood if

there's a heavy rain upstream. You'd be swept away. You can't go climbing down into that gully."

"Sure I can. I do it all the time."

Rafe grabbed her by both shoulders and turned her to face him. "You're going to get yourself killed over a fish carcass."

"Fish *fossil,* and I won't get killed. You fret around like a baby with a wet diaper."

Rafe's brows shot up.

Audra stepped around the corner of the house at that minute, Maggie in one arm, picking up kindling out of an undersized woodpile. That drew Julia's attention away from the thought of sweeping Rafe away with a flood of cranky, bossy words.

CHAPTER 7

"Julia?" A woman's voice pulled Rafe's attention away from the beautiful half-wit he was escorting home.

Then Rafe saw a very tiny, bedraggled blonde, toting a baby on her hip and another inside her belly. The woman gave a cry and then came up with what looked to be another batch of tears. Rafe had seen and heard and been soaked by more tears in the last half a day than in his whole miserable life. Looked like more were on the way.

"I hate crying," Ethan muttered beside him.

"Audra!" Julia raced down the trail.

"Julia!" The blonde ran toward them.

Rafe went after Julia and toward a very run-down, undersized cabin.

"Where's Julia's pa?" Ethan asked from where he followed after Rafe.

Rafe looked back. "No man would send his woman out with a baby to fetch wood."

"His woman who looks to be about to have a new baby," Ethan added.

"Yeah, and his woman just screamed and he hasn't come out to see why. Even though his daughter has been missing all night. Any decent man would be on edge. Must mean trouble." Rafe planned to find out just what was going on. The women flew into each other's arms just as he caught up to them.

The women were chattering so fast that Rafe couldn't follow it. The baby started hollering. Rafe heard the words "He's hurt" from one of them — he thought Audra.

He took a second to wrap his head around the little fairy princess being Julia's stepmother.

Julia took the little one from Audra, and then the two women dashed around the cabin. Rafe went after them. Hard to protect a woman who was always leading the way into trouble.

Rafe went into the miserably small cabin to see Julia kneeling on the floor beside an unconscious man sprawled flat on his back.

John Gill.

"Trouble sure enough," Ethan muttered from right behind him.

Julia still held the baby, a little girl who looked a lot like Audra, except bald as an egg.

"What's the matter with him?" Rafe knelt beside Julia, who was closest to the door. The blonde was on the man's other side. It was definitely John Gill from Rawhide.

"He just passed out. I . . . I . . ." Audra looked up, blushing, guilty, worried.

"You what?" Rafe asked.

"I hit him." Tears welled in Audra's eyes.

Rafe reached for the man's flushed cheeks. "You hit him so hard he got a fever?" He shook his head. "I doubt it."

"This is my stepmother, Audra Gilliland."

"You're Julia's mother?" Ethan dropped down beside Audra. "I doubt it."

She was like no *mother* Rafe had ever seen. She was young and beautiful. That seemed to run in the womenfolk in this family. But Audra was frail. Her round stomach almost overwhelmed her body. This woman did *not* knock Wendell Gilliland down.

"No. He . . . I guess he already had a fever. I just didn't know it when I hit him." Audra gave a guilt-ridden look to Julia.

Who surprised Rafe when she said, "Good for you."

Rafe had a fleeting moment of sympathy for poor old Wendell. His wife hit him and his daughter's response was "Good." The man was not well liked in his home.

"Don't you want to know why she hit him

before you side with her?" Rafe asked.

"I know my father really well. He deserved it. Besides, I've seen the way Audra gives Maggie a licking."

"Julia, hush." Audra's cheeks pinked up, and she rested a delicate, pale hand on her belly.

"One swat on the fingers when Maggie tried to grab a butcher knife. Maggie laughed at her. We just learned to keep the knife up high. Audra wouldn't be able to knock a fly insensible."

Temper flashed in Audra's eyes. It was *not* a scary sight. "I would so."

She might knock a fly out, Rafe decided, but it'd be a near thing. Audra appeared to be about as mild as milk. Which meant . . . "So Wendell's sick."

"Yes. I . . . I guess he must be. I've been so worried since I knocked him down."

"You did *not* knock him down, Audra," Julia scolded.

"You didn't come home, and I thought you must be . . . must be . . ." Audra broke down, bent forward until she'd have folded in half if her stomach hadn't gotten in her way. She turned loose of her tears and cried her heart out. Way more upset about her missing stepdaughter, who was right in front of her and just fine, than her unconscious husband.

Ethan, kneeling beside Audra, gave her a purely terrified look. He reached out his hand as if to pat her on the back, then snatched his hand back and turned to Rafe, helpless.

Rafe could sympathize. "I met your pa, Julia. I'm on Audra's side." He looked around at the rickety cabin. He wanted to get away from it right now, before a strong wind blew it into kindling. Which wouldn't be all bad. They could use it to build a fire and Audra wouldn't have to go get wood.

Ethan pulled a kerchief out of his back pocket and thrust it into Audra's hands.

"What about an injury?" Julia handed Maggie to Rafe. Which caught him so by surprise he almost dropped the baby on her unconscious pa.

Julia turned her attention to Wendell, moving her hands over his head, then onto his neck in a manner far more medical than affectionate.

"An injury could bring on a fever." Audra rested one hand on her husband's forehead, her lips turned down with worry.

Rafe decided that having these two beautiful women fussing over him wouldn't be such a bad deal. Wendell was doing all right.

With confidence and skill, Julia continued

checking Wendell.

"Something was wrong with his arm yesterday in town," Rafe said.

"Yes," Audra said. She straightened, wiping tears from her eyes with Ethan's kerchief. "He was doing everything with his left hand." Audra tapped at two metal cylinders about six inches long and an inch wide, stuck in the breast pocket of Wendell's shirt. "He even smoked left-handed."

Julia reached for Wendell's right arm. When she touched it, the unconscious man groaned and tossed his head.

"Let's get a look." Julia rolled up her father's sleeve.

Rafe's stomach twisted. He tore his eyes away from the ugly wound and looked from Julia to Audra. "When did he hurt himself?"

"I didn't know he had. I haven't seen him since Monday morning, and he was fine then." Julia's throat worked as she studied the red streaks that stretched up past his elbow and down to his wrist.

"It's so swollen." Audra covered her mouth and looked nauseated. Rafe hoped she didn't decide to empty her stomach. One more indignity for poor old Wendell.

"He's been outside more than in from the minute he got home last night. He was searching for you, Julia." Audra offered it as if to assure Julia that, yes, her pa had cared about her.

"I'd say this wound is close to a week old," Rafe said. Maggie distracted him by yanking on the brim of his hat. He handed the little girl to Ethan, who looked mighty shocked.

When the tyke squeaked and bounced in Ethan's arms, he said, "It must've started out as a scratch and turned septic."

Julia pressed gently on the reddened area around the cut. Her pa moaned but remained unconscious.

"Eth," Rafe said, "you get —"

"We need hot water." Julia rose from her father's side. "Rafe, get a basin full of it. Audra, tear up some strips of cloth. We need to get that open and drain the infection."

Surprised to see Julia taking charge, Rafe jumped to his feet and headed for the fireplace only to find the fire had gone out. Audra tried to stand and almost tipped over. Ethan caught her one-handed. With Maggie in his left arm, he helped Audra to her feet. Ethan had his hands full for a fact.

"I've got an old dress I can tear up for bandages." Audra left the room.

The fireplace was empty and cold. There was no kindling to be seen in the cabin. Even the sticks Audra had been fetching when they'd arrived had been dropped and left behind. "I'll be a while heating water."

Julia rushed for the water and poured a basin of it. "I'll do the best I can with cold water until you get that fire going. Ethan," Julia snapped, "take this cold cloth and keep it on Father's head."

The trembling, clinging woman he'd pulled out of a cavern had turned into a general ordering her troops. It occurred to Rafe as he dashed for the door that he really didn't know Julia at all. Not under what a man might call normal circumstances.

He found a mighty small stack of wood that wouldn't last long. Julia didn't need to give the next order. Rafe could see he needed to chop wood, probably haul water — and while he was at it, he should hunt. He hadn't seen much food in the house and a little broth would be all Wendell would be able to eat for a while.

Rafe knew from the look of the wound, Wendell Gilliland was in a world of trouble.

He filled his arms with wood, which as good as emptied the pile, and hurried back inside to find Ethan bathing Wendell's flushed face while holding a baby in his lap. Ethan was plumb handy.

Julia worked on her father's arm. Audra stood tearing a faded blue gingham dress into strips.

Rafe went to work starting a fire. While everyone was busy, he said, "Mrs. Gilliland, tell me what's happened here since Julia went missing." He thought of that rope that had been moved. There was more going on here than a scratch that'd gotten putrid and a night of worry over a woman who didn't return from her walk.

It was hard to demand much of Audra Gilliland, though. Hard to even call her missus. She looked like little more than a child. He thought Julia had said her stepmother was only a few years older, but she looked younger.

A cry from Ethan's arms stopped Audra from telling her story. "It's time to feed the baby."

Rafe felt his face heat up, and he saw Ethan blushing and looking at the little baby as if she might explode.

"Give me the dress. I'll finish tearing." Julia stood quickly.

Rafe noticed the bloodstain on the dress Julia still wore. There'd been no time to change. They should've torn up the one she was wearing because it was ruined.

The kindling caught and began licking at the bigger pieces of wood with an encouraging crackle.

"Rafe, get over here. Let's get Father into his bedroom. Audra, take Maggie so Ethan can lift from that side."

Wendell being sick didn't stop Rafe from being amused by the orders Julia was firing at everyone.

Rafe's eyes met Ethan's across Wendell's feverish body, and Ethan arched his brows at Rafe before sliding a look at Julia, who stood near her father's head. He handed Maggie to her ma. Maggie clung to Ethan and her hungry whimpering turned into a shriek. Ethan had to peel the little girl's hands off his neck.

"She's a bossy little thing," Ethan muttered.

"Julia or Maggie?" Rafe asked.

Ethan smirked as they lifted together.

If Julia heard him, she didn't say anything.

"He doesn't weigh much," Rafe said. "Let me carry him. One of us can get through that door with him more easily than two."

"Audra, get the door." Julia, in charge. Her stepmother obeyed with alacrity, which told Rafe a lot about how this household worked. "Ethan, if you're not needed to help carry, get the water started heating, then move Audra's chair into the empty bedroom so Audra can have some privacy."

Audra led the way down what couldn't

really be called a hall. It was a space about six feet long and so narrow Rafe had to walk sideways to get Wendell to his room. The little hallway divided the cabin in half with a door to the left and right. Audra swung the droopy door to the right open and stepped out of the way.

Rafe, Wendell in his arms, went past the fragile-looking mother who'd knocked her husband down, and stopped in the doorway. "How many kids do you have?"

"Just one." Audra's cheeks pinked up again and she patted Maggie's little tummy. Maggie went to crying in earnest. "She needs to eat."

He gave her belly a significant glance.

She placed her hand on her belly. "Well, two counting this one."

"And how old are you?"

"Rafe, hurry up. You're blocking the doorway." Julia shooed at him like he was a flock of chickens.

Rafe left off questioning the young mother and turned into the room. He stopped, and Julia ran into his back. "This is a bedroom? It looks more like a lean-to."

"Get in there." Julia shoved and Rafe went in. The ceiling sloped, and he only had room to stand upright right against the wall. Julia had to bump against him to get in, too.

Then she pulled the door mostly shut, and Rafe could tell by the slightly more quiet crying that Audra had gone into the other bedroom.

There was barely enough floor space for two people to lay side by side. Several nails on the wall held a scanty supply of clothes. Blankets thrown on the floor were all there was of a bed.

"Is the other bedroom this size?" Rafe hunkered down with Wendell in his arms and laid the man on the floor.

"Exactly this size." Julia knelt beside him. Shoulder to shoulder, they all but filled the room. Wendell lying down, Julia and Rafe on their knees at his side.

"Where do you sleep?"

"With Maggie in the other room. Audra sleeps there too when Father isn't home. It's cold in here at night."

"Have you got the same bedding in that room?"

Julia quit frowning at her father and gave Rafe a disgruntled look. "Why do you think I've been pushing my father to get out of here? This is no place for children to live. Yes, that bedroom has the same pathetic blankets. There's no mattress. No bed. No crib. We loaded everything we could carry on a single packhorse and in our arms. We walked to the nearest train in the middle of the night. We got on the first train leaving the station and headed west. When we reached the end of the line, Father bought a covered wagon and we didn't begin to fill it up, even though it was small. Pa said we'd get all the things we needed when we got settled. We're still waiting for him to bring proper supplies home and help us build some furniture."

"But if it gets cold at night, how do you — ?"

"It *does* get cold at night. No *if* about it. Can we focus on helping my father for now? You can question me about this pathetic shack and our complete lack of bedding, firewood, and food later."

The sound of the baby's crying finally stopped. Audra must have gotten the little one settled down. When Rafe thought of exactly how she'd go about that, his face heated up again. He'd never been around babies. His own little brothers didn't count because he didn't remember them being babies.

"You don't have food? Julia, I —"

"Rafe!"

"Okay, okay. Later."

"Go on out. There's not room for you to be in here while I work. Get that water heated up. I need to open this wound to drain the infection, and I'll need the hottest water I can get."

Rafe started to obey her but then stopped, there on his knees beside her, and looked at that ugly wound. Wendell's arm was swollen to nearly double the normal size and it was deep red, with darker streaks spreading up and down. His skin had a shiny, almost waxy look to it. A small scratch seeped yellow.

"This is real bad." Rafe looked to see how she'd take that.

"Really bad." Julia blew a long breath out and closed her eyes; then her shoulders squared and her chin lifted. "My father . . ."

For a while Rafe didn't think she'd go on.

"He's always made my life a lot harder than it needed to be." She opened her eyes and looked at her father's still face. "And not just since we moved west. Being his daughter wasn't easy. But he could be kind. He knew I liked exploring caves and learning about fossils. I had a teacher who encouraged my interest and suggested some books. Father bought a few for me. He kept me supplied with paper and pencils, and he'd mail my articles when I'd write them.

"He was an angry man. But he wasn't angry really with me. He was just angry with" — she spread her arms wide and almost whacked Rafe in the nose — "the whole world."

Julia shrugged as if it didn't matter, but her eyes were sad. "I decided I could put up with it. Hang on until I could grow up and get away. I almost made it. Figured once I was old enough, I could do something. Teach school, write about my fossils, maybe. Whatever it took to leave him and live on my own." Her voice dropped to a whisper, and Rafe knew she didn't want Audra to hear through the thin walls. "Then he got married. Audra can't be alone like I was all those years. Not with babies to care for."

"Alone? But you had your pa."

"No, he left me alone like he does here. Worked in town, came home on Sundays. I can't leave now. Not ever."

Rafe heard near desperation in her voice.

"My pa was a hard man, too." Rafe didn't want to say that out loud, because his pa's hardness was Rafe's fault. He'd never been an easy man, but he'd gotten so much worse after the accident in the cavern. Rubbing at the scar on his temple, Rafe thought for the thousandth time that if he had just stayed out of there . . . been more trustworthy from the start . . . taken better care of his little brothers . . . Pa wouldn't have been so cranky. He wouldn't have started staying away more and more until he seemed more of a visitor to the Kincaid Ranch than its owner.

Rafe almost told her. It might help to know she wasn't the only one.

Before he could, she went on whispering. "But I couldn't regret him marrying Audra. Things got so much better. Not with Father. He's always been difficult. But having Audra . . ." Her voice softened with affection. "Things got better for *me*. She was like having a sister. With her, the house became a home. When Maggie was born, Audra and I had such a good time with her that Pa's grouchiness didn't seem to matter much."

"How long have they been married?"

"Not quite three years."

"They had their children fast. How old is she?"

"She's far closer to my age than Father's." Julia's shoulder brushed his as she leaned close to him and dropped her voice even lower. "But Audra should *never* have had another baby so fast. It would have been okay if we hadn't moved. And I adore Maggie. But Audra's so delicate, and with no milk cow, Audra is still nursing. I'm afraid

118

the babies are taking every bite of nourishment she eats."

Rafe thought of that fragile flower of a woman and had to agree, though she'd survived, and here was tough old Wendell in a world of hurt. "You can't always judge toughness by looks."

Julia's gaze met his, and for a moment they weren't in this shabby little room with a sickly man and trouble in their past and their future.

Before Rafe was anywhere near done looking, Julia shook her head and broke the spell.

It took some doing, but he remembered what he'd been wanting to say. "Your stepmother has survived in a hard land — and I'm counting Texas as well as Colorado. She's delivered her first baby, and Maggie is alive and well."

"True. But it isn't wise. My father doesn't seem to care about much but himself."

Rafe hated how lonely she sounded. He had to tell her she wasn't alone in her struggle with her parents. "My ma was a big strapping woman. Broad-shouldered, broad-hipped. Gave birth to three young'uns without much trouble, least I never heard of any. But she wasn't tough in her mind and her heart. There was an accident. My fault." Rafe ran a finger over his scar. "We almost lost Seth."

"Seth?" Julia interrupted. "Ethan said Seth's Cavern."

"Our little brother. He got hurt. Bad hurt. For a while we didn't think he was going to live. Ma . . . It seemed like she just took to her rocking chair and quit the family. Pa started staying away. He'd always gone off to do some trapping every once in a while, but he ran his ranch, too. After Seth's accident, he starting leaving more and more to me, until we boys were doing everything and he barely lived with us anymore."

Rafe had thought many times of how — before the accident — he'd run wild. Explored the cavern. Ma couldn't keep up with them and Pa was busy with the cattle or gone trapping, and Rafe had done as he pleased. After the accident he'd grown up, but it was too late for his family. When Ma died, it had been sad, but they'd buried her and the family went on as always because she hadn't really been part of it for a long time. Rafe had decided long ago that this land wasn't right for women. Now here were Julia and Audra, living proof that a woman ought not to try to settle here.

"We should never have settled here." Julia looked down at her father. "We weren't exactly happy in Houston, not with Father's temper, but we had a good roof over our heads and food in the cupboards. He wasn't around all that much, so we put up with him on the weekends and he'd go away and we'd have our happy home back. I have no idea what possessed him to head west. As usual he didn't explain himself."

"I know why." A voice turned Rafe around. Audra stood in the doorway. She pushed the door open, looking about as strong as dandelion fluff.

Julia stood. "Really? He's never said anything to me."

Rafe got to his feet and watched the two women. Worrying about what would become of them without a man.

"He told me just before he collapsed. I think he was feverish, not thinking clearly, or he'd never have said anything. He stole some money from a dangerous man and ran. That's why we left so abruptly."

"He stole money?" Julia's brow furrowed. "But we've always moved on short notice."

"Maybe it wasn't the first money he stole." Rafe gave unconscious Wendell a disgusted look.

"There's more." Audra told them about the gambling, and about how her father had as good as sold her to repay a debt.

Ethan appeared behind Audra, just peeked around the corner with a baby in his arms. The little one was sitting up, looking at Ethan and grinning.

Audra looked over her shoulder, then smiled shyly at Ethan. "Thanks for holding her. Let me tear up a few more rags and then I'll take her." She turned, but Ethan took up too much space. She stopped, facing him.

Rafe thought his brother was a mite too slow about stepping back to let her go past.

Once Audra was gone, Ethan went back to standing more behind the doorframe than in front of it. The young'un leaned sideways to peek into the room. Rafe moved, hoping to block the little girl's view of her sick pa.

"Water's hot." Ethan's complete lack of haste in delivering that news told Rafe his brother had heard Audra's story.

"I'll get it." Julia edged past Ethan.

Rafe couldn't quite take his eyes off her as she whisked her bossy little self out of the room.

He watched her vanish, and his eyes lingered on the spot where she'd been before he looked to see Ethan and his stupid smile. Ethan always smiled too much.

"What'd you see here that's even a little

bit funny?" Rafe was surprised by the urge to yell at his brother, tackle him and punch him. At least wrestle him to the ground. They'd spent most of their childhood in some kind of battle, usually laughing through it all. Their wrestling matches were another thing that had ended after Seth's accident.

"Not a thing, big brother. So, have you ever seen a woman before? Least ways one you're not related to?"

Rafe clenched his fists. Then the little girl peeked around the corner of the door again and saved Ethan's mangy hide.

Ethan seemed to know it because he showed no fear. In fact, his smile got wider. Fighting with Ethan might help Rafe work off the strange turmoil in his gut, but how was a man supposed to tackle his brother when he held an innocent child?

The little girl started bouncing and drew Rafe's attention. Rafe wasn't going to be able to swing a fist. But that didn't mean he couldn't land a punch of another kind. "You look real nice holding a baby."

Then a thought came to him. "This cut is . . . is . . ." Rafe didn't want to say that Wendell was going to die, especially in front of the little one. Especially if Audra was within hearing distance. But Ethan knew as well as Rafe that only a miracle stood between Wendell Gilliland and the Pearly Gates. And from what Rafe had heard, Wendell and the Almighty weren't on the kind of terms that earned a man a miracle.

Of course, who ever really deserved a miracle? So anything was possible.

Ethan nodded and spoke very quietly so the women in the room only a few feet away wouldn't hear. "Not the kind of thing a man recovers from most times. Short of using a hacksaw."

The little girl slapped Ethan in the face.

Ethan couldn't help but smile at the little angel.

Hacksaw and a smile.

This was one of the strangest days of Rafe's life. Of course, his life was mostly normal as the sunrise. Work and eat and sleep, then wake up and work again.

Strange was kind of nice for once. Except for Wendell being close to death, of course.

"So if we do . . . that." Rafe didn't say cut his arm off with a hacksaw. "If it *saves* him, they're gonna need a lot of help for a long time. And if it doesn't . . ." Rafe gave Maggie a deadly serious look and dropped his voice to a whisper. "Her ma is gonna need a new husband."

Ethan was darkly tanned, but Rafe thought

he turned a slight shade of green. He glanced over his shoulder and whispered back, "Why are you lookin' at me when you say that?"

"Was I looking at you, brother?"

"Look at yourself. Except, wait, you got eyes for a pretty redhead, don't you?" Ethan looked sideways again, clearly checking to see if Julia or Audra were listening. "Pick either of them and you end up with the whole brood." Ethan shuddered and ran away as if he were being chased by a pack of rabid wolves.

Rafe noticed he held on to the baby, though.

Turning back to Wendell, Rafe looked at that arm. The red streaks went up as high as his sleeve could be rolled. Julia came bustling back in the room with her basin of hot water, and Rafe didn't know what to tell the woman. Hot water wasn't going to make one bit of difference.

If they were going to have a chance of saving him, the arm needed to come off. Rafe felt sick. He'd never done such a thing and wasn't sure he could. Then he thought of Steele back at the Kincaid Ranch. A tough man who'd spent time in the war.

Steele did what doctoring got done on the ranch. He'd never talked much about the war, but he was a man who might have at least seen an infected wound like this. Julia stood with the steaming water, frowning at her sick father.

"I'll leave you to it." Rafe turned sideways so she could get past.

"Are you leaving?" She blocked the door as if she'd tackle him if he tried.

"No." Julia had too much hardship in her future. Rafe wouldn't leave her alone to deal with it. "No, I'll stay and see you through this. All of it. Get your pa fixed up, make sure you're safe — whether you go or . . . stay."

She said, "Thank you," so quietly Rafe read her lips more than heard the words. Turning to her father, she slipped past Rafe, knelt by her pa's side, and set her basin of steaming water on the floor.

Rafe turned and went after his brother. "Ethan!"

Ethan wasn't in the tiny cabin, but he appeared at the outside door holding the baby . . . still. Ethan didn't seem to notice he had a child in tow.

"Did you spend time fighting in the war?"

Audra was bending over a pot of steaming water hanging from a hook at the fireplace. She gasped, then dropped her pile of rags and rushed over to snatch her baby away from Ethan, as if he were going to war at that moment and taking Maggie along.

Ethan studied Audra for a bit too long, then turned to Rafe, his brows arched. "You want to talk about that now?"

"No, I just wonder if you've seen any . . . any doctoring that might help us."

"I didn't go to war. I went north. Spent time logging here and there. Went on to California and sailed the ocean some. War didn't interest me."

"Okay. Then, I need Steele. Ride back to the ranch and get him."

Ethan flashed that charming smile. But there was a look in his eye that reminded Rafe his little brother didn't like taking orders. Not one bit.

"Do it." Rafe looked very deliberately at Audra, who stood watching every word that passed between them.

Rafe pushed Ethan outside and around to the back of the house.

Rafe could make out Julia moving on the other side of the thin, sagging wall, so he spoke quietly.

"There's something I hope Steele can do that I can't." He hated to admit he couldn't do something, but . . . amputating a man's arm. Well, any notion of how to go about it was better than none, which was what Rafe came equipped with.

"It'll be hours going there and back."

"I know."

Ethan leaned close. "He may not have hours, Rafe."

"I know that, too, but I don't think I can do it. We don't even have what we need." *A hacksaw.* "Tell Steele what's wrong, and he'll get the . . . supplies." *A hacksaw.* "Then get back here." *With a hacksaw.*

Ethan gave Rafe a long, quiet look.

It took everything Rafe had to admit, "I don't know what else to do, Eth."

"Neither do I." With a jerk of agreement, Ethan left to cross the creek.

Rafe went back inside.

"Julia." Rafe got the little general to come out from the bedroom. He looked between her and Audra. "There's no way to say this except straight out." Rafe tried to figure out a way to soften the news. "Wendell's arm is too badly infected. If we want him to live, we've got to . . ." Rafe swallowed hard. "His arm . . . It's . . . If we don't do . . . something drastic, he'll die."

Audra reached an unsteady hand out, and Rafe caught her wrist to steady her and relieved her of the baby. "You mean . . . ?" She lifted her chin and squared her shoulders. "Cut it off?"

Julia's face went bone white, and she sat in a chair a bit too suddenly. Rafe braced himself to catch her if she fainted. If he wasn't careful, he could be trying to catch all three females in the next few seconds.

"I sent Ethan for Steele, the foreman at my ranch. Steele served in the War Between the States. I hope maybe in the war he saw some doctoring like this. He knows some healing tricks. I don't know how to do what I'm sorely afraid needs to be done. I'd probably kill him trying to save him. Plus, I need a . . ." *Hacksaw.* Rafe suppressed a shudder. "A tool you don't have. I can't image how I'd handle this with what's on hand. And maybe there's something we can do short of . . . of . . ."

"Amputating his arm." Audra said it with a steadier voice than Rafe. He decided that maybe he'd underestimated how much strength she had. Or maybe she just really didn't like her husband and didn't mind the thought of causing him a load of pain.

"I'm hoping Steele can help."

"I expect we'll need a new batch of hot water." Audra turned to the fireplace.

"Audra . . . Mrs. Gilliland, what ails your husband is beyond what hot water can cure."

Audra didn't turn to face him. She stood

by the fire, not moving for far too long. At last she reached for a basin, protecting her hand with a small towel, and began ladling from the steaming pot that hung from a hook over the crackling fire.

"Until there's more to do, we'll do what we can."

CHAPTER 8

Julia prayed — prayed hard — while she bathed her father's arm.

She unbuttoned his shirt, and her hands bumped against his stupid cigar cases. She lifted her eyes to glare at a wooden box full of cigars. It sat in the corner of this room, in a house that barely had food and clothing. Disgusted, she jerked the cigar cylinders out of his pocket and tossed them against the far wall. They rolled into a crack between the wall and the floor, and Julia was glad to see them drop out of sight.

But she knew how much her father loved his precious cigars and he was never without them, though there used to be just *one* case. As those cylinders disappeared, it struck her hard that she would never have dared to discard those cylinders if she had any hope.

Then she slipped her father's shirt off.

And it got worse.

Red streaks reached up to his neck and

leeched out onto his chest.

Amputation wasn't going to do any good.

As she worked over it, the wound opened and she daubed at the poison until it ran red with blood instead of the ugly yellow.

She'd been at it so long that her knees were aching and her back protested her bent-over position. Her fingers were bright red from the hot water. As she pressed on the wound to open it more and drain every ounce of the poison from it, she thought of the pain she was causing and, wishing she could apologize, looked up to see her father's eyes flicker open.

He tried to pull his arm free and groaned, clutching his wounded right arm with his left hand. "Stop your fussing. Let go."

"You're awake." Julia quit doctoring and dropped her cloth in the hot water. She reached for the basin of cold water, wrung out the rag and laid it on his forehead.

"What's going on?" He lifted his right arm to push her away but checked the movement with a groan of pain.

"You've got an infected cut. You're running a fever." She might be having one of her last conversations with her father.

"I love you." She wasn't sure if that was true anymore. But it had been once. Before Mother died. "I'm sorry I worried you and

Audra. I got in a . . . in a tight spot out hiking." No sense burdening the poor sick man with details.

His bleary eyes cleared, and he looked at her, really looked at her for the first time in what seemed like years. His sullen expression faded, and Julia remembered he'd been a kinder man once.

"A rancher found me and brought me home." Now wasn't the time to discuss any of what she'd learned about her father in the last day. Now was the time for another kind of talk.

"Do you believe in God?"

They'd never attended church. She'd learned of God from her mother, and she read her mother's precious Bible daily. Once Audra came to live with her, they'd worshiped together.

Ignoring her question about faith, he said, "You've got the look of my mother's family, the red hair. But I see your ma in you, too." He reached for her and gasped in pain. The pain brought him back to the present, and he scowled. "Where's Audra? I need to talk to her."

"Father, you're very sick. You need to decide where you want to spend eternity. You need to believe in Jesus as the Son of God. You need to confess your sins to Him

133

and —"

He tossed his head restlessly. "I don't want you nagging at me. Audra knows when to shut up."

"She's making soup for you. While she dishes it up, I want to ask you to make a confession of faith to God. Father, you may not get another chance."

"Get her in here." He looked half mad with fever and rage. "I don't want soup." He fumbled at his pocket with his left hand. "What happened to my cigar case?"

"I laid it aside. It's here."

"I want it."

"You can't smoke now, Father. You're barely conscious."

"I want Audra in here. She'll mind me." His voice rose to a shout. "Audra!"

Julia gave up, for now. "Audra, he's awake."

Audra was at the door, holding Maggie. Julia had heard all that her father had admitted to Audra and that Audra had hit him, though Julia knew better than to think Audra carried much power in her fists. But that didn't mean her father wouldn't be cruel.

"Get out, Julia. I want to talk to my wife."

"No." She'd been protecting Audra from her father almost since the day they'd been married. "I need to see to your arm. Go ahead and —"

"Get out!" Wendell's roar barely bothered Julia. She'd heard it many times before. It had always shaken Audra badly, though. Maggie jumped and started to whimper.

"Go on, Julia." Audra spoke quietly, but with a strength Julia hadn't heard before. "We need to have a talk, your father and I."

"She'll mind me whether you tell her to or not. I'm the head of this house." Profanity laced every sentence as he ordered Julia out. He lunged at her but was too weak to even sit up. Julia turned, kneeling at Audra's feet. She saw Audra studying those ugly red streaks. Their eyes met. They knew whatever talking was done now might be the last.

"Please, go. Take the baby." Audra extended her heavily laden arms.

Julia rose to take Maggie just as another stream of filth came from her father's mouth. Tears rolled down Maggie's face and she cried louder. But Audra looked calm and unruffled.

"I'll be praying for you, Father." Julia gave him one last look, then clutched her precious baby sister in her arms and slipped past Audra just as Rafe appeared in the doorway.

He looked with contempt at Wendell, who

was still shouting at Audra. Then Julia saw his eyes go to those lines of infection. He understood everything. Including why Audra was putting up with the shouting and Julia was following the vile orders.

"Audra?" Rafe's voice distracted Father from his yelling.

"Who are you? What are you doing here?" Wendell demanded. "Don't I know you?"

"What is it, Rafe?" Audra ignored Wendell. And Rafe didn't waste his time reminding the man of their brief meeting yesterday in Rawhide.

"I'm just outside. I won't put up with him hurting you. All you need to do is holler."

"Thank you." Audra turned to Wendell. "This is Rafe Kincaid, the man who brought Julia home."

Rafe stepped back to let Julia pass, then followed her outside.

Rafe looked at Julia with the baby in her arms and was confused by how pleasant it was. He had no memories of his ma and babies. Seth was close enough in age that by the time Rafe could remember much, they'd all been running wild outside, winter and summer.

Rafe and Julia walked away from the house. Downhill rather than up toward the creek that led to the cavern. The cabin was in a pretty spot. The mountain they were on swept downward, then rose up again to a flat-topped mountain a few miles away to the west. Rafe saw the slender trail that led around it and no doubt went into Rawhide. Julia was right. It was probably only about five miles away.

A ledge with a level path topping it led to a small corral where Wendell's horse stood grazing. Rafe guided Julia toward the corral to put some space between themselves and the house.

"If . . . No, I mean *when* he dies . . ." Julia lifted her chin and held the little one close.

Rafe's heart beat hard to see a woman stand strong. His ma had never lifted her chin in her life. She was more the slumped shoulders, bowed head type. But here Julia stood, her shoulders square, her green eyes fierce, her messy red hair wild and alive and fiery.

She still hadn't cleaned up from her ordeal in the cavern. Blood on her dress, her hair in snarls. She'd been too busy tending to business, caring for her father and step-mother and baby sister, to take care of herself. Too busy ordering Rafe and Ethan around, too.

"We'll have to figure out where to go. Back

to Houston? Into Rawhide? North to Denver? What about the men he stole from?" Julia shook her head. "All I know is, we can't stay here."

"You don't have to make any decisions right away. When is Audra's baby due?"

"Maybe two months." Julia shrugged. "Maybe one. Maggie's just over a year. This one came along so soon." Julia turned to give the baby a gentle smile and tickled her little sister's soggy chin. "Audra's not sure when it . . . when it . . . began." Julia glanced at him, her cheeks faintly pink, then looked down at the baby in her arms and drew one finger over the child's tear-streaked face.

The little girl grabbed for her hand with a happy squeak, then bounced. All the fear brought on by her father's cruelty forgotten. Rafe stopped, out of hearing distance from the cabin.

"I don't know how strong Audra is," Rafe said. "But she looks like a wind would blow her over. A long journey right now might be more than she can take. I think you should come back to Kincaid Ranch. We've got room there. You can stay until the baby comes and Audra has regained her strength. Then decide."

"We can just stay here." Julia caressed the

baby's back and the tyke's eyes drooped. She leaned against Julia's chest and nodded off as quickly as if someone had snuffed out a light.

"Do they always fall asleep like that?" Rafe didn't know much about babies.

"Maggie does. She's the only baby I've ever been around. Let me go lay her down." Julia vanished before Rafe could stop her. He suspected she went back in as much to check on her pa and Audra as to put the baby to bed. She was back right away.

"How's it going in there?"

Julia shrugged. "I heard them talking quietly. The door was closed, so I left them some privacy."

"Julia, it's not safe for you and Audra to stay out here alone."

"I know." Julia ran her hands up and down her arms like she was cold. The day was warm, even though there was a light breeze. So her chill must have come from inside. Rafe knew how that was.

"Father started doing this not long after Mother died. We moved real suddenly. That was the first time. I know he had a general store back then because I'd been in it. He bought a house in the country and had his store in town. He'd come home only Saturday nights and Sundays. I got myself to school — if I could find a school near me — and lived alone after school."

"Completely alone?" Rafe wondered at such a lonely life. He'd been terribly lonely since Ethan and Seth had left, but he'd been a man grown, and he'd had the hands and the ranch. He wasn't truly alone.

Julia gave him a rueful smile. "Being alone was usually preferable to being with Father. I was glad to see him head for work. Before he married Audra, it didn't matter."

Rafe thought of a little girl, growing up too much alone. It *did* matter.

"I got so I roamed the hills. I was about ten when my mother died and old enough to see to myself and the house, at least after a fashion."

Rafe remembered being ten. He and his brothers had run wild just like Julia. But they'd come home to a warm meal and two parents — except when Pa was gone tending his traplines. One was a grouch, the other cried too much. But at least they were there. And there were hired hands around the place. Not the same at all.

"After Mother died, we moved to Illinois. Father set me up in a house way out of town. He left me. Said he'd be back in a week. I found a cavern there and started to explore. That's where I found my first fossil. In my wandering, I also found a school. It was a long walk, but I showed up at the door every morning and they let me attend. I had a teacher who loved geological things, and he was full of stories of rocks and caverns and ancient beasts that roamed the earth and were now long gone. He let me borrow books from him and he even gave me my first copy of the *Proceedings.* I took that interest with me wherever we went."

"Fossils, huh? Old bones. Never figured those were of much use."

Julia smiled and shrugged one shoulder. "Maybe not of much use, but definitely of some interest." Her eyes flashed with sudden excitement that dispelled the sadness weighing her down. "In the cavern here, the one you call Seth's Cavern, there is so much to study. I could spend a lifetime down there."

"No, it's dangerous."

"If we stay here, I'll be able to continue exploring. I'll be able to write papers on what I find. I'll get them published and earn money that way. This is a really fascinating, unique cavern, Rafe. I could find fossils maybe of some creature that's never been seen. And if I could find proof that this mountain was once underwater, that would —"

"I told you I'd take you down there one more time. Then that's it. You can't keep going."

"Of course I can. I have to. That's the main reason I hate the thought of moving. I need to explore that cavern."

"What about that rope?"

The fire went out of her flashing green eyes, as if he'd drowned her excitement in ice water. He had a talent for bringing coldness to the world. He hated doing it to this fiery woman.

"Who could have done such a thing?" She raised her hands to clutch her wild red curls.

"I don't know. But I aim to find out." Rafe suddenly thought of Ethan. Ethan was always easygoing. Always happy. But deep things stirred in Ethan. Old pain that was trapped inside him. Ethan had come home at the same time someone had played a cruel, possibly deadly trick on Julia. And Ethan hated that cavern.

Rafe shook off the thought. Not possible. Ethan wasn't capable of such a thing.

"But how can you find who did it?"

"The *how* will come, but while I'm figuring it out, I'm going to make sure you're safe."

"So you'll come down with me?" Her excitement flared to life again.

Rafe couldn't stand to douse it. "One more time."

She looked a little doused. "I need more than once."

Rafe was silent for too long. "I'll let you have a good long look around. Maybe if you see something you think needs to be studied, we could go back again."

"Oh, Rafe. Thank you." She threw herself into his arms.

He wrapped his arms around the grateful little thing. "You like that idea, huh?"

"Very much."

"So, all I've got to do to keep you happy is . . . let you do anything you want?" Rafe pulled back just enough to see her smile.

His eyes flickered to her pink lips. What came to his mind was more dangerous than anything he'd ever faced. But he wanted to *feel* something.

He tightened his hold on her and lowered his head.

Fast-moving footsteps pulled Rafe's attention away from Julia. His Colt was out and cocked by the time he moved between her and whoever approached. Ethan rounded the corner of the house from the back. Steele was right behind him.

"Good, you're here." Rafe holstered his pistol and started for the house — doing his best to ignore the remembered warmth of her arms and the frost that was softening in his heart.

As he came around the house, Ethan noticed Rafe standing way too close to the pretty lady he'd pulled out of the belly of the earth.

Rafe had saved her. Ethan could imagine how good that felt. Saving someone, coming through, was a yardstick Ethan measured himself with. He always came up short.

"I don't think there's much you can do for him, Steele." Rafe strode toward them, ignoring Ethan to focus on his ranch foreman. Rafe would pay attention to Ethan when he had some orders to issue. That twisted Ethan's temper, but he covered his anger with a smile.

The ranch foreman was right on Ethan's heels, carrying a pack as big as Ethan's. He was spry for an old-timer.

"Tell me what's wrong." Gray brows lowered over eyes as black as a raven.

Rafe gave a quick, cold outline of Wendell's condition.

Ethan didn't know medicine and he didn't know Steele Coulter. But he knew hopeless.

His thoughts immediately went to the

fragile woman who must be inside with her husband. With a quick glance at Julia, he asked, "Is Audra with him?"

"She's in there." Rafe looked grim.

"I'll go look at the arm. Doubt there's anything . . ." Steele's eyes slid to Julia. "Sorry, miss. It sure sounds like things are serious for your pa."

"Let's go in." Julia started toward the cabin.

Rafe turned to take the lead, as always, but Ethan grabbed his arm. "Wait a minute."

With an impatient glare, Rafe said, "We should be in there."

Julia went inside with Steele tagging after her.

"There's not room for us to be in there, and you know it."

"There's room. They might need something." Rafe jerked at Ethan's hold.

Hanging on doggedly, Ethan said, "Let Steele have a minute alone with the family."

Rafe's jaw tensed, but Ethan was right.

"I saw your chain ladder tossed on the ground beside the cave. And the rope is lying there, coiled up. So nobody can be down there, right? There'd have to be a rope or ladder hanging down. That's the only way in or out."

"Unless someone went down and another person pulled up the ladder."

"Which would mean two people hiding around here. And they couldn't be together because whoever trapped Julia would've also had to trap the other man. Not real likely."

Nodding, Rafe glared at Ethan as if he were only holding himself out of the cabin by pure force of will.

"So, whoever scared her and stranded her is out here." Ethan looked around and felt the forest pressing on him. Someone could be watching just a few yards away.

"He's got to be around somewhere."

"Maybe ducked down in a clump of scrub pines or hiding behind a boulder or over that ledge." Ethan jabbed a thumb to indicate all the possible places a man could conceal himself. "Did you get any idea who'd done it? Did you see any tracks?"

"No. I didn't take the time to track anyone. It was full dark and I was busy with a hysterical woman."

"Anyone low-down enough to do that to a woman is a danger to all of us." Ethan looked at the cabin, thinking of the hacksaw Steele had packed. He felt as if the cabin held the terrors of Hades. Not unlike that cavern.

All that grief, crying, bleeding, dying.

Ethan didn't want any part of it.

He didn't want any part of the cavern, either. But tracking — *that* he could do.

"I'm going to go see if there's a trail. Try and follow it."

"You're needed here, Ethan."

A sudden cry came from the cabin — must be Audra. Steele must have just given his opinion of Wendell's wounds.

"I'll be back after a while." Ethan ran from the commotion inside that cabin. He was good at running. Good at being useless when someone needed him.

Julia came out of the cabin carrying Maggie just as Ethan dodged toward the back of the cabin.

"Ethan, you get back here." Julia's voice froze Ethan in his tracks.

Dreading the thought of Audra sobbing over her no-account husband, Ethan turned to see Maggie sniffling, tears running down her face.

His panic subsided. A baby crying. He could handle that.

The baby snuggled against Julia and her heavy eyelids dropped shut. With a couple more whimpers, she fell asleep.

He slid a wary look between the baby and Julia. But he stayed.

"Where are you going?" Julia rubbed

Maggie's back.

"I'm gonna try and pick up the trail of the man who trapped you in the cavern."

Julia looked from the baby to Rafe to Ethan to the cabin, and whispered, "If Maggie stays asleep, can I come?"

"No, you can't come. Tracking's a one man job." Ethan took a longing look over his shoulder, toward that cabin and the trail behind it.

"Steele wants to tend Father for a while. Maggie woke up, but she hasn't been asleep nearly long enough." Julia rested a gentle hand on the baby's face. "I need to get out of the cabin. Every move I make bothers Audra or Maggie."

"But Steele will bother them." Ethan was looking forward to going off on his own. He had half a notion to just keep going, get away from all of them.

Then Ethan thought of the homecoming hug Rafe had given him and how long it'd been since anyone, even someone as bossy as his big brother, had cared if Ethan lived or died.

"Steele's being quiet, working on the wound. It was me moving around that was the problem." Julia took a close look at Maggie. "She's out. Let me put her down." Julia was looking straight at Rafe. "You wait for me."

More orders.

Ethan looked at Rafe, who shrugged.

"Okay, go lay her down. Steele will look after your pa until we come back."

Julia nodded eagerly and went inside.

"Tracking is a quiet business, Rafe. If we follow the tracks until we find someone, there could be trouble."

"After this many hours, we'll be lucky to even read his sign, let alone follow him back to wherever he's hiding. If it looks like we might be coming on him, you can take Julia back and I'll go on after him."

"Why don't you just give me a rattle to play with." Ethan smiled at Rafe, when he wanted to growl. But nobody could out-growl Rafe, so why bother to try?

Rafe opened his mouth to say something bossy, Ethan was sure, just as Julia came back out. They set off.

"You really have to leave the house every day?" Ethan headed around the cabin and up the slope and down.

"Yes, that's the only way Audra gets a good rest. She shouldn't be having another baby so soon. She's gone into labor at least three times since we left home."

Ethan wasn't real sure how a woman went into labor, then didn't go ahead and have the baby. He knew better than to ask — for fear Julia would answer. In detail. He crossed the stream and climbed.

"The first two times didn't amount to much, but the last time I thought the baby was coming. I've been trying to keep Audra still as much as possible, and I give her time to sleep whenever I can." Julia almost caught Ethan, but he moved fast enough to stay ahead of her. Julia was going to lead this expedition if she could manage it. Even though she had no idea where they were going.

"That's why you found the cave?" Rafe brought up the rear.

"I'm used to being by myself wherever we lived. Wandering, exploring." Julia was right on his heels as Ethan rounded the duck rock. "Father always left me on my own. I wonder if he had a false name in all those towns."

"Audra had to know the right name." Ethan glanced over his shoulder as they reached level ground. "She married him."

Julia's brow beetled. "You know, now that you say that . . . The first time I met her was when Father brought her home after the wedding."

"Your pa didn't *tell you* he was getting

married?" Ethan shook his head. "Surprise, huh?"

"Big surprise. I was within a few months of moving out. I'd told him I was going to find a job, be a schoolteacher, maybe. I hadn't been to school much, but I read a lot and thought I could do the job." Julia caught up to Ethan as the path widened at the top of the gully. "I wasn't sure how to make it all work, but I was more or less on my own anyway. I thought I'd just as well get on with being an adult."

Ethan saw the four Kincaid horses grazing where he and Steele had picketed them.

Rafe caught up. "And right after you told him you were leaving, he brought home a new wife?"

Julia's jaw went all tight, and she nodded with one quick jerk of her head. "Anyway, Audra said something about being Mrs. Wendell. I corrected her. 'You mean Mrs. Wendell Gilliland.' She acted embarrassed and laughed about getting her own name mixed up."

"You think your pa was calling himself by the last name of Wendell in Houston?" Rafe walked straight for that pit, and Ethan could go along or be left behind.

"Maybe. And when Audra was told he was Mr. Wendell, then found out that was wrong, it would be natural to just think she misunderstood it. I've never thought about it before." Julia looked up at Rafe with a start. "If Father used a false name, is their marriage legal?"

"I wouldn't worry about the details at this point."

Julia grimaced and neared the cavern entrance.

"Stay back!" Ethan snapped. He flinched at his tone. A man didn't need to shout to the whole world that he was a coward, now did he? And anyway, he didn't care. Not at all. Speaking more calmly, he added, "You're going to mess up any tracks that're left."

Julia and Rafe stopped, and it occurred to Ethan he could toss an order around, too.

Ethan felt a flush of embarrassment as he studied the black hole and saw that rope lying coiled beside it. Rafe's chain ladder was still out, too. He always packed it back away, or he had when they were kids. Rafe took good care of all his things. Always organized. Always in control of everything and everyone.

Ethan looked at Rafe, knowing his brother could read him too well; it was all a man could do to keep the carefree smile on his face. "We both know I'm a better tracker'n you, right?"

"You couldn't out track me on your best day." Rafe's temper flashed.

Which gave Ethan a stab of satisfaction to get under Rafe's skin, so the smile came easier. It reminded him to stop taking everything so seriously. Of course it was mighty easy to get serious with a man dying a slow painful death, a woman left stranded in a pit, and another woman threatening to have a baby before her time. But Ethan was tough. He could manage it.

"Stay back. No sense adding your footprints and Julia's." Goading Rafe by telling him not to be careless suited Ethan. His homecoming so far seemed to just fall back on the old ways. Rafe giving orders. Ethan going along. When Rafe had hugged him, it had felt so good that at first Ethan couldn't manage much beyond being glad to be home. But it was time Rafe knew that Ethan had done all right on his own and he wasn't going to fall in line and take orders anymore.

"I should be able to separate them out. We didn't go close last night, so the only tracks should be yours and hers from when you brought her up" — *from that dark, deadly hole* — "and whoever left her. Just pat the pretty little lady's hand and let me do the work."

Julia looked at him and rolled her eyes. At least she'd be a pretty little thing if she ran a comb through her hair and took a nice bath and quit giving orders with every breath.

Ethan approached the hole, glad to leave Rafe behind. This way his big brother couldn't see the smile shrink off Ethan's face.

It took about ten seconds to spot a set of man's footprints that weren't Rafe's. Ethan crouched down and studied them. "He's got a pair of boots that are barely hanging on his feet."

Ethan looked at his own battered boots. A worn-out pair of boots wasn't hard to find in the West. He tried to keep his eyes on the footprints, but they kept straying to that black hole. It was like a gaped open mouth. It might as well have called out to him. Taunted him, sneered at him for never going back.

Fighting to ignore it, the tension threatened to choke him. A soft whistle of breeze seemed to flow down into the maw, laughing at him, calling him a coward.

He needed to go closer, but his feet wouldn't move. He decided he could see enough. Crouching near a well-shaped print that was neither Rafe's nor Julia's, he studied it, then, pivoting on his toes, he stayed low to follow the line the tracks made.

"His boots are about my size and the stride is long, which means long-legged because I can tell he isn't running. The impression isn't deep, so he's not a heavy man."

"Tall and skinny," Rafe said. As if Ethan hadn't just said that.

On the rocky ground, a clear trail wasn't visible, but there was enough to tell him where Rafe had tied his horse last night. Right next to their picketed horses brought over yesterday and the one Steele had added today.

Rafe had walked that way, obviously carrying Julia because she made no tracks. The skinny man had walked straight into the forest from that pit.

"Nothing fresh here. He climbed out of the cavern, pulled up the rope, and walked that way." Ethan pointed in the direction opposite Julia's cabin. Toward the Kincaid Ranch. "But he doesn't stay on the trail; he went into the woods."

Ethan stood, opening his senses wide. There was more to tracking than finding footprints. Ethan listened for any sound out of the ordinary. He smelled, knowing man could leave his own scent. He looked for twigs freshly broken or grass and weeds snapped over.

"Let's go." The cavern was at his back now, and he felt chased until his jaw was too tense to crack a smile, even though Rafe could see him. So he moved out to get in the lead again, hunting the low-down coyote who had left Julia to die. Ethan went braced for trouble.

Rafe and Julia were gaining on him again. Ethan ducked into the thick woods and stopped so suddenly that Rafe bumped into him.

"What's the matter?"

"Watch it." A reaction he couldn't control made Ethan turn and shove Rafe back.

"Get out of the way and let me take the lead." Rafe's fist clenched.

Ethan could see Rafe was in a hurry to track down the man who'd done Julia wrong, which explained most of his temper. That black hole accounted for Ethan's.

It would have felt almost good if Rafe took a swing. Let Rafe start it and Ethan might just finish it. They'd cleared the air with their fists many times as boys.

"I'm not your little brother anymore, Rafe." The terse words were like letting steam out of a boiling pot. It helped a little.

"You'll always be my little brother, Eth." Rafe's reasonable sounding words were really an insult, if Rafe would just think about what he was saying.

"No. I'm your *brother,* nothing little about me anymore. You ran me for years until you ran me off the ranch. Now you're doing it again."

"I never wanted you to leave. You know that."

"I know your word was law. I know we did things your way. It was your ranch. It still is. I'm an adult man who's not interested in taking orders every day for the rest of my life. There's no place for me on Rafe Kincaid's ranch."

"It belongs to all of us. Pa left it to his sons."

"You built that ranch more than Pa. You built the herd while he went fur trading."

"You worked right beside me. So did Seth when he wasn't haring off."

"You sold beef to the gold hunters so you could buy more acres while Pa was trying to chisel money out of stone."

"Everything was in Pa's name. When he died, it was divided three ways between me and you and Seth."

"It was in Pa's name but he didn't even

157

care about it. And I've been gone for five years. You're the one who stayed. You've earned it. It's not my home anymore." It felt like home, though. Ethan had been so lonely for so long. And now he was back and all he could do is fear that cavern and resent Rafe's orders and remember why he'd left.

"I want you here. I want my family back."

Ethan felt some of the rage fade. "I should have never come home. Maybe I'll go hunt for Seth."

"How're you going to find him when you don't know where to even start looking?"

"He fought in the war. There'll be a record of where he served."

"You're not going anywhere." Rafe rested his hand on Ethan's shoulder, and Ethan knew he should just take that order. Just agree. Make peace. Smile big. He tried. He really did to just go along, get along. Obey Rafe.

Ethan clenched a fist instead. "More orders, big brother? Well, I'm not taking them anymore. I go where I please, when I please." Rafe always did things his way. Always down in that cavern. Always leaving Ethan behind to feel like a coward. "You don't get to tell me what to do anymore."

"I just ran things to hold them together

158

for us. Someone had to do it. Pa wasn't here and you sure weren't going to take charge. And someone had to chase after Seth and protect him. You were too busy laughing off every reckless stunt he pulled to be any help."

"I wasn't going to risk my neck following him into danger. Just because *he* was stupid didn't mean I had to be. You didn't have to be, either."

"You'd have let Seth die," Rafe said, jabbing him in the chest, "because you were too yellow to go down into that cavern."

Those words cut right to the bone. All he could think of was making Rafe eat them. Ethan itched to plant a fist in his face.

"And you'd have let him kill you both because you wouldn't stay out of there." He rammed his hand flat against Rafe's shoulder, and Rafe staggered back, then came up with a cocked fist and surged forward.

Ethan hauled back his fist.

"Stop it!" A soft hand slapped flat against Ethan's face. "Stop it right now."

A startled Ethan didn't take a swing. Having a woman standing in front of his fist averted that.

Julia shoved Rafe back the same way and forced her way in between them. "We don't have time for this now. And if you can't

159

settle your differences without fists, then both of you get out of here. Go back to your ranch and leave me to tend to Audra and my little sister alone. I've got enough to worry about without two muleheaded men making life more difficult."

Ethan clenched his jaw against the hot words he wanted to say.

With visible effort, Rafe gained control of himself. "We started this because I ran into you. Why'd you stop?"

It took Ethan a few seconds to remember. Then he pointed to the clearly visible prints. "I didn't want to mess up the ground before I could study those."

"The ground here is softer, even I see these tracks." Julia quit standing between them, and Ethan's eyes met Rafe's for too long. Nothing much was settled between them, but Ethan could always leave tomorrow. He had things to do today.

Julia must have figured she'd given her orders for the two naughty boys to behave and no further effort on her part was needed. She was intent on the dark stony soil of the forest floor. "It's as if he walks right up to that tree and . . . and . . ."

Ethan followed her pointing finger and saw it, too. "Vanishes?" Ethan swallowed hard.

"Climbs the tree?" Julia suggested.

They all three looked up together.

"He could have. There are branches enough." Rafe looked back at the ground. "But why?"

"He's not there now." Julia turned, looking overhead in all directions.

"He had to come down somewhere." Ethan approached the tree and looked around the sides of it.

"I suppose he could have climbed along in the treetops." Julia began looking around on the ground.

"Must've, but why not just keep walking?" Ethan weighed the possibilities. "These tracks are at least a day old and it's not like we were hot on his trail. We need to split up. I'll go toward the stream. You two go north."

"No." Rafe was telling Ethan how it was going to be, as always. "I want us together. It's safer."

"We need to cover some ground, Rafe." Ethan glared at Rafe, daring him to override his decision.

"We shouldn't leave Audra alone too long," Julia said.

Finally, Rafe nodded. "It'll save time, for a fact."

Ethan didn't imagine Rafe had made that

decision out of respect for his little brother; rather he'd let Julia sway him.

"I'll go to the east." Julia took a step forward.

"No, not you." Rafe's voice stopped her. She arched a brow at him. "You stay with me."

Ethan decided to let the two tyrants work that out on their own. "I'll go toward the stream."

"Watch yourself, Eth. Remember he might be overhead." Rafe caught Ethan's eye, and they both nodded. That pit might bedevil them, but they'd grown up in a harsh land with little adult protection. Rafe might not want Ethan to be in charge, but he trusted him to be competent.

Rafe and Julia went north, bickering, and Ethan headed west, searching for the spot where a tree-climbing man might come back to earth. Looking back through the trees, he could still see that gaping cave mouth opened wide to swallow a man whole.

A shudder racked Ethan's body as he thought of Seth and what Ethan had done to him that day. After that day, Ethan had never been able to say he really cared about much of anything again. Or maybe it was more fair to say he didn't deserve to care.

And he didn't deserve to have anyone care about him.

He shook off the memories and fixed a smile on his face, then turned back to his tracking. Walking deeper into the woods, he concentrated on the dense forest, his senses on full alert.

Then he heard a twig snap. His gun was drawn and aimed before he made a conscious decision to move.

Julia led the way, though Rafe had to tell her which way. They'd moved about a hundred feet and Rafe had seen no sign of the man they trailed.

Suddenly Julia stopped and gasped.

Rafe had his gun drawn and aimed before he made a conscious decision to move. He grabbed for her to push her behind him, but she dropped to her knees and his hand closed on empty space.

"Look at that!"

"What is it?" Looking in all directions — including overhead — he couldn't see anyone coming at them.

"It's a fossil." Julia reached her hand for the rock. She was kneeling before it with a reverence Rafe thought she oughta save for prayer time.

He squinted to see what in the world she

was looking at. "It a rock. A big old chunk of mountain that tumbled down here."

"No, don't look at the whole rock." Her finger traced along an uneven line. "This, right here. It's ancient. I need to get back here and make a rubbing of it and write about —"

She squeaked when Rafe grabbed her wrist and dragged her to her feet. "We don't have time to look at rocks right now."

"Fossils, Rafe. That leaf —"

"Fossils, then. Julia, there's a man out here that tried to kill you." He didn't even get her attention. She was looking wistfully at that dumb rock. "Don't you have a lick of sense?"

"I told you I was interested in geology."

"Geology?" Rafe held her captive with one hand and checked his gun with the other. He swung the cylinder out with a practiced flick and lifted it to eye level to make sure it was fully loaded. "You said that word before. What is that?"

"It's the science of soil and rock. Rivers and forests."

"Sounds like ranching." He'd known it was fully loaded, but a man learned to check and double-check. An empty cylinder could mean the difference between life and death. He snapped his gun shut. "Should've called it Ranchology."

Julia's chin came up and her eyes shone. "You might be able to help me. You have practical knowledge I lack."

"You lack at being practical — that's for sure." Rafe reholstered his gun.

That comment didn't even slow her down. "You could help a lot when I write my paper about the cavern. And it would be something really different. They'd be sure to publish a paper about a find this important. I've done quite a bit of studying. But in all I've seen in my life, nothing has fascinated me like that cavern. It's a treasure."

"It's dangerous."

"I have to study it, and I *will* write about it, Rafe. You can't come up with a single reason important enough to stop me."

"How about staying alive?" There, she couldn't avoid admitting that.

"I disagree."

Unless she was really stubborn.

"You're right in the short term."

"Short term? What's that mean? If you die in that cave, well, death is real long term."

"In the *geological* sense that cave is more important than my life."

Rafe didn't bother containing a grunt of disagreement. Since she was ignoring him anyway, he might as well make any rude

165

noise he wanted.

"I'll give you a bit of time to find the scoundrel who trapped me, but I've got to go back down. I need to make rubbings of the fossils. I think I can chisel a few of them out without harming them, but mostly I want to describe what's down there." Julia frowned. "I'd make sketches, but that's never been my gift. Shame. Can you draw a picture?"

"No." Rafe picked up his pace.

"Fine then, we'll have to skip the drawing. I'll get a paper published, even without sketches. This is a scientific age, Rafe. We are discovering wonders all the time that tell us more about God's creation." She stumbled.

He caught her before she pitched face-down onto the stony surface of God's creation. "You can't even walk in the woods; down in that cavern you'll fall into a hole and die."

"I need to go back to the cabin, Rafe. Audra might be awake by now."

"We're not going to find anything." Rafe combed through his hair with one hand. "Maybe Ethan had better luck. Let's go."

They started back. The oak and pine were so dense it was hard to walk side by side.

Rafe didn't like her lagging behind or getting ahead, though, so he did his best to stay close.

Jumbled rocks were scattered everywhere, and Rafe knew if they went very far to the west they'd come to that same stream, cutting them off. The stream had cut a deep, narrow canyon. He suspected an avalanche had broken down the side of the canyon and left those stones Julia crossed. Rafe hadn't considered trying to cross up here for years. There was a much easier ford a few miles to the north of his cabin. That winding route was what made Rawhide such a long trip.

Julia kept yammering about fossils while Rafe watched the ground for something that might've gotten here a lot more recently, like a killer.

"We're almost to the spot we split from Ethan. Wonder how far he's gone."

"I can see the entrance to the cavern," Julia said.

He saw tracks. "We're here. Let's give Ethan a few minutes to show up."

A gunshot cut through the quiet forest.

Ethan came to a sharp drop-off where the stream had cut a gully fifty feet deep. He skidded to a halt, glad he wasn't moving fast, or he'd have pitched over the edge. His attention was drawn across the gully. A man vanished into the woods on the far side. And he saw something else. Something he'd never seen before, nor thought of.

He fired his gun to signal Rafe and rushed toward the swaying rope that dangled over the rushing water. It was tied to an overhead limb that stuck out so far it nearly spanned the gorge.

Considering the situation for only a moment, he started climbing.

He'd definitely heard that twig snap on this side of the stream and now that man was on the other side. And this rope was swaying more than could be explained by the wind. That man had gotten across using it. And if he could do it, so could Ethan.

He shinnied out on the branch until he reached the rope. He was all the way out, looking down in the white water of the stream, twisting and dancing over rocks. Well, it was caverns Ethan didn't like. A rushing stream lined by stony cliffs didn't bother him all that much.

He grabbed the rope, scrambled backward, and climbed down.

"Rafe, where are you?" He yelled just because it seemed like the kind of time when a man oughta do a little yelling.

He thought of Rafe, Julia, and himself on

this side of the gully, while the man who'd very likely left Julia in the cavern was on Audra's side of the gully, and not that far from her cabin.

Steele was there and he was a solid hand. But was Steele properly on the lookout? Might Audra have gotten up and taken Maggie outside?

Ethan dismissed the idea of waiting for Rafe. All he'd do is order Ethan to watch over Julia and get to Audra.

Left behind with the women and children and invalids.

That didn't suit Ethan one bit.

He got to the ground, held that long rope in his hands, and looked at the far side of the stream, then took another hard look at the water rushing at the bottom of the gully. He drew his gun and shot off another round. Jerked hard on the rope to make sure it was solid, then quit lollygagging. Jamming his gun into the holster, he flipped the loop through the trigger to tie the gun down, tested the rope one more time and adjusted his hold, then took a running start and swung out into midair.

A shout escaped his lips as he sailed through the air. Part terror, part pure joy.

The rope was longer than he'd reckoned it'd be and he swung down a long way

169

toward the water, then swooshing up, he soared far and high. He reached the end of the long swinging arc and began going backward. Against every speck of common sense he possessed, he let go and hoped he hadn't held on too long.

If he'd picked the wrong moment, then he'd have time to regret it. It was a long way to the water and the jagged rocks below its surface.

"That's Ethan screaming." Rafe didn't let go of Julia, but he picked up his speed — not easy in the thick undergrowth.

The woods thinned. He emerged from the forest right on the edge of a cliff. Skidding, Rafe grabbed Julia and threw her down on the ground. The leaves and sticks and stone poked and scratched at him as he slammed into the ground. He did his best to protect Julia from their sharp edges. They stopped in time. He started to sit up and saw his legs dangling over the cliff.

Scooting backward, with his grip still iron-hard on Julia's arm. He saw movement and something hit him in the face. Looking around for whoever had done the shooting and whatever had made Ethan scream, he saw a rope swinging past his face, then swoosh back toward the gorge.

Following it with his eyes, he looked across the stream to see Ethan picking himself up off the ground.

Ethan wasn't that far away, but he might as well have been in another state. He'd gotten over there . . . Rafe saw that swinging rope and shook his head.

Ethan turned to Rafe and raised a hand to his mouth. "Get back to the cabin. I saw a man. He could be heading there. I'll try and catch him from this direction."

Ethan whirled and ran into the woods and was gone before Rafe could say a word.

Rafe's heart was still pounding hard from nearly pitching over the cliff. Hot blood raced to the coldest part of himself, and it was a fight to stay in control.

"Let's go." Julia jumped to her feet and ran back in the direction they'd come — only she picked wrong and headed north instead of south.

With a sigh, Rafe caught her and dragged her around. "This way."

She trusted him apparently, because she was soon leading in that direction. But Rafe put on more speed, tripping and dodging around fallen trees and limbs, boulders, and ditches. He reached the trail and sprinted toward the crossing.

They were down that gully and back up,

and running down the trail toward the cabin without saying a word. They rounded to the front door just as Audra stepped outside holding Maggie.

"Oh, there you are." She smiled, all calm and a bit puffy-eyed from sleep. Not in danger at all. "That man doctoring Wendell wants to talk to you, Rafe. He won't let me stay."

With a heaved breath of relief, Rafe felt a tug on his arm and realized he was still holding tight to Julia's hand. He had to have let her go when they went down the steepest part of the gully but must've caught hold again without noticing.

Strange how easy it was to hold Julia's hand.

"I'll go." Then he thought of what Steele might want him to do. Torn about leaving the women outside or letting them come in and hear an ugly conversation, he scanned the area and made a decision. "You two stay close to the house." He did his best to singe Julia with a look, and he could see she understood his worry. "Pay attention. If you see or hear anything that worries you, get inside. Keep an eye out for Ethan."

She nodded. "We'll stay close."

Rafe gritted his teeth and went inside.

"I should be in there." Audra took one step toward the cabin.

"I don't want you to see what they might do." Julia didn't want to see it either, but she'd do what needed doing. Julia's heart still pounded from fright and from their long, desperate run. And now here she stood, everything fine. But Ethan was out there chasing a man. It had to be the one who had frightened her and left her stranded in the cavern.

"You can't protect me from everything, Julia."

"I know." Julia respected Audra's heart and knew she was a smart woman, but she wasn't tough and she wasn't decisive. Audra needed someone to be in charge. "But it would be a terrible thing to see."

Audra gave Maggie an absent kiss on the head. "Talking about it does no one any good, so let's don't."

Julia was used to Audra's way of dealing with the world. Remain calm. Keep the peace. Respond to wrath with a soft word. Very biblical. Very different from how Julia attacked life. Of course, Julia had taken a lot of long walks to keep the peace, too.

"Why are you breathing so hard? What happened?"

Julia explained quickly while she waited for her father to start screaming.

There was only silence.

"Shouldn't Ethan be back by now?"

"Not if he's trailing the man. Did I tell you that Ethan's been gone for years?"

Audra arched a brow. "Too much has been going on to even think about Rafe and his brother, beyond being grateful for their help. I don't know a thing about them."

"Ethan returned home last night. Things aren't easy between him and Rafe. And there's another brother who fought in the war." Julia told Audra what she knew about Seth.

"Our family needing so much help couldn't have come at a worse time." Julia shook her head, and a red curl whacked her in the face.

Audra reached up and plucked a twig out of her hair and held it up so Julia could see it. "You've got leaves, too. You need to go change your dress and clean up. What a day."

Maggie started to wiggle, and Audra put her down so the little one could toddle around.

Rafe came back out shaking his head.

"The infection's spread too far."

"We already knew that." But it still hit Julia. Hard. She'd been coiled up tight, bracing herself for the screams. Then nothing. Now this death sentence. She thought of the times she'd walked away from arguments with her father to keep the peace. These days it was for Audra's sake, and Maggie's, but she'd always done it, even as a young girl. Solved her problems by taking long walks. Her feet itched right now to walk away and find just a few minutes of peace — and distance — and loneliness.

She had lived so much of her life alone, she wondered if she'd ever truly be comfortable with people close at hand all the time.

"I hoped there was something . . ." Rafe sounded like he pitied them. Julia didn't like the pity. She'd received a fair amount of it over the years when schoolteachers asked about her parents and neighbors worried over her father being away so much. She'd become more and more guarded about her living situation to avoid that pity. In these circumstances, she understood how Rafe felt, but she couldn't help but want to escape it.

Rafe went on in his gentle tones, completely at odds with his usual take-control bossiness. "I hoped maybe Steele would know some medicine to draw out the poison."

Maggie gave a happy squeal, then ran toward Rafe on wobbly legs and slammed into his knees. Rafe gave her a faint smile, reached down to steady her when she'd have sat down hard. He ran a big hand over the girl's head in a way that made Julia's heart clutch. Had her father ever touched her so gently?

"So you won't even try . . . what you —" Audra cleared her throat — "planned to try?" Her jaw was clenched so tightly, she could barely speak.

"Steele says no. Wouldn't do any good to . . . to . . ." Rafe hoisted Maggie into his arms and was silent for too long. "No sense putting him through it."

Audra closed her eyes and rested a slender hand on her stomach. "I have to go to him. Make sure he's comfortable. Try and pray with him. I'm sorely afraid my husband isn't ready to meet his Maker."

"Julia wasn't real sure when the baby would come. Do you know?" Rafe's question stopped Audra.

Steele came out just as Rafe asked. Julia knew how shy Audra was. She wouldn't want to speak of such things in front of strange men, however kind and helpful they'd been. And she'd already told Rafe enough.

Julia opened her mouth to take over.

"I've got . . . um, a month or . . . well . . . I'm not positive." Pink colored Audra's cheeks. "The usual . . . signs . . ." The pink darkened. "It's hard to judge."

She fell silent, as if speaking exhausted her.

"I wish we could ride out of here." Rafe looked at the trail that led down the mountain to Rawhide. "Wendell's got a horse. We could get you to town, but there's no doctor and no fit place for you to stay. Or we could get you across that creek and come with a wagon most of the way to give you a ride to our ranch."

He looked around as if prepared to take charge of everything.

Julia bristled. "Do we dare to move Father?"

Rafe hesitated.

Steele said, "Moving won't make his condition worse, miss. He can't get much worse."

Audra inhaled suddenly.

"But it will be painful for him." Rafe spoke quickly. Julia suspected he did it to head off tears. "So we'll wait."

Until he dies. Rafe didn't say that out loud,

but Julia got the message.

"I'll get some wood chopped, then haul water. Ethan spotted a man in the woods. He's on his trail. Steele, can you take Wendell's horse down the trail toward Rawhide for just a little ways. Ethan was heading in the right direction to cross the trail. See if you can find him and give him a hand if he needs it."

"Sure, boss." Steele pulled on his gloves.

"If he doesn't turn up soon, we'll have to get serious about hunting him. And I want you back at the ranch soon. I need someone in charge. I may be out here a while."

"I can keep the place running for however long it takes." Steele headed for the horse picketed down the trail on a grassy slope.

Rafe turned to look between Julia and Audra and opened his mouth.

"Are you preparing to give us orders, too?" Julia braced herself. "Maybe you'd like to put the baby to work."

"We'll need an evening meal." His eyes shifted between her and Audra, and she knew he was deciding which one of them to assign that chore to. She couldn't stand it. She just needed a few minutes.

"Audra and I know full well what needs to be done around here." She put enough starch in her words to make sure Rafe knew he wasn't the only one who could give orders. Then she closed the few feet between her and the man who was acting like the crowned king of the Gilliland home.

"But I need a few minutes alone." She cut her gaze to Audra. "I need time. To pray. To walk."

"I'll go along," Rafe said.

"No. Alone, I said. We've got time before I need to start cooking. Just watch Maggie for a few minutes while Audra sits with Father. Then I'll be back to take the baby, tend Father, and see to a meal."

Steele came riding up the trail from the corral with Father's horse. The grizzled old man turned to head downhill again toward Rawhide.

Rafe looked doubtful. Like he was afraid she couldn't *walk* unaided. He pointed to several packs Julia hadn't noticed by the door. "Ethan brought some supplies. I haven't looked at 'em, but Ethan will've brought plenty of food."

Julia set a hand on Audra's back. "Will you be all right for just a little while?"

"Yes, you go. Get away from here. Clear your head. Pray, cry if you can."

Audra knew her so well.

"Did you get any sleep last night?"

"I've already had a nap. I don't need

another." Audra's cheeks, fiery red when she'd talked about her baby being birthed, had faded to milk white, but she looked determined.

"Before I go, I'll get a chair set up in Father's room and you can sit with him." They headed inside. Julia pointedly ignored the tyrant in front of her cabin.

Audra trailed after her. "Maybe he's beyond our help, but he's not beyond God's. I'm going to go care for him with hot water and prayers."

Audra's words were calm, but Julia heard exhaustion. "I won't be gone long." Julia picked up the canvas bags of supplies as they entered the house. Neither of them had taken the news about Father's death very hard. It was a sad testimony to a man's life. She helped get Audra settled in a chair by Father's side and stepped outside to see that stubborn mule of a Kincaid standing in her way.

"I don't like you going off alone, Julia."

"I'll just go along the trail your foreman just came on from the corral. It can't be dangerous. Just, please, Rafe. A few minutes is all I need."

He didn't like it, that was plain as day, but he let her go.

■ ■ ■ ■

He'd been in the dark for so long. How long? A week? A month? He'd gotten so used to it, he'd forgotten there was light.

He moved well in the dark, as if blindness were his natural state. His childhood had prepared him for this cavern.

Touching the scars was a reminder.

Now he spied on Wendell Gilliland's house and watched and waited.

Slipping from rock to rock. Hiding in the shadows, he saw no sign of Gilliland. Better anyway to take one of the women. Hold her until he could force Gilliland to talk. He preferred the redhead. The blonde, far gone with a child, would be too much trouble.

But the redhead would be tough enough to not collapse when he pulled her down into that cavern. He didn't want her hurt. He just needed her to get Gilliland's cooperation.

He crawled up, over the lip of a ledge near the corral to see the redhead walk straight for the place he hid. He slid his gun out. One blow to the head and she'd be silent. He'd take her away, hide her in the dark.

She strode along, dressed in green, which made her hair seem vividly red by contrast. He crouched, ready to spring. She got closer and he heard her muttering. Then closer still, and he heard prayer.

"Hold my father in the palm of your hand. Save his soul, Lord. Bless him, forgive him."

He coiled to lunge, but . . . he couldn't. It was as if her words were ice and they froze him, crouched low, like he was cringing before God.

He tried to focus his strength, break through the ice. She rushed by, and he shook free of that unnatural stillness and could move again.

"Julia, wait!" Rafe picked up his pace, determined to catch her before she hiked all the way to California.

Julia stopped and turned. She planted her hands on her hips and scowled at him.

Something shifted behind a pile of man-sized rocks, and Rafe stopped to look in that direction. He had his gun in his hand before he was even sure what he'd seen, if anything.

He kept his eyes on the rocks but talked to Julia. "Get back here. I don't want you out alone."

"I just needed a few minutes of peace and quiet, Rafe." She crossed her arms and tapped the toe of her little boot fast and loud. "Are you planning to shoot me if I don't obey you?"

He had to fight back a grin as he holstered

his gun and walked to meet her. "Now, don't be upset. I didn't know you were going to go so far from the cabin. If you need to walk, let me come with you. I promise to be quiet."

The noise Julia made was pure rudeness. Rafe grinned. Which was a mistake.

"I said I wanted to be alone."

"So I'll walk a few paces back."

"Go away."

"No." They stared at each other for far too long.

Rafe had no idea what she was thinking. Dismemberment probably.

Suddenly, she relaxed from that defiant stance and walked toward him.

She drew even with him and would have walked past, but Rafe's hand shot out, almost against his will.

Their eyes met, and Rafe saw so much. Grief. Anger. Confusion. Strength.

"I just needed to ask God to give my father a chance for salvation. I know I can't judge a man. But it's impossible to look at my father's life and not fear the worst. It's a terrible thing to fear that your father might not make it through the Pearly Gates."

"In the end that's his choice. God gives us all a chance."

"I know. And I know my father's had

183

plenty of chances because I've talked with him myself. We had an ongoing tussle over Sunday services at our home. I usually just went outside and spent time with God alone."

"Like you're doing now?"

Julia nodded.

"I can't let you stay out here when there might be trouble around. So I'll walk with you, or you can come back and sit apart from us but well within my reach." Rafe looked at those big rocks and frowned. "I don't like it out here. I don't like the feel. I don't see anyone around, so it's probably just eating at me that Ethan saw someone. Probably the man in that cavern with you, but he wouldn't have come this way if he knew Ethan was on his trail. But it don't matter if the itch I feel is real or imagined, I'm not leaving you alone."

Glaring at him, she seemed to gauge her chances of winning a fight. She must've gauged it right, because she folded without any more bickering. "Fine. Let's go back. I've said to God what I needed to say. Any answers will be between Him and my father, anyway."

Rafe reached out, and after a moment's hesitation, she slipped her hand into his.

"When are you going to take me back

down into the cavern, Rafe? You promised. Don't even pretend I'm going to forget." They walked back together.

"Soon, Julia. Now's not the time."

"Why not?" She tugged on his hand, not to be free but to draw his attention. Well, he didn't mind looking at her one bit. "We could get away for an hour or two, you know that. Leave Ethan with Audra and the baby. Ethan could promise to check on us after a while in case something happened to the ladder."

"We'll see. Maybe we can do it tomorrow. Now quit asking me questions. I thought you wanted quiet." Rafe looked back over his shoulder and wished he could be sure it was just an overactive imagination that had drawn his attention to those rocks.

"I wanted to be *alone.* That's different." She turned her cute little nose up as if to prove to him she wouldn't say another word.

He seriously doubted she could sustain that.

She seemed determined to pretend he didn't exist. Rafe kept quiet, but he sure couldn't forget she was there.

They were planning to go back to the cavern.

He'd have to wait and take her in the dark. She would come. Her determination was

185

clear. It was only when he made that decision that he realized how badly he wanted to go back into the darkness.

The couple moved out of sight, and he slipped over the ledge and slid away. He wanted to be back underground. It felt like home there. He could force Gilliland to admit where he'd hidden the money if he wanted to see his daughter alive again.

He rushed for his dark home in the nether-world and felt his spirits — evil spirits, he re-alized — burn with excitement. Burn as hot as Hades.

CHAPTER 9

Living with Julia was a little like being a child again with a bossy mother. Audra loved her stepdaughter dearly, but there was no denying who was in charge.

When Julia came back from her walk, she checked on Audra, who was sitting down, the baby on her lap.

Julia cocked her head as she studied Audra, as if trying to decide if Audra was tough enough to have a toddler sit in her lap. "Has he spoken to you?"

"No. He's stirred a few times, and muttered, but he's never opened his eyes or responded when I talked to him."

"I'll get supper on. You stay with him. Give me Maggie."

"No, go on." Audra thought she sounded quite stern. "I'll keep her. She's fine with me."

It hadn't taken Audra long to learn their lives were more peaceful if Audra did as she was told. So Audra did the few chores she could get to before Julia forbade it and otherwise minded her . . . daughter.

It pinched.

Now, she sat by her husband. Her dying husband. Her husband who would not leave a single person behind to grieve.

He was sleeping, or unconscious. Audra glanced over her shoulder to make sure Julia wasn't watching, then scooted off the chair to kneel at his side, urging Maggie to sit on the floor beside a basin of clean, cool water. Wendell's shirt was off and a blanket covered most of him. But his arm with its small ugly wound was uncovered, red and swollen. Audra saw nothing she could do for that, so she bathed his forehead.

At the first touch of the cold rag, he tossed his head and muttered, "Stop . . . go away."

Leaning forward, she pressed the cloth to his brow and cheeks. "Wendell, you're very sick. We need to get your fever down."

Wendell's eyes fluttered open. They looked glazed and seemed to have a film over them.

Bending toward him, she twisted so she could look him in the eye. "Wendell, I'm sorry you're so sick."

She meant it. She had no affection or respect for the man, but he'd given her Maggie, and Julia. He'd given her life meaning whether he'd intended to or not.

Remembering her hasty wedding turned her thoughts to Carolyn. Audra's little sister was too young for a husband right now, but her father might well have new gambling debts building up. Audra had to find a way to save Carolyn from a husband of Father's choosing.

Looking down at her husband, she felt guilty for her uncharitable thoughts. She wanted him to *change,* not die.

"Pray with me, Wendell." Audra set the rag in the basin and moved the water to her right so Maggie couldn't reach in and splash. Taking Wendell's right hand in hers, she said, "You are very sick. We need to pray. That's the only hope we have. We need a miracle to stop this infection."

"My arm hurts." He tugged against her hold, but she hung on, and only because of the pain, he didn't fight her.

"You've got a cut. It's infected." Audra was careful not to move his arm.

"Just a scratch. Scratched it on a nail at work. Nothing. Need to be up."

"Pray with me, please. We'll pray for healing and we'll pray for your soul, Wendell." She braced herself for the cruel words she feared would come. "If we don't get a miracle, you'll be facing your Maker very soon. You need to make your peace with God."

"Struck it rich. Hid it. A fortune."

Startled, Audra leaned forward. "What about a fortune?" Then she realized what was really important. "We'll talk about that later. First we need to —"

"No one'll find it. No one. Not my stubborn daughter. Not my stupid wife." Wendell laughed, weak and rusty but with a satisfied air. "Stuffed it in deep. Deep and dark."

"Hush about the money. If you want to tell me about it, we'll do it later." She hoped they had *later*.

"I'm not telling you where it is. I put it in a hole. No one'll find it." Wendell fumbled for his shirt pocket, and found no shirt. "Where're my cigars?"

"Let's pray." Audra moved one of her hands so she could hold both of his.

Maggie sat quietly in the corner, chewing on the hem of her little dress. The little one sitting quietly was a miracle in itself.

"Need my cigar case. Where is it?" Wendell's eyelids drooped as if they were too heavy to keep open.

Audra felt tension in his grasp, so she hoped he was still awake. She prayed aloud for him, hoping God could soften this hard-hearted man.

She stayed with him, in prayer. She thought his lips moved with hers a few times and prayed fervently that God would reach the stony soil of Wendell's soul. Finally his hands went slack and he slipped into unconsciousness.

Audra stood, her knees aching. A wave of dizziness swamped her. For a moment Audra thought she might lose the contents of her belly. She sat in her chair to let her head clear, and just as her stomach began to settle, something else hit her. Pain. A solid wall of pain that tightened across her belly. She'd felt it a few times before. Once when Maggie was born. Several times with this child.

But it would stop if Audra would just stay quiet. It always had.

Maggie got up from her quiet play and came the few steps to Audra. The little one slapped at Audra's lap. "Up!" She reached her arms for Audra in such a sweet, loving way, Audra nearly cried with the pleasure of it. "Up, mamamama."

It might not be Mama, but then again it might. Maggie made that same sound for a lot of things. But one of these times, someone was going to have to admit Maggie could say *Mama*. The tension left her stomach and, wondering if she should exert herself even this much, she pulled Maggie onto her lap.

It was mealtime for Maggie, so Audra took the moment of privacy as an opportunity to nurse her. The pains came again several times while Audra sat feeding Maggie, but they eased off and Maggie finished, and Audra hoped it meant things were fine again.

When Audra was sure she could stand, she rose to go help Julia, knowing Julia wouldn't let her do a thing.

She felt useless and protected and loved. A strange combination.

When she entered the front room, Julia looked up from a steaming pot and smiled.

"Rafe brought in four rabbits. We'll have fresh meat tonight."

Julia set aside the potatoes she was cutting into chunks to stew with the rabbit. She saw Audra's wan face and rushed into her father's room, got the chair, brought it out and sat it beside the table. That was all the furniture they owned. Nails on the wall to hang the single dress each of them owned, to be taken down and replaced by their nightgowns. A makeshift table created by jamming split logs into cracks in cabin walls.

"Here, give me Maggie." Julia took the little sweetheart and eased Audra down. She felt Audra's shoulder tremble. This life was too much for her fragile stepmother.

"That rag I tore up this morning was an old skirt of yours, but the shirtwaist that matched it is still in the ragbag. You need to change your shirt and wash up, Julia. You're a mess." Audra smiled to take the sting out of that rather rude opinion.

Though Julia knew it was no opinion but rather the absolute truth.

"I'll clean up as soon as the stew is on. I'll be a while washing up and getting a comb through my hair." Julia was made of sterner stuff by far than Audra. She'd moved many times, beginning soon after her mother had died. She knew how to make the most of the three carpetbags and two wooden crates she and Father could carry.

A skillet, a pot, plates and a spatula, a few tin cups, staples from the cupboard, blankets. And of course her precious few books, papers and ink, and the magazines she loved. Julia knew some might call those frivolous, but she refused to part with her books and her copies of the *Proceedings.* Her father had bought them for her. Those books and Father's help mailing off her articles were the only ways he showed any kindness to her. They meant more to her than simply something to read and study. She'd often thought that if she could get one of her articles published, her father would be really proud.

She'd learned to be ruthlessly practical during a move. But she couldn't bear to give up the books and the few tools she had for her exploration.

"I can hold her, Julia. You can't cut up vegetables with a baby in your arms."

Julia smiled. "That's about the only thing I can't do. Let's let her run a bit. I can block her from the fireplace."

Audra nodded and gave Julia a grateful smile. "Okay. I just have a bit of an . . . an . . . uh . . . upset stomach. You do so much for me, Julia. Thank you."

"I've had some practice." Julia set Maggie down on the floor. "Now, you be careful of the fire." She tweaked the little sweetheart's cute chin and went back to preparing the stew.

When the stew was assembled and needed only time to get tender, she rushed into her room and changed into a clean, if faded and worn, shirtwaist that clashed with her skirt.

She washed a bit. The water from bathing

her face and neck and hair was pink, tinged with blood. She struggled to tidy her hair for a few moments, but worry about Maggie and the fire and poor tired Audra had her doing a poor job of taming it.

When she returned to the kitchen she found the rabbit was simmering nicely. She'd made a huge pot and planned to dish up some for Audra as soon as the vegetables were tender. A little tough rabbit wouldn't do any harm. Then she'd skim off some broth and try to coax her father into eating. Then she'd see if Rafe was ready to eat. If there was time, she'd take Maggie outside and let her run a bit. Then she'd —

The door swung open, and Ethan Kincaid entered. Julia had forgotten about him.

"How's Wendell?" His attention was all for Audra.

And why not? She was the one who needed attention. Maggie made a break for the door.

"He's sleeping." Audra rose from her chair, steadied herself by gripping the back, then headed for Maggie.

Maggie saw her coming, squealed and toddled faster, laughing. She loved the game of *chase me.* Ethan scooped her up, and Maggie giggled and hugged his neck. Ethan looked down at the baby with a disconcerted expression. "Go 'head and sit down. I've got her."

Audra narrowed her eyes in a way Julia didn't understand. She almost looked angry, but why? The woman needed help. She should be relieved and grateful.

"Did you find that man?" Julia thought of being stranded in the pit. The fear combined with the lure of that cavern was almost maddening.

"No. I never caught up to him. I followed him until he hit a stretch so rocky I couldn't pick up the trail after that."

Rafe came up behind her. "Could he have been heading for Rawhide?"

"Maybe. But it was . . . odd before that."

"Odd?"

"Well, the way he wandered, it was odd."

"Odd how?" Julia gripped Rafe's arm tighter. "Odd like . . . crazy?"

"No." Ethan frowned at her. "What makes you say that?"

"Moving that rope, well, whoever did it knew I was down there. But a regular person, an unprincipled one, might take a chance like that to rob someone or even kill . . ." Julia shuddered.

Audra gasped.

Forging on, Julia said, "But just moving the rope, there was no point to it." She whirled back to the fireplace, poked a carrot with a fork, and decided it was tender enough for a bowl of soup for everyone. The meat wouldn't be tender, the vegetables still a little on the crisp side, but it was still tasty. The smell of it made Julia's mouth water. Father always brought enough food, but none of it was very good.

"Tell me what made this guy odd, Eth." Rafe's voice turned Julia from her cook pot to hear what Ethan had to say.

"Well, he went in circles a few places."

"Maybe trying to lose you," Rafe suggested.

Julia stuck a fork in a potato.

"I don't think so. The movement was more random than that. I don't think he knew I was trailing him."

"You sure you were following one man?" Rafe's brow lowered.

"Yes, I'm sure. I'd've told you if I wasn't. I'm better on a trail than you, Rafe."

"No you're not."

Ethan grinned.

Julia remembered how the brothers had clashed and knew there was no humor behind that smile.

Rafe looked at the tippy table Julia had contrived.

Julia saw him judging her home harshly,

but he didn't say anything. He just shook his head and leaned against the wall. Julia hoped he didn't fall through it and bring the roof down on their heads.

She might be judging her home harshly, too.

"I met up with Steele. He already crossed the stream and is headed back to the ranch. He said he'd ride around, going across the ford we take to Rawhide and bringing some horses to corral over here. He'll have more supplies, too."

Julia hoped the ranch foreman didn't get back at mealtime. They didn't have a bowl for him. "It's been a long day. Let's eat this soup."

Ethan, Rafe, and Audra could eat while she used a cup to feed Father. Then she'd wash dishes and eat herself. She was starving. Except for the bread last night at Rafe's house, she'd yet to eat since being trapped in the cavern.

"I made a big pot thanks to your hunting, Rafe." She began scooping, using a tin cup for a ladle.

"How's Wendell?" Rafe quit leaning and came the whole five paces across the room to take the bowl from her hands.

"Careful, it's hot."

Rafe moved fast, setting it down on the

table. "Told me that a little late."

"Father is mostly asleep. His fever is steady, no sign of it going down." Savory steam curled up from the pot as she pushed a towel into his hands and filled the next bowl. "I'm going to see if I can get him to take some broth. You three go ahead and eat."

"We'll wait for you." He took the third and last bowl they owned.

"No, go ahead." She turned to skimming liquid off the pot for Father. She used one cup, poured into another, because the edges of her ladle-cup were messy.

"We'll wait."

Glaring at him, she felt embarrassed to admit the truth. "We've only got three bowls. Eat now. I'll have to wait anyway or eat out of a cup."

Rafe looked around the tiny cabin. He muttered, "I have to get you out of here."

Julia slammed both cups she held down on the table. "*You* have to get me out of here? You have nothing to say about where I go and what I do, Rafe Kincaid."

Maggie whimpered in Ethan's arms. Audra sat up straight, as stiff as one of Julia's fossils.

"I have as much to say as any decent man. I'm not leaving you here with precious little food, a cabin that barely slows down the wind, and a lunatic climbing around in the treetops."

When he put it like that, her whole life sounded as bad as her cabin.

Julia didn't bother to argue. She didn't want to upset Audra or Maggie. She clamped her mouth tight shut and picked up Father's cup and a spoon. At least they had four spoons so the others could eat.

"We'll discuss this after I've seen if Father can take any nourishment. Please eat so I'll be able to when I get back." She swished around Rafe, conscious of her messy hair. But she needed more time to deal with it. Maybe after everyone went to bed tonight.

She entered her father's room and saw him sleeping. With a prayer, she knelt by his side.

CHAPTER 10

Rafe and Ethan slept outside, to guard the front door, and the next morning they did every chore they could think of short of building a new cabin. Rafe waited until Julia had finished her midday meal and Audra and Maggie settled for a nap. Through cracks in the cabin wall, Rafe saw Steele ride up. Ethan went out, and the two of them unloaded the pack animals, then led the horses away to graze.

When Julia finished tending her pa, Rafe said, "Come outside."

Julia followed quietly. Rafe enjoyed this moment of obedience, knowing it was only because of the sleeping baby.

"I'm going to ride out to the west this afternoon. Come with me."

"No, I need to stay close in case Maggie cries."

"So you can snatch her out of the room so Audra can sleep the afternoon away."

"And so if Father wakes up, I can check on him and try to get some food into him."

"If Maggie or your pa wakes up, Audra can tend to them." As much as he didn't care for Julia's bossy ways, he'd learned that she felt the need to protect and care for everyone else, leaving herself for last.

"Then can we go down into the cavern today?" Her eyes flashed with excitement.

"No."

"You said we could go back down into the cavern." She jammed her fists on her hips, her excitement replaced by temper. "When are we going to do that?"

Rafe thought she was about the prettiest little thing he'd ever seen. "After we catch whoever stranded you down there."

"You said we could go." Her green eyes flashed. "Ethan could guard the entrance. Steele could stay here and guard Audra. We'd be fine."

"We're not going down there until we find that man."

"I'll stay here, then." She crossed her arms, a pretty picture of pure female stubbornness.

Steele and Ethan came walking up to the house. Steele gave Rafe a quick report on how things were going on the Kincaid spread. Rafe had a ranch to run. He really

202

couldn't stay over here much longer.

"I saw tracks on my ride over. A man's footprints, no horse. Could be the same guy Ethan was tracking." Steele gave Rafe the details.

"I want to have a look at those tracks." He leaned close to Julia. "And I need to have a word with you about all this in private. I don't want Audra to overhear."

He didn't particularly care if Audra overheard, but it was the kind of thing that would make Julia cooperate. She gave a short, hard jerk of her chin in agreement. Before she could think of some new way to be stubborn, he grabbed her by the hand and led her to the horses. It took the work of a few minutes to strap leather on two of them and toss her into the saddle. When she didn't slap him, he figured he'd won. He mounted up and they rode away.

Rafe set a fast pace in the direction Steele had seen the tracks. The time to talk to her would come when they were far enough from her cabin that she wouldn't just turn around and go back.

They skirted the ledge to the west of the house and wound down a mountain trail. There was some open space at the bottom. A trail curved along the base of a massive flat-topped mountain higher than the one they'd just descended, and Rafe thought to follow that a mile or so to the point it split west to Rawhide and northeast toward home.

Before he'd gotten far down the trail, and before he'd even started the serious talk he needed to have with Julia, he saw the first footprints.

"What's wrong?" Julia came up beside him. Rafe was impressed at how quickly she'd caught on to trouble.

Pointing, he said, "A track right next to that talus slide." The slide had spilled down the side of the mountain Rafe had planned to ride around. But the footprint was climbing right up the slope.

"Someone walked up that?" Julia looked doubtful. "Wouldn't the footing on a slide like that give?"

"It could. I wouldn't've thought of going that way if I hadn't seen that track." He looked up to the top of the slide and saw a black slit in the mountain. He couldn't tell if it was dark-colored rock, a shadow, or a cave big enough to hide a man. "Let's see what's up there."

Rafe couldn't imagine anyone going up that way, but according to Ethan, they were dealing with a crazy man. Rafe swung off his horse and took a mighty careful step onto those shattered rocks.

They were as solid as . . . well, as solid as a rock. "I think these will hold. Lead your horse. Move easy." He took a step toward Julia to help her down but didn't get there before she was already on the ground. His fingers itched as he realized how much he'd been looking forward to getting his hands on her.

They really did need to have a talk. Rafe had some plans for the future concerning her and her little family.

"I've climbed a few talus slides in my day." Julia fell in behind Rafe. The hooves clopped with a hollow sound as they scaled the slope. "If they're old enough, they're very safe. Looks like these are old."

"The rocks work almost like stair steps. They're easier to climb than if the side of this mountain was clear." The stones didn't slide or give a bit. They were packed together and worked into the ground beneath them. He climbed, alert and cautious, expecting any minute to feel the ground give under his feet. When he reached the top of the slide, the first thing he saw was a level trail leading into a black slit. It seemed to be a passageway into the heart of the mountain.

"Another cave." Julia sounded so excited,

Rafe prepared himself to lasso her and haul her home over his saddle.

Then he saw footprints.

He drew his gun and cracked back the hammer.

Julia came up to his side, her eyes wide. "What?"

"Someone's in there." Rafe eyed the ground. There were tracks going in only. Boots distinctive enough he was sure it was just one man. And the prints looked fresh. "I need to get you out of here."

"You think that's the man who left me in the cavern to die, don't you?"

"Could be." Rafe tore his eyes away from the ground and looked at Julia. She was mad clean through, no sign of fear. "These are the prints of the man we tracked yesterday."

"Let's go have a talk with him." Julia urged her horse forward so suddenly, Rafe didn't have a chance to stop her.

He caught up just as she entered the cave. "Wait a minute." He grabbed her wrist. "You need to get out of here. Let's go back to your place. You stay there with Steele and I'll come back with Ethan."

He'd wanted to see the tracks, but mostly he'd wanted to get Julia off by herself. Women could surely mess with a man's ability to control a situation.

Julia shook her head. "We may have this one chance to corner him in this cave and put a stop to him running around hurting people. We don't dare take an hour to ride back to my cabin, and you know it."

Rafe did know it.

"At least let me lead the way." He let go and surged ahead. The cave was too narrow for them to walk two abreast.

"Why, so you can take the first bullet?" She was sounding stubborn again.

"No, so the one with the gun — me — can defend the one without the gun." And also so he could take the first bullet. But he was smart enough not to admit that. "How am I supposed to shoot back if you're between me and the lunatic?"

Julia shrugged one shoulder. "I guess that makes some sense."

"Let's keep the horse between us and anyone who's in there."

"I wonder how deep this cave goes into the mountain." Julia sounded like she was lagging.

"Keep quiet. We need to sneak up on whoever's in here." Rafe looked over his stallion's shoulder.

Julia had stopped and was running her hand over the wall. "This looks like a vent for a volcanic flow of lava."

"What? I've heard of a volcano. They're a lot hotter than this."

"Yes, if they're active. But this may be an old one that hasn't blown for a while." Julia gasped so loud it echoed in the tunnel. "Wait a minute. This is a fossil."

Rafe moved toward his horse's back end, running a soothing hand on its chestnut rump. The animal wasn't that happy to be walking into this cave, and Rafe didn't want to earn a kick from iron-shod hooves.

"Jules, we need to keep moving. If this is anything like that cavern back by your cabin, someone could be hiding in any one of a hundred places. We need to keep our attention focused on finding the man we're trailing."

She ignored him like he was a buzzing gnat. Pulling a knife out of her skirt, she used the tip of it to pry on the wall.

"What are you doing?"

"This is a bone. Look at this. It looks like maybe a jawbone" — she leaned so close, her nose almost touched the wall — "with a fang of some kind attached to the jaw. A large sort of triangular tooth."

"So you found a long-dead wolf. So what? We need to pay attention."

"No, maybe not a fang. Rafe, this looks

like something I found in Seth's Cavern. I think this might be a fish, too."

"More lunch?"

Julia turned and glared at him. "This is no trout."

"I've seen some pretty big ones."

"Hmmph." She turned her back on him and began chiseling with more energy. "If this is an old vent for a volcano, we could find some perfectly preserved fossils in here. I've done extensive studying on fossils and this doesn't look familiar." She looked up, a smile so bright on her face that Rafe hated to insist she use the brain God gave her.

"Have you ever heard of *dinosauria?*"

"What?"

"The writings of Sir Richard Owens contain reference to many creatures, now extinct. He called them 'dinosauria.' There are people doing research on them all over the world. If I could discover a new species, they might even name it after me." Julia looked away from her chiseling, and even in the dim light of the cave, Rafe could see her excitement, and maybe just a touch of fanaticism. Well, as fanatics went, liking old bones wasn't such a bad thing.

Unless people were apt to start shooting at you.

"If he named them, why didn't he name

them Owensauria, instead of dinosauria?"

"Because dinosauria means *terrible lizard.*" Julia went back to chiseling as if he hadn't spoken a word.

"Okay, then we should name this Terrible Trout." Rafe leaned closer. "That tooth looks more like a pig tusk. Terrible Pig, what word would that be in geologist talk? Wait, you want it named after you. So, Julia the Terrible Pig." Rafe was going to have to drag the stubborn little thing away from her wall. "Does that sound like a good idea to you?"

"Look at the size of this fang . . . tusk . . . tooth. Oh, I need to study this. I have to refer to my books. And there are several articles in my copies of the *Proceedings Quarterly.* I can read about — Rafe! Oh, Rafe, look!" The tap and scrape of a knife on rock echoed throughout the whole cave, like she was begging someone to come find her and shoot her. But just in case it wasn't enough, now she'd gone to yelling. "The jaw. It could definitely be another fish. Up this high. Do you realize what this means?"

No. But he didn't say so out loud.

"Look, I can see part of it. I think I can get it out in one piece if I —"

"Leave it for now." He hissed the words and heard them echo. "Julia, *come on.* We need to stay on our guard."

"Yes, yes. Coming." She chipped away at the stone. Bits of rock spit out from the wall.

She was absolutely *not* coming.

"Just give me one more second. I wish I had my mallet and chisel."

"I thought you had to pack fast because your pa decided to move suddenly."

"I did." She kept tapping away.

"But you brought copies of fossil books and a chisel?" Anyone with a lick of sense would have grabbed another dress or a few more bowls, or maybe a chair.

"This knife isn't enough. I need my tools."

Rafe's jaw tightened, and he clenched his fists to keep from dragging her away. "It will still be there later. It's obviously been there for a long time. Let's —"

"Here's where the fang attaches to the jaw. I've never seen anything like this before." Then suddenly Julia gasped, quit with her knife and stepped back.

Rafe went for his gun. "What is it?"

"I was too close." She was still looking at the stupid pig or fish or lizard or whatever it was. It looked like part of the rock. "I can see more of it. We need lanterns. If only I was a hand at drawing a sketch."

"That does it."

"Then I could — Ah!"

Rafe grabbed her and dragged. "We don't have time to dig up a whole animal right now."

Julia looked at him, fuming. With a huge effort, she nodded. "You're right, of course." The longing glance over her shoulder almost made him smile. "It's just . . . that's not like any bone I've ever seen before. It's definitely not a pig. From the shape of the little bit of jaw, I think it might be —"

"Julia, let's *go*."

"I have so much research to do in the other cavern. And now this one might —"

"We'll come back, I promise." Rafe regretted saying that the minute it came out of his mouth. "But for now, we've got to pay attention. There's a curve up ahead." He leaned to speak into her ear. "We've got to assume he can hear us since you've been yelling your head off. Let me go ahead until I can see around that bend."

Julia swallowed, sneaked a peek at her fish-pig, and nodded.

"You hold the horses. And keep your attention on this *cave.* You want to live long enough to dig your *Julia-pig-osauria* out of the wall don't you?" He gave her the reins. Maybe it'd make her feel useful. He eased his back against the wall, his gun pointed toward the cavern roof and — one sideways step at a time, his eyes wide open for trouble — looked around the corner to find . . . another corner. He looked back to see Julia coming. She hadn't minded him about waiting, but at least she hadn't gone back to chiseling.

Thank you, Lord God.

He kept moving, feeling like he was walking right into the belly of the mountain. At least here it felt like he was walking in through the wall of the belly, instead of sliding down the beast's throat like the cavern on Kincaid land.

They left sunlight behind, and Rafe wished for a lantern, although it might have revealed more bones and that would've slowed them down. He couldn't see well enough to be sure if the tunnel divided. He prayed as he moved that, in the darkness, he wasn't missing someone hiding.

Julia came steadily behind with the horses. The tunnel was wide enough for the horses to walk single file with their heads up, but that was about the limit of the space. Rafe hoped it didn't narrow. When he went around about the fifth curve, he saw the tunnel grow lighter ahead. Blinking in disbelief, he kept moving. The tunnel was visible again, the walls smooth and solid with nowhere for anyone to hide.

Rafe rounded yet another bend and blinked at . . . sunlight.

An exit.

Had they curved around so much they'd gotten back to where they'd started?

When he reached the mouth of the cave, he stopped, stunned.

Julia came up behind him. "What is this place?"

The cave opened to a valley, the likes of which he'd never seen before. A valley so lush, his heart hammered in his chest.

Rafe clamped his mouth shut, aware it had gaped open. "It's beautiful."

They were standing in a bowl. A massive bowl created by a huge scoop taken out of the top of a mountain. He could see for miles across waving grass and stands of stately oaks. Spinning and quaking in the wind, aspens climbed the walls that closed around the valley. Water splashed out of cracks in several places, cascading down, running together, forming a brisk creek that cut across one corner of the place.

"It's a caldera."

The strange word gained Rafe's attention. "A caldron?"

"Caldera. This mountain was a volcano. When all the lava spits out, sometimes the top of the mountain sinks and forms a bowl like this."

They were standing about halfway up the side of that bowl. "And the tunnel we just passed through was a . . . did you call it a vent?"

"Yes, I'm sure that's what formed it. The lava flow goes out the top of a volcano, but sometimes the pressure explodes a hole, or maybe many holes, in the sides of the mountain, to let lava escape. When the volcano is spent, everything cools."

"Where did you learn all this stuff?"

"I told you I study geology."

She had said that. He needed to start listening to her better.

"I study land and plants and animals. I subscribe to scientific journals when it's possible to get mail. I particularly like the *Proceedings*. It's a quarterly journal from the American Philosophical Society."

He'd start listening later. Right now she was really boring.

"Ben Franklin founded it. One of them contained information about dead volcanoes. Christian Leopold Von Buch, a paleontologist, wrote that —"

"Okay, okay, we'll talk about Ben Franklin and Leopold later. For now we need to remember that someone else is in this caldron."

"Caldera."

"Whatever. Keep your eyes open for trouble." Could someone live here? Was he so intent on believing the footprint belonged to the man who'd abandoned Julia to her fate in that cavern that he'd ignored the simple possibility that someone lived in this bowl? He could surely understand if someone found it, they'd like to stay. He'd like to stay. The Kincaid spread was covered with trees with occasional open meadows. But this was a beautiful expanse of lush grazing.

"I'm going to step out slowly," Rafe whispered. "There are places a man could lie in wait."

She leaned forward so she was pressed against his back, and whispered in his ear, "Be careful."

Rafe was momentarily distracted from life and death by the feel of Julia and the tingle in his ear. Very distracted. He shook his head. "Give me the horse. I'll use him as a shield."

He patted his stallion on the shoulder in apology. He liked this horse better than most people he knew and hoped very sincerely he didn't need the old boy as a shield.

Rafe stepped out.

There was no gunfire. He looked around and saw no one lying in wait.

An eagle screamed overhead, and though it distracted from his normal caution, he couldn't stop himself from looking up. The eagle soared down into the bowl of this canyon and skimmed the gushing stream at the far end, rising up with a fish in its talons. "Fish in that water. Where did they come from up here?"

"It's possible that after the volcano cooled —"

"Shh." Why wasn't he surprised that she had something to say about everything?

A sudden movement brought his gun around, and a doe and two spring fawns darted out of a copse of trees on the far side of the caldron. The threesome ran across a stretch of the belly-high grass. A soft summer wind made the grass nod and dance and ripple like waves on an ocean of green water. It rustled through the trees as if God himself was running a loving hand over this hidden mountain meadow. It was possibly the most beautiful place Rafe had ever seen.

And that's when he realized that, without hardly being aware of it, he'd been forming a new vision for his life from the moment he stepped out of the cave. He thought of Ethan and his resentment. How Ethan didn't feel like the Kincaid Ranch belonged even in part to him.

This valley could solve that problem. As that vision came into focus, it warmed him, a warmth that seemed to have its source in the way Julia had pressed against him when she'd told him to be careful.

He didn't want to be warm inside. He didn't want to thaw. It frightened him to remember the terror, the helplessness, the lack of control he'd felt when Seth had been hurt. He never wanted to feel that way again.

Rafe decided right then he'd marry Julia. It was a commonsense thing to do.

He could marry her, care for and protect her. Staring at this valley changed his vision of the future. Then that hand God ran across the grass seemed to brush across him, too. It eased his fears, gave him courage to face his weaknesses without the ice in his veins. He breathed deeply of the cool, thin air, and his lungs felt stronger, his thoughts clearer, his faith purer.

Ethan could have the Kincaid Ranch. Rafe would stake a claim to this mountain. They'd find Seth and get him back home, and he could buy up the land in between the two places and the Kincaids would control a vast stretch of this rugged, mountainous land.

But first he had to find the man who had endangered Julia in that cavern.

"Do you see anyone?" Julia came up behind him and whispered again. He really liked it when she whispered.

Turning to her, Rafe smiled. "You were supposed to wait inside the cave."

He had a feeling she'd never mind him worth a lick.

Well, he had a whole herd of longhorns that acted just like that, and he'd learned to handle them, hadn't he? Life wouldn't be boring.

"I waited quite a while. You're just standing out here looking around." Then another eagle dipped down to the rushing stream and she gasped. "It's beautiful. The grass goes on forever."

Rafe pointed at a spot beside a nice stand of trees far enough to the center of the bowl edge to give a house a full day of sunlight, despite the edges of the caldron. "I think I'll build a house right there." He shifted restlessly as he thought of Julia in that house, with a baby or two or three gathered around her knees. He thought about holding her and being warm in her arms and he wanted it all to be true right now.

"Don't you already have a house?"

Rafe slipped one arm around her waist,

and after one last careful check for danger, he lowered his head and kissed her.

"Rafe." She pressed the flat of her hand against his chest. "What are you doing?" She turned her head aside.

"You're right. Now's a bad time." He caught the back of her head in one hand, turned her back and kissed her again, longer. Then he eased back on his own, without her mentioning he should.

"Behave yourself while I take a look around." He found he liked scolding her. Even more, he liked kissing her to quiet her yapping mouth. If she was obedient, he'd never have a chance to do that, now, would he?

He noticed she wasn't looking at anything but his lips, and when she looked up finally, she seemed a bit dazed.

To get her head to working again, he said, "Someone came in. But no tracks go back out. Which means he could be here. Of course there could be other vents. Let's see if we can pick up his trail. Stay between the horses, Jules. Be careful."

She blinked at him and shook her head as if to clear it. "Stop calling me Jules." She glared at him, then wrecked the sternness by glancing at his lips.

"You make me think of jewels. Ruby red

hair, shining emerald eyes, pearl white skin. Everything about you is colorful and pretty in a rare way. Just like jewels."

His gaze locked with hers and he couldn't look away. Finally a gust of wind snapped him out of the daze, and he looked down. Footprints.

"Let's go." How could he lower his guard for even a minute? He looked down the slope and saw a single trail heading into the valley.

A chill tingled up Rafe's arms and shoulders as he mentally chided himself for allowing the beauty of this place, and his interest in Julia, to distract him. He welcomed the cold because he could think better.

"Pay attention. And stay between the horses." He didn't look back, because that's what had gotten him in trouble before. The descent into the meadow was easy. It went down about fifty feet before grass began to grow and the ground leveled.

Rafe kept the horse between him and any area that provided cover. A clump of aspens was the only place within firing range. They were walking in waist-high grass, and Rafe knew well that anyone could be ducked down just waiting. He'd played this game with his brothers enough times.

He paid close attention to the grass, those aspens, and his horse. His horse would warn him before Rafe noticed anything.

He forgot everything but caution, watchfulness, and ice-cold control.

CHAPTER 11

Julia watched him walk away. The big dumb ox had already forgotten all about kissing her.

So she would return the favor and forget about everything but that fossil.

She peeked over her shoulder. Imagine. She'd thought the cavern she got stuck in would take her a lifetime to research and write about. Now she found something else. It was a wonderful land.

She tried to quiet the pulse of pride that getting published would give her. No *Julia-pig-osauria,* but maybe the Gilliland Cavern.

She only followed Rafe because the horse sort of dragged her downhill.

Her whole attention was back on that fish fossil. She didn't fully realize that until she walked into Rafe's back.

"Hey, be careful." He gave her a disgruntled look, and she noticed he had his gun drawn.

"What's the matter? Did you see some-one?" Julia gave herself a mental shake. She really should be looking around for slink-ing, rope-moving, tree-climbing lunatics, even if she would rather be riding for home to fetch her chisel.

"Stay between the horses."

Looking to her right, she saw nothing but the steeply sloped side to this bowl. That was when she realized there could be other vents, other fossils. Suddenly she was very alert looking for cave entrances on the slope. More places to explore! If that helped her spot a lunatic, all the better.

As they reached the first clump of aspens, Rafe moved into them and looked around in all directions. "There's a trail here that leads straight to the water. I can see where this grass has been bent."

Julia looked at the grass. It just looked like grass to her. No bending except that it swayed in the wind.

She turned to study the trail they'd just come down and spotted a darkened area behind her, mostly concealed by aspens, below and off to the south of the cave they'd just come through.

"Rafe, look, behind the trees. Another cave." Julia pointed to the barely visible opening. "We need to go look."

"We need to check it out."

Julia turned to look at Rafe to see him turning to her. He said, "We agree on something."

"That's a first. So let's go. There could be more fossils."

"He could be in there." Rafe spoke at the same moment. He visibly relaxed and smiled.

"Why would you smile when we disagree?"

"I was just worried is all. Afraid you might be rubbing off on me. But now I see we still think different. It's a relief."

"I want to see if there are more fossils in that cave. We could find —"

"Julia, will you pay attention." Rafe lowered his dark brows until they formed one straight line.

"To what?"

His broad shoulders seemed to slump as if he were bearing too much weight. "We aren't going in there to check for *fossils*. A man who could have *killed* you might be in that cave. He could have a gun trained on us right now. Can you please pay attention to what's important for just a few minutes?"

"Fossils are important." Why couldn't the man understand that?

He growled — clearly not understanding.

"Fine. I'll be very alert and mindful of danger while I stay with you ahead of me and the horses on both sides. But what if danger comes from behind?" she asked with all the sarcasm she could muster.

"Overhead, too. Danger could come from overhead." Rafe didn't seem to get that he was being mocked.

Julia clamped her mouth shut and tagged along as he led his horse to the trees sheltering the cave opening. She glanced behind her and above her compulsively now, though there was nothing to see.

Once they gained the shelter of the trees, she sensed Rafe relax a bit. He positioned himself behind the most stout of the aspens and studied the cave.

Because he was right in front of her, blocking her view of the cave, Julia looked across the saddle of his horse into the valley.

"Oh, Rafe, look." She rested a hand on his back.

Turning, he saw another opening. Much larger. Halfway up the south side of the caldera. Sunlight poured through it and the sky shone blue. A jumble of rocks and a heavy stand of trees had shielded it from their sight until now. There was a solid arch of stone over it, but it was a clear trail out.

"I wonder why no one has settled in here. I was already worried about driving my cattle through that narrow cave. Figured I could do it somehow, but it wouldn't be easy. Instead we can go through that opening."

"Maybe there isn't a good way down."

"Or maybe the trees are thick on the other side, too, and it's hard to spot." Turning to her, Rafe smiled. "We'll check. We'll explore this whole valley before we're done."

Since she agreed completely, all she did was smile back, though she did wonder, *Before we're done with what?*

"Let's see if this is a vent going all the way through or just a cave. This direction should lead back toward your place. I hope there's one on the west side. That would cut a lot of time off the trip to Rawhide. Going around this mountain to town must have been a slow trip for your pa. Going straight through it, if there's a passage, I'll bet you're mighty close. There's a circuit rider who comes through. I wonder when he'll be in Rawhide next?"

Rafe hadn't talked much about going to church. She was glad to know he was a believer. "I'd love to hear some preaching. But we can't go into town. Father said Rawhide is dangerous. Or no, wait, he just

227

said that to excuse leaving us out here alone." Shaking her head, one of her ridiculous red ringlets escaped from her braid and slapped her in the face. "I can't keep track of all of Father's lies." She reached up to shove the coil away from her eyes, but Rafe beat her to it.

Their hands touched as he tucked her hair behind her ear. "You're a beautiful woman. You know that, Julia?"

She didn't know that. "I seem to remember you worrying that I might be sixty years old when you first found me and went to kissing me."

"I got over that real quick, if you'll remember." He cupped her chin and took a kiss now, as if she'd asked for one.

"I do remember." Julia really had to insist he stop kissing her. She'd never been kissed before Rafe, had never felt much interest in the activity. Had never expended a bit of effort avoiding men, since there were never any around. And now, the man was just taking a kiss any old time he wanted. She'd insist he stop it very, very soon. Not right now, but soon.

A snap drew her attention to the cave ahead of them. Julia looked past Rafe's shoulder and saw a heavily bearded man poke his head out and spot them. She gasped.

"What is it?" Rafe turned around. The man vanished back into the cave.

"A man! Didn't you see him?" Julia was talking to Rafe's back.

"I saw him all right." Rafe raced for the entrance.

Julia quickly lashed the horses to the aspen tree. They went to munching on the leaves and grass and she hurried after Rafe.

The cave swallowed Rafe. By the time Julia got to the dark entrance, he was gone. She took two steps inside and heard footsteps running away. A few more steps and she came to the first split in the tunnel. One seemed to go down at a steep slope. The noise came from that direction. Straight forward, in a nicely arched passageway about two feet over her head, was the best chance of passing through to the outside of the caldera. She might follow it and wind into the mountain and end up going down or up or sideways or nowhere in the pitch-darkness. And if the tunnel split off again, she might become hopelessly lost. She knew enough about exploring caverns to be very careful to mark her path and always have a lantern on hand. But she had none of the necessary equipment today.

Which way had Rafe gone? Which way had that bearded man gone? Now that the footsteps had faded, she wasn't positive she'd heard them from the downslope tunnel.

Was that the man who had left her in Seth's Cavern? Swallowing nervously, Julia prayed for guidance and wisdom, and absolutely no assurance came to her about which way she should go. That might well be a sign she should go nowhere.

Rafe would be upset if she followed. She would be very upset if something happened to him and she'd stayed behind. Staying would be the cautious thing to do, and Rafe seemed to be very much in favor of her being cautious. He had a gun. She was unarmed.

That wasn't true. She was not unarmed. She had a small knife best suited to chiseling stone.

She looked back at the entrance to the caldera and that was when she saw it.

Another fossil.

This one of some strange creature she'd never quite imagined before. It looked like a bear maybe. A very large bear. Or a wolf. Or maybe a big cat.

Would God send a fossil to keep her from following Rafe into the bowels of the earth?

God might well do such a thing. She got her knife out of her boot and took a closer look at the strange beast. With a prayer for Rafe's safety, and an afterthought of prayer for her own, she leaned closer to the fossil to try and decide where to start. Raising her knife, she felt her spirits lift to the sky.

She was so in love with this place, she felt like bursting into psalms of praise.

"I hate this place."

Ethan chopped wood and muttered. He hunted and brought down a mule deer and muttered. He skinned the doe and started smoking the meat and muttered. He hauled water and muttered. All the muttering was about tending to a weeping woman, great with child, her overly friendly baby, and the fiery, bossy stepdaughter who went along with the package.

And doing it all right next door to that stupid, ugly, dangerous cavern.

He should have stayed in California.

"Ethan, Wendell's awake. Can you help me feed him, please?" Audra Gilliland came around the cabin, belly first, and Ethan wished he'd have gone ahead and built on. Chopping and hunting and skinning and smoking and hauling weren't enough. He needed something more to keep himself occupied — especially if it kept him away from the house. Even with all the work of tending this family he'd gotten stuck with, he had plenty of time to help with Wendell.

Too bad.

He'd've mounted up and ridden back to his own ranch, except his whole family . . . which these days was only Rafe . . . was over here.

Maybe he should try and get to know Steele a little better. Seemed like a good man. Then he could stay at the Kincaid place and not miss his brother much at all.

Turning the strips of venison hanging in the billowing smoke, he grabbed a roast and carried it with him into the cabin. "I can get this started cooking before we feed him if you want."

Maggie cried from behind the bedroom door.

Ethan plunked the roast in the Dutch oven, poured some water over it, put on the lid and nestled it into the red hot coals to cook.

"Audra, keep the baby quiet and get in here!" Wendell was the lowest kind of snake that crawled on the earth. Unkind to women and children — worse, unkind to his own woman and child. He might as well slither along on his belly on the ground, he was so low-down. Only the fact that the man was so sick kept Ethan from teaching the old buzzard some manners.

Just as Ethan washed the blood off his hands, Audra came out of Maggie's bedroom carrying the whimpering baby, looking distressed because of Wendell's shouts.

Her eyes. She could stab him to death with them. She was so frail. With her delicate bones, fine blond hair, fair skin, far too pale, she reminded him of thistledown. Ready to blow away with one good puff of wind.

Every instinct he possessed told him to protect her, shelter her, set her like delicate china on a high shelf so she wouldn't break. He'd bring her food. He'd care for her child. He'd carry her from place to place on a satin pillow.

He considered ramming his head into the wall of the house just to clear his thoughts.

"I really hate this place."

"What did you say?" Audra blinked those beautiful, fragile, tearful blue eyes at him.

"I said, give me the baby while you see what he needs." Ethan snagged the toddler from Audra's arms. "If he needs something that takes both of us, Magpie here is gonna have to come whether Wendell wants her in there or not. I swear that man does more crying than the baby."

"Thanks, Ethan." Audra got a little flush of pink in her cheeks.

"If it'll make you happy, I'm more than willing to say nasty things about Wendell full time."

Audra smiled while Wendell called for help.

This was not an ideal marriage.

Ethan propped Maggie on his hip.

Audra went to Wendell. It was with some dim-witted amount of pride that Ethan got the fireplace stacked with kindling, a nice fire crackling to keep the meat roasting, all with a baby in his arms.

"I'm gettin' good at this, aren't I, Magpie?"

She bounced and grinned at him. He wasn't all that thrilled to be acquiring the skill of doing chores with a baby in tow, but he had to admit he was learning the way of it.

The house was starting to have the smell of cooking meat when Audra came back out. "He's asleep again."

All that pretty pink was gone from her cheeks, and there was no smile to be seen anywhere. Her eyes looked haunted. Ethan had gotten the message that there was no grief in this household for the loss of

Wendell the grouch, but that didn't mean it was easy to watch a man die slowly.

"How is he?" Ethan shifted the baby away from the fire.

"Give her to me." Audra relieved him of the toddler.

"Mamamama." Maggie bounced and whacked Ethan in the face.

Their hands tangled together as they handed off the little girl. His got very gently pinned between the baby and Audra's belly. A sudden jerk shocked a gasp out of Ethan, and he only stayed close because he was afraid he'd drop Maggie on her little head.

His gaze met Audra's, and something strange happened inside him.

Deep inside.

Ethan didn't let anything touch him inside. Caring deeply about someone was a good way to get your heart torn out.

"I . . . I felt the baby move." Ethan couldn't seem to block that tiny show of life from taking a grip on his heart.

He didn't know what it meant. He didn't understand how it could be true. But it was. That bit of life — well, not bit; she was getting close to having the baby after all — was in there. It was another person.

"That's strange to have a baby inside you, isn't it?" Ethan stayed right there, Maggie blocking him from getting any closer to Audra. He was surprised to find that bothered him.

"It doesn't seem so strange." Audra smiled. Her eyes were usually sad and tired. She was so fine-boned, he worried that she'd snap like a twig. But her eyes flashed blue and strong. Ethan felt every protective instinct roar to life inside him.

Ethan was only distantly aware of leaning down, slowly closing the distance between him and this delicate, beautiful princess of a woman. The one thought that echoed in his head was that she needed help. She needed him.

Maggie swatted him in the face again. It woke him from whatever madness had overtaken him.

Audra's eyes widened with shock and confusion, and maybe a bit of dawning horror as she realized he'd almost kissed her. A married woman. And he saw clearly that she'd been fully prepared to kiss him back.

He'd have run screaming from the cabin if he wasn't afraid he'd drop the little one. "Have you got her?"

Audra's pretty blue eyes dropped to Maggie, and she nodded without speaking.

Ethan felt her hands tighten on her toddler, and he slipped his hands away from her — and her belly — and stepped well away from her — and her lips.

"I'm . . . uh . . . going to . . . uh . . . go. Somewhere." Ethan forced himself to meet Audra's eyes.

Lucky for him she was currently fascinated with straightening Maggie's little dress.

"Hunting." No, he'd just butchered a deer. But he was cooking it, slowly over a smoky fire, for hours. It didn't need him to stand there watching. He hoped Audra didn't know that. "You'll be okay?"

Audra looked up. A bit of temper flashed in those pretty eyes. "Yes, I'll be okay."

Her cheeks were pink with embarrassment. Her dress was faded and worn. It looked like her two babies would be too much for her to bear. But she had gumption.

Ethan thought gumption was probably a mistake for Audra, who clearly needed to be careful with her fragile health. But for better or worse, she had it.

"You know, Ethan, sometimes it gets really old having everyone treat me like a delicate hothouse flower."

Ethan suspected that was the absolute truth. "You seem upset. Why don't you see if you can get Maggie to take a nap so you can lay down yourself for a few minutes? I think I'll build you a rocking chair."

A growl of frustration surprised Ethan. She sounded a little like a wounded mountain lion. Which was odd because she seemed more the baby-kitten type.

"I'm not weak! I've never been sick a day in my life."

"You're expecting a young'un and you've got another to care for." He spoke quietly, coaxing, not wanting her to get even more upset. "That's a lot for any woman."

"Stop talking like that."

"Like what?"

"Like I'm equal parts sickly, childlike, and stupid." Her little pointed chin lifted in the most adorable expression of defiance.

"Well," he said carefully, "I don't think you're *stupid.*"

"Just sickly and childlike, then?" The kittenish mountain lion was getting growly-er by the second.

"Not sick and you're certainly no child." He wouldn't have almost kissed her if she'd been either. "I'd say more delicate and very young."

"How old are you?"

Ethan hadn't thought about his age in years. "I guess twenty-three? Maybe?" Ethan fished around for his smile. He always smiled. Just to make sure no one ever suspected he cared about anything.

"So am I. So, would you like to sit down, maybe take a nap? Let me go out and finish smoking the deer, then chop more wood so you can rest. After all, you're very young."

"I don't need to rest." He frowned and leaned forward, insulted.

"Well, neither do I." She leaned right back toward him. "Yes, Maggie is a lot of work, but I'm managing nicely, thank you. Julia takes such good care of me, it's a wonder she doesn't tuck me in a crib at night and feed me baby food at mealtime."

"Julia's a bossy little thing, isn't she?" A few of her orders still stung. But lucky for him, Ethan was used to being bossed around by Rafe.

The blue fire flashed in Audra's eyes; then an unexpected laugh escaped from her pretty pink lips. "She certainly is. I love her. I love her more than anyone I've ever known. She's my sister, my best friend, but if I'm not careful, she starts acting like my mother. I . . . I do need help. Or at least I'm very grateful for it. But I'm all right. I don't need to be treated like you treat Maggie."

"Maggie hits me about five times a day. I don't treat you one bit like I treat her."

"In some ways you do. Tell me, Ethan,

how many women in the world have a toddler and a baby on the way?"

Ethan thought that was a dumb question. "You want me to try and guess?"

"I'll tell you how many." Audra took a step toward him, and he wished very badly that she'd stay far away. "Most of them. Pretty much all of them. Only the old ones — and they did it when they were younger, and the ones who are children themselves — and they'll do it when they're older. Spinsters don't. That's it. And most women end up married whether they like it or not. And *none* of those many, many mothers get to spend their lives sitting around."

His mom did. Ethan's main memory of his mom was of her sitting in a rocking chair, quiet, head down. Ethan realized Audra was close enough that it would be easy to fetch that kiss he'd almost taken from her.

Married. She's married. Remember she's married.

Not for long. Wendell doesn't have much time left.

Doesn't matter. For now the woman is married.

Later, then.

Later, definitely.

No, not later. Well, maybe later. No! Defi-

240

nitely not later, not ever.

One good crack of his head against the wall. Just one. Just to shut his thoughts off and figure out how to smile through this so she knew he didn't care.

He couldn't conjure the smile so he decided to run. Something else he was good at. "I'll go finish smoking that deer and start tanning the hide. Then I'll build you a rocking chair. You just take care of things in here by yourself." He did his best to sound very uncaring about abandoning her. Let her know she was on her own.

She smiled.

"But call if you need anything, okay?"

Her smile twisted into a scowl. "I'll be fine. But I will call, if I need your help. Now go."

She was really cute when she was angry.

Ethan almost told her that.

He thought better of it and ran. He had things to do. He had to watch meat smoke. And he had to envy Rafe getting out of here.

He thought of Audra and suddenly wished he hated this place a whole lot more.

CHAPTER 12

It went pitch-dark.

Rafe heard footsteps ahead, running in this black tunnel. Was it the man who had moved that rope and trapped Julia in the cavern? It sure could be.

How many sneaking strangers who liked caves could there be?

But who? And whoever it was, why did he want to harm Julia?

It had to be someone brave enough — or crazy enough — to run through a tunnel in the pitch-darkness.

Or did he have a lantern? He might have been far enough ahead that Rafe wouldn't have known. Whether he had light or not, running in this tunnel spoke of either crazed recklessness or complete familiarity with this cave. Or both.

The ground sloped until Rafe was afraid he'd start sliding, fall forever. Inching along, Rafe tested each step, the memory of that eggshell-thin floor in the other cavern haunting him. He kept one hand on the wall to feel if the cave tunnel had any branches he couldn't see.

Rafe thought of how long he'd lived in Colorado. He'd have told anyone that he knew the land around his ranch very well. He'd seen this mountain plenty of times — of course, the whole world was mountains in this part of Colorado. The trail he took to town was to the north, so he hadn't done much riding this direction. But he knew the mountains. And he'd had no idea this one was any different than the others.

He paused over that thought. What if it wasn't different? What if there were a lot of mountaintop valleys like this one? Rafe itched to find out. He hadn't done enough exploring.

The fading footsteps suddenly stopped.

Rafe's hand went to his revolver. He continued on. Maybe there was light ahead. Maybe this tunnel led through the mountain to the outside like the vent they'd entered the valley through.

Surely that was why the footsteps had stopped, because they'd gone outside, run into grass instead of clattering on stone.

The light never came. Rafe took each step slower, more cautiously. He had a sudden vision of the cavern floor shattered under Seth's weight. Rafe took one more step and his toe hit a stone. It bounced, then bounced again, still moving along fast. Then suddenly silence.

Rafe froze.

Finally that stone hit a long, long way down. His knees wobbled, and he dropped as the stone bounced.

The dark of the cave suddenly pressed on him. The cold inside him was crushed by blackness, until he feared the ice would crack open and all his worst, most childish fears would explode free.

As he fought for control, he heard something that turned him aside from the encroaching panic. Something scratched. A sound so faint he thought he might be imagining it. On his hands and knees, he reached forward to find a ledge, just inches in front of him.

A ledge he knew dropped off forever. A ledge just in front of the path those running footsteps had taken. How had someone run across this? Impossible. But he'd have heard it if someone had fallen. And he'd come inches from falling himself. Just like so many years ago when Seth had nearly died.

The shock bowed his head. One more step and he'd have gone over the ledge.

The pressure of the black pit ground him down, squeezing and crushing. Rafe grimly battled to overcome such weakness.

Rafe heard that rustling sound again to his left. He reached for it and his hand scraped against a boulder. Or maybe one of those stag-tight things Julia had talked about. But the noise — what was that? He ran his hands around the rock, closing in on the sound by touch . . . and felt a rope.

A rope that moved. A taut rope that even now someone was using to climb down into the pit.

Or up.

The image of Satan erupting out of the underworld, grabbing Rafe, dragging him down, broke what was left of his wavering control. He whirled, still on his knees, leapt to his feet, and ran.

His throat closed or he'd have shouted with fear. He felt the devil gaining, coming, burning. This was how he'd felt when he abandoned Seth so long ago.

Rafe slammed into a stone wall and rapped his head so hard he saw stars. Staggering, he barely remained on his feet. He slapped his hand on the tunnel to keep himself in contact with something, anything solid. Running like a coward, racing for a way out of this nightmare.

Abandoning his brothers to save himself just like before.

He had to get out. Get out or die.

It was his chance. At last. He fought down the urge to laugh as he inched forward. He'd gotten very good in this cave. Very good. Silent.

Any bit of sound carried and echoed. A boot sliding on rock. A hand brushing on stone. A hard breath.

She was making a fair amount of noise chipping on the stone, so he could move more swiftly if he wanted. But he was too smart, too careful. And the man with her was busy running in the wrong direction. Laughter bubbled up, but he fought it. Stopped it in time.

He'd hidden the horses. Glad now he'd thought of it. He hadn't expected anyone to come here, not besides his friend, of course. He slowly, silently eased forward, mindful of each step.

She muttered and chiseled, completely focused on the stone. And she was his path to the money, to success. He might not go back once he had it. Oh, the boss had tentacles that reached a long, long way. But it was only his tracking skills that had gotten him this close. Anyone else the boss sent would never find this place.

So he might take the money. And this

woman was the key to finding it.

She chiseled. Another step closer. The next step would take him out of the dark. She'd be able to see him, then. He could keep inching along until he was close enough to grab her.

Surprise her.

He'd like that. Time now to forget about silence and move fast so she didn't have a chance to scream and call her guardian back.

He resisted the urge to laugh and prepared to spring.

Julia heard thudding footsteps. She dropped her knife as she whirled to face whomever or whatever was coming at her so fast.

She leaned down and scooped up the only weapon she had, a knife with a two-inch blade.

Rafe appeared around the bend of the tunnel, and she breathed a sigh of relief and turned back to her chiseling.

"Now." He grabbed her arm in midchisel and dragged her after him. "We're going now."

"Rafe, what in the world . . ." She stumbled as he rushed her along, until she was running to keep from being dragged. She couldn't even see his expression, but she read terrible urgency and hurried to keep up. They reached the horses, and Rafe tore the reins loose from the aspen and lifted her up onto her saddle.

"Tell me what —"

Rafe vaulted into his own saddle, and holding her reins raced his horse up the steep slope at such a reckless speed, Julia quit talking and clung to the saddle horn. Rafe charged for the vent they'd entered through. When they reached it, he swung down, dragged her off the horse, and that was when she finally saw his face.

He'd seen something terrible.

"Stay right behind me." His eyes met hers as if asking for complete, blind obedience. "I need to go out the entrance on the other side first." He scowled and looked back in the direction they'd come. "Wait. No, I should bring up the rear. But wait. No, I need to go first in case . . ."

Rafe, the strongest man she'd ever known, was scared to death of something that he'd seen in that cave tunnel. Her heart started thudding in matching fear. As always when she was in a tight spot, she took charge and started issuing orders.

"You go first. Lead your own horse." It's just that she'd never thought she'd need to do it with Rafe. "I'll stick close leading mine. No one would be able to get to me with my horse behind me. Let's go."

He hesitated another second and then jerked his chin in agreement, leading his horse into the dark tunnel.

With her own fear ignited, she wanted to get away just as badly as he did.

Except she wanted to come back, too. Yet she had a bad feeling, based on the way he was acting right now, that Rafe wasn't going to want to bring her.

As the light vanished, she rested her hand on the cool rock wall, let it scratch gently at her fingertips and wondered what she was touching. Her horse trailed her, its iron-shod hooves echoing. What had gone on to create this caldera and this vent and leave behind the fossils? She could imagine the power of a volcano. She could see the explosion, ripping a hole in the side of the mountain while the top exploded with fiery lava, then collapsed to form that beautiful crater. In the pitch black, she felt the glory of God in a way she often did while she worked with fossils.

It was all a wonder, a mystery, a gift from a God who created things both wonderful and terrible.

The thought of God's power calmed her. The clopping of Rafe's horse guided her. Before she knew it, they were out of the cavern and into the sunlight.

"Let's go." Rafe turned to grab her.

"Stop!" Julia held up her hands and backed away from him. Rafe's horse slowed him down and he missed when he tried to snag her. "Stop it, Rafe, right now!"

Either the yelling penetrated his fear or he'd just finally calmed down enough to be sensible. He stopped. He stood in front of her for a long moment, his chest heaving, his tanned face flushed. Then his eyes slowly fell shut. He dragged a deep breath. His tense shoulders relaxed and he opened his eyes.

"Okay. I know I'm acting like a locoweed. I know it." He looked at the tunnel. Julia stepped off to the side so he had a clear path to stare into the black oval of stone.

"I just — just — I had to get out of there. I thought, that is I heard . . ." He swallowed as if he had half an apple stuck in his throat.

Julia came forward and caught his hand. "Tell me what happened."

Rafe looked away from that tunnel entrance and nodded. "I just went back — back in time." He scrubbed a hand over his face as if to wash away the memory. "Inside my head. I went back to a really awful time and place. Something that happened when I was young. No, not *that* young. I was too *old* to have been so scared, so weak."

There was something in his eyes that edged its way into Julia's heart. He looked young and scared and almost defeated. Julia had always taken care of herself. She'd taken care of her mother when she'd gotten sick and died. She'd taken care of whatever house her father had set her up in. Lately, she'd gotten the duty of taking care of Audra and little Maggie. Now she couldn't stop herself from taking care of Rafe.

She moved forward quietly and took him into her arms. Hugging him tight, she felt him tense. For a man who had taken far too many liberties with her, he didn't seem receptive to her touch and she wondered for a moment if he'd push her away.

The pain was shocking, the fear. Though it didn't seem possible, Julia knew she loved Rafe Kincaid.

Maybe not a man and woman kind of love. Maybe just the love God called every believer to show for others. But whatever it was, it was real and solid and she didn't want to let it go.

And she was terrified Rafe would reject her. That was a man's way, wasn't it?

Then suddenly his arms came around her hard, so hard they hurt. A wonderful kind of hurt that Julia knew she'd remember and cherish for the rest of her life.

They stood there on that mountain slope, the breeze buffeting them. One of the horses tossed its head and the metal in its bridle clinked. Cool, dank air breathed on her from the tunnel while the warm afternoon of a Colorado June warmed her, even though the sun had slipped over the mountain at their backs and cast them into shadows.

The moment was one of the sweetest of Julia's life. It reminded her of the day she'd been there to bring Maggie into the world. With no idea how to do such a thing — and Audra knowing even less — Julia had attended the arrival of a new life. And this embrace felt like new life, too.

Finally, Rafe's grip eased and he raised his head. Their eyes met.

"Can you tell me what happened?" Her question was a whisper, soft enough that if he wanted to ignore it, turn and move, he could pretend that he hadn't heard her and she'd let him.

"I — I just had a hard look at a terrible part of myself. A failure. Out of control. It's shameful." The harsh laugh was nothing Julia had ever heard from Rafe before. "Like a whining little girl."

That pinched. "Hey, I'll have you know little girls can be as tough as they need to be." Julia knew from experience just how tough a young girl could be.

That brought Rafe's head around and she saw amusement in his eyes, though he couldn't quite manage a smile. "You're right. Sorry."

"Just tell me." Julia hoped and prayed he would.

Rafe nodded. "Let's go on down while we talk."

He started out down the talus slide, and Julia kept up rather than be left behind.

"We ran pretty wild when we were kids. Ma was . . . sick, I guess you'd say. She just sat around, quiet-like. She'd cook meals at least part of the time, but mostly she sat in her rocker. She cried a lot. And Pa was building the ranch, and he trapped furs too, and hunted gold. He'd go off, sometimes for weeks at a time. Seemed like he was gone longer and longer as the years went by.

"He wasn't kind to Ma, yelled at her a lot, and he seemed to want to do things on his own rather than have us boys tagging after him. We had chores. He'd leave us to them and go out alone." Rafe shrugged. "That left us pretty much on our own."

Rafe was describing Julia's life. Her mother sick. Her father gone. She'd have loved above all things to have a couple of little brothers or sisters. But what if she'd had them and led them into danger. She shuddered at the thought. Instead there'd been only her. And she ran wild, hunted in caverns she probably had no business in, found peace and contentment — as much as possible — in nature and her own company.

"We got in the habit of exploring that cavern you love so much. It's a dangerous place, but I didn't realize it at the time, or maybe I just didn't think it through. It was spooky and beautiful and fun. I was all for hunting around down there."

Rafe picked up the pace. Julia hurried along, hoping he wouldn't forget he was in the middle of a story.

"Then one day we had trouble. Bad trouble." They reached the bottom of the slope where Rafe stopped, turned to her and grabbed one hand. He squeezed her fingers until they hurt. "You need to stay out of there. It's deadly. I didn't stop Ethan and Seth from going down. I encouraged them. I wanted to be down there." Rafe's breathing picked up. His gaze seemed to look through her. Then he closed his eyes and shook his head as if to clear it.

"There was trouble and I — I —" He ran

a hand over the scar on his forehead.

"Is that when you got the scar?" She reached up and her hand touched his as she drew her forefinger along the jagged wound. His hair was short enough that it showed all the time, but she mostly forgot about it. That scar didn't change the fact that he was the most handsome man she'd ever seen.

"Yes. Every time I touch it, I remember how badly I failed my brothers."

It was his habit to rub on that scar. Which meant he remembered all the time. "What happened, what trouble?"

"I found out the truth and I — I am not an honorable man. I can force myself to do the right thing, but in my heart I couldn't control the selfish need to take care of myself no matter who suffered."

"No, Rafe."

"Yes." His eyes blazed. "And today there was a pit in that cave. I almost fell into it and it brought that day back. I heard something or someone, climbing up out of that pit. I felt like something was coming for me. I — I suppose it was just that man we saw. Of course it was."

Rafe scrubbed his face again. "But for just a few minutes, I could have sworn the devil himself was climbing right up from the underworld to grab me and drag me down.

And I ran. Today I ran just like all those years ago. I thought I'd gotten control of myself, but I haven't. I'm the same weakling I always was."

A chill raised goose bumps along Julia's arms. "There's a pit in this cave? And someone was in it?"

"Yes. I might have let my imagination run wild with thoughts of the devil, but I didn't imagine that someone was there. It was pitch-dark. I heard a sound, felt along and found a rope hanging over the edge of a hole. It was moving, pulled tight, as if someone was hanging from it. That's where the man we saw must have gone, but I lost control in there. I ran scared."

"I'd have run, too." Julia launched herself at Rafe and he stumbled backward with a grunt.

He held her tight. So tight.

"Anytime you need to talk, I'll listen."

"Thank you." Rafe kissed her.

She knew she shouldn't be kissing him, but he needed her. When the kiss ended, she whispered, "I'm so glad you told me. Talking about it has to help and I want to help."

"Good, then it's settled." His callused hands rested, one on each cheek. "I'll see to it."

"Settled?" Julia's eyes weren't fully focused. And neither were her thoughts. "See to what?"

"See to —"

"Rafe!" Ethan's voice lashed them like a bullwhip. "Julia, come quick."

Julia stepped back and bumped into her horse. She and Rafe were standing between their two mounts. She peeked over the back of Rafe's to face Ethan.

Bracing herself for what she'd learned was a steady stream of irreverence from Ethan, Julia wondered just exactly what Rafe thought was settled.

Ethan galloped up, lacking his usual incessant, vacant smile. And he was looking straight at her.

With sympathy.

"Julia, I'm sorry."

She knew before he said it what was coming.

"Your pa just died."

Rafe's hand came to her back to support her.

"And Audra went into labor."

Julia jerked away from Rafe's touch.

"It stopped. She says it's happened before and she's fine now, but I convinced her to go to bed." Ethan swung down, and that was when Julia noticed that Ethan had

Maggie in a little pack on his back.

"Good grief, where'd you get that thing?" Julia hurried toward the baby.

"Steele had seen one before. An Indian woman carried her baby this way. He made it while I stayed inside worrying over Audra."

The baby was facing backward, her arms and legs waving.

"Give her to me."

"No, it takes a while to get it rigged. Just mount up and let's go."

Julia nodded. "Yes, of course. I have to get home."

She turned to her horse and was galloping before she'd given it a thought. Then finally she did think and she realized she was riding for Audra, to help her. Worried about the baby falling out of that strange pack. There was no grief, and that in itself was a terrible sort of grief.

Thundering hooves told her the Kincaid men were right behind her. She glanced back and a movement far behind her drew her attention to that vent they'd just come through. A man. Was it the same man? This one didn't look just the same. He had a beard but something else. He was too far away to see for sure, but she thought he wore an eye patch. Then he was gone and

Julia wasn't sure what she'd seen. She looked forward to guide her horse.

Who was that man?

And what had Rafe meant when he'd said he'd see to it?

And what in the world did he think was settled?

Gilliland was dead!

He cursed the luck. He wanted to shriek and swear and pull his gun and kill and kill and kill.

Staring at the three people who rode away, he considered the possibilities.

He could follow a trail. Rubbing his sweat-soaked hand over the scar that had made him so ugly, he wondered how to handle this? The boss wasn't one for excuses.

A letter. He could use their system and leave the boss a message. Then what?

Quit?

If a man died, his secrets didn't necessarily die with him. He left a trail.

If anyone would know the truth about a man's secrets, it was his daughter.

The daughter looked over her shoulder and saw him. He deliberately stayed in view for a few seconds, enjoying revealing himself to her. After a few seconds, he ducked back into the cave and back into darkness where he belonged.

Nothing had really changed. He needed the daughter still. Only now, instead of using her to drag the truth out of Gilliland, he'd find the truth within her.

And again he had the urge to laugh. This time he didn't try and control himself.

CHAPTER 13

The only salt water Old Wendell Gilliland had earned with his miserable life was the sweat of Rafe's brow from digging a hole.

"I'm riding to town." Rafe finished dumping dirt over the old scoundrel and turned to Julia and Audra. Audra leaned heavily on Julia. The baby was sleeping in Julia's strong arms. Julia bearing the weight of this whole family. Audra's face was white, her jaw rigid, her eyes dry as a bone. The women looked upset and worried, but there was no grief.

Rafe wanted to ride into town for the parson before he started doing all that he saw needed doing. He wanted to haul Julia along with him, to get time alone with her, to have that conversation that had been interrupted by Wendell's death. But she'd been inseparable from Audra, and Rafe didn't figure he'd have much luck getting her away.

Which meant he'd have to handle it all

himself.

Which was fine.

He turned to Ethan. "Help me get my horse saddled."

Ethan's brows rose in surprise. Ethan would know good and well that Rafe could saddle his own horse, which meant they needed to talk alone.

As soon as they were out of hearing distance, Rafe said, "Audra isn't up to being dragged miles across country to get her to our place and there's no sense taking her to town. I didn't even like letting her stand up for the funeral."

"Agreed." Ethan strode along beside Rafe, and it warmed Rafe's heart to have his brother back. Now he just needed to get settled in that mountain valley with Julia, convince her that cavern was no place for a lady, give Ethan the homeplace, make sure he was running it right, get Audra's baby safely into the world, and find Seth.

And then everything would be fine.

Rafe explained quickly about the man Julia had seen ducking into the cave. "Whoever that was may be dangerous. I need to go to Rawhide. You're on guard duty until I get back with the parson."

"The man's already buried, Rafe. Besides, last I heard the only parson in Rawhide is a circuit rider. He might not show up for a month. No sense bringing a minister all the way out here for the funeral that's long over and done."

"No sense at all." Rafe dropped a loop over his chestnut, grazing in the deep grass alongside Ethan's and Wendell's horses. He kept busy slapping leather on his horse, thinking of all that needed doing, and then he swung into the saddle and turned to his brother.

Ethan didn't ask any more questions, but that was Ethan. He did a good job of not letting anyone know he cared.

"I'll make it a fast trip. Hope to be back by dark. If I'm delayed, be careful. Whoever that was in that hidden canyon, I think he's up to no good. Otherwise why run like that? Why not just come on out and say hello?" Rafe didn't confess to the way he'd acted in that tunnel. It was too shameful.

"I'll keep an eye out."

Rafe spurred his horse.

He strode into the cabin just as dusk was turning to dark.

The evening meal was over, but a plate sat covered on the table, and he knew it was for him. Audra sat in a new rocking chair that Ethan must have made this afternoon. Rafe

wished he'd done it. He loved fine woodwork and would have made something pret-
tier, but Ethan had beaten him to it and the
chair rocked and kept Audra's backside off
the floor. That was all a chair really needed
to do.

Audra lifted her head when Rafe came in
and blinked at him so owlishly he knew
she'd been dozing. Julia sat in front of the
fireplace in the only other chair. She had a
large flat book on her lap and was using it
as a desk. An ink bottle balanced on the
book, and she was writing diligently by
firelight — no doubt about her *Julia-pig-
osauria.* Ethan sat on the floor, one knee
drawn up, his head leaned back against the
stones that surrounded the hearth.

It was a homey sight, and even though the
cold night wind whistled in through the
ramshackle walls, Rafe was glad to come in
from the dark to this place of light and, best
of all, a woman who was waiting for him.

"Someone saw the circuit rider in the next
town over from Rawhide. No idea how long
he'll stay there, but his next stop is Rawhide,
so he oughta be out here soon."

"That's nice." Julia looked up from her
writing. "We haven't had a visit from a
parson in years."

"He can say a prayer over Wendell's

grave." Audra started her chair rocking.
"And baptize Maggie."

"Yep, after he marries us." Rafe hung his
hat on a nail and turned to see three heads
come up. Red, blond, and brown. Their eyes
locked on him.

"What?" He couldn't imagine what was
going through their minds.

"Marries . . . ?" Audra's voice was a barely
audible squeak.

"Yeah." Rafe pulled his gloves off and
tossed them on the floor beside his hat. It
had gotten chilly tonight on the ride home.

"Marries who?" Ethan asked, sounding
on edge.

Rafe smiled at Julia, who was riveted on
him. Her pen frozen in midair. The firelight
glinted on her red hair, and Rafe longed to
touch those fiery curls. He intended to have
the right to do just that very soon.

"Marries Julia and me, of course." He
smiled at Julia's nonsense. "I told you that."

"No, you didn't." They all three spoke at
once.

Audra gave a tiny shudder and said, "I
was afraid he meant me."

Which wasn't very nice.

"You never learn, brother." Ethan grinned,
his eyes sliding between Rafe and Julia like
he was afraid he'd miss something.

Julia very slowly rose, set her book with the paper and ink on her chair with almost painful precision. She capped the ink and turned to Rafe.

"Clear this up, Julia. Tell 'em."

Julia's eyes got a squinty look that was better suited to a hired gunslinger. "Are you telling me" — she spoke so slowly, no one could miss a word — "you asked a parson" — she breathed in and out far too slowly — "to come out here" — she clasped her hands together in front of her in a way that sort of looked like she was strangling someone — "to perform a wedding ceremony . . ."

Rafe heaved a sigh of relief. The woman was getting the message.

". . . for the two of us?"

"Well, sure. And while I was in town, I bought that mountain valley for us to live in."

He turned to Ethan. "They have it listed as wasteland, nothing but rugged mountain. They have no idea all that lush grass is in there. And I've never staked a claim, what with the ranch bein' Pa's, so I got a lot of it free. Then I bought the rest for next to nothing. You can help me build a cabin over there, and then have the Kincaid ranch house for yourself. Now, I'm not happy about seeing that man in the tunnel, Eth. You and I need to search —"

"Rafe!" Julia's voice cut him off.

He turned back to her. "What?"

Her head tilted slowly, a fraction of an inch at a time to the left, as if her brain were out of balance and she was trying to bring her world to a level place.

"You thought . . . You really mean . . . What makes you . . . ?" Her eyes fell shut and her head straightened. Her clasped-together knuckles turned white. Her chin came up, reminding him she was a stubborn little thing.

"You said yes." Really, it was like she couldn't keep two thoughts in her head at the same time. She was probably thinking about fossils now and couldn't summon anything else.

"No."

"Sure, we talked about it."

"We did not."

"Why would I ride to town and get the parson for a wedding if we weren't getting married?"

"That's a fascinating question." Her green eyes flashed such fire, Rafe thought he might have singe marks on his shirt front. "Why *would* you ride to town and get the parson for a wedding without even discussing such a thing with me?"

"We talked at the vent of that caldron."

"Caldron?" Ethan looked at the pathetic assortment of pots and pans in the house.

"Stay out of this," Rafe said, glaring at his smirking brother. Then he looked at Audra. "And what do you mean you were *afraid* I meant you? You need a husband, too. I'll figure that out as soon as Julia and me get hitched and settled."

Audra's jaw dropped.

"Rafe, where in the world did you get the idea we were getting married?" Julia jammed her fists on her slender hips, and Rafe thought of getting all that fire in his life. He might risk warming up all the way through once he had her permanently in his home and in his arms and his bed.

"I got the idea when you let me kiss you." Rafe scowled.

Julia blushed.

Ethan grinned.

Audra gasped and looked at her step-daughter. "Julia, really?"

"And when we came out of that caldron—"

"Caldera, not caldron." Julia took two steps toward Rafe, which brought her really close, considering the puny size of the room. She hissed, "And you'll not speak of such a thing" — she sneaked a look at Ethan, who was listening to every word, and her voice dropped — "in front of others."

Rafe snaked one arm around her waist and said, "Okay, let's go sort this out in private."

He swept her out the door, slamming it hard enough that for a second he was afraid it might shake off its hinges. Which wouldn't matter a whole lot because he wasn't planning to stay much longer. But still, no sense having the front door lying on the ground in the week or two it'd take him to build a better house. He must have surprised her, because she let him take her quite a ways before she started struggling.

"Let me go. I'm not marrying you, you big, dumb *umphh* —"

Rafe kissed her. It was the only thing he could think of to keep her quiet. She froze, and Rafe was suddenly afraid, as afraid as he'd been when he'd knelt beside that hole and felt that rope trembling and believed something terrible was coming straight for him from deep in the belly of the earth. Afraid she really meant it when she said she wasn't marrying him. Afraid he'd be alone and cold forever.

Then she thawed.

Her arms went around his neck and he

had her tight in his arms. He lifted her until her toes dangled, and when at last he pulled away, he spoke, his lips still touching hers. "How could you not know —" he broke off talking for a minute to kiss her — "we were getting married? How could you kiss me like this a single time and not believe we had to join our lives?"

He pulled away far enough to meet her eyes in the moonlight. They looked slightly unfocused.

"Say you'll marry me, Julia. We need to get married. We can't go around kissing like this if we don't, and I like it too much to give it up."

Relaxing her iron grip on his neck, Julia laid her hands flat on his shoulders and pushed gently but firmly to get away. Her gaze seemed to clear. He lowered her to the ground, sure now she would be reasonable.

"Let me go, please."

When he did, all the cold rushed back into him. Only when it returned did he realize just how much he was feeling while he held her.

They stood, face-to-face in the dark. Starlight cascading down on them. Her red hair and green eyes lost their color in the night and cast her in a shade of dark blue that made her seem too beautiful to be true.

Rafe searched in his head for what he could tell her that would make her his. He needed to take control fast before she got her say in.

"Rafe, you never asked me to marry you."

Flinching, Rafe knew he'd waited too long to start. "Julia, are you telling me you've been kissing me like a house afire with no notion that I might have . . . have . . . serious, honorable intentions toward you? Do you think that little of me? Do you kiss men like this all the time?" That caused a flash of heat that crawled up his neck and got hot under his collar.

"Of course not."

"What then? Why wouldn't you expect to marry me?"

She got that squinty look in her eyes again. Rafe did his best to keep his face straight, but he was disgusted that the woman didn't make sense. He was going to insist she be logical once they were married.

But for now, he decided to play along with her strange notions. "Okay, so you're not one bit serious about me? You just like kissing any man who's to hand — is that it?"

Her arms crossed and she began tapping her toe. "No, that's not it. Don't act like this is my fault."

"But it is your fault. What's more, it's just common sense that we'd get married."

"Common sense that I marry a man I've known for only a couple days who invites a preacher out, buys land" — her voice started to rise — "and plans to build a house and move me in . . ."

Rafe thought he could count this as shouting now.

"*. . . and does this all without mentioning it to me?*"

Definitely shouting.

Rafe found he had no taste for being hollered at. "You need someone to take care of you."

"I take care of my*self*. I always have."

"You always had your father."

Julia snorted in a way that was purely rude. "My father —"

"Even if he wasn't around much." Rafe cut her off. "He bought the cabin."

"It's a wreck." Her hand flew wide. "It can't have cost anything."

"He brought supplies for you." Moving closer, he glared down at her shadowed face. Rafe knew how to control a situation, and he knew he had a glare that made grown men take a step back.

She took a step forward. "He brought barely enough for us to get by."

She was a brave little thing. Rafe had to admire that. Although foolish might be a fair description instead. "He earned the living for your family."

"Which he never shared with us." The look in her eyes was the next thing to shooting burning Apache arrows into his hide.

"Can you hunt? Can you bring down a deer and butcher it and tan the hide? Can you snare a rabbit or even catch a fish?"

"I can fish and I can plant a garden."

"Mostly you just sit and write about old bones, and climb around in dangerous caverns."

"I can earn money with that writing."

"Money you can't get because you can't get to town without leaving Audra alone while you ride out in a dangerous country."

Her jaw got so tight, Rafe worried that she might break her teeth.

"If you survive the ride to town, and get your money for your writing, you've still got to chop enough wood to keep you warm and cook your food."

"I can swing an axe."

"Can you build a better cabin? That one" — he jabbed his thumb over his shoulder — "is going to be pretty small for the four of you. And even if you don't mind the size, it's too drafty to keep you warm through a

273

Colorado winter, no matter how much wood you chop and burn. Can you do *any* of those things while you've got a frail stepmother, one baby in your arms and another around your knees? You've got one horse between what will soon be four people. You couldn't ride anywhere for help now, not all of you. And come winter you'd have to do it with snowdrifts higher than your head. You won't be able to go for a doctor if one of the little ones gets sick."

"Audra isn't that frail."

"You need a *husband.* A woman in the West doesn't survive without a husband. And if not you, then Audra. And considering all the smooching we've been doing, I thought marrying you was the better choice."

She gasped, and Rafe noticed she'd made a fist. He braced himself for her to let it fly. This wasn't the marriage proposal of a man's dreams. Of course, maybe it wasn't what a woman dreamed of, either.

He forced himself to control his temper. He pulled in a deep breath and blew it out. "Julia, honey, I don't want to argue with you. I want to marry you."

The fist relaxed. The temper faded from her eyes and she got a sad look, hurt. It reminded Rafe too much of his mother, and he realized he'd rather have her yelling at him than crying.

He realized that at the exact same second the first tear streaked down her face.

"Now, Jules, don't go crying. I don't like it when a woman cries."

She sniffled and swiped the back of her hand across her face. "A woman wants nice words when a man asks for her hand. Not orders. Not talk of common sense. Not being informed that the preacher is coming before the man so much as asks for her hand. She wants kindness and affection. She wants to hear talk of *love,* Rafe. I lived all my life with a father who never said a word about love, and now you want me to give myself over to a man for the rest of my life who talks of marriage with less excitement than he talks of buying a mountain meadow."

"You want me to bring you presents? Or posies? You want talk of love?" Rafe was real disappointed in her. She seemed like such a sensible woman. "You're a practical, reasonable woman. I think we're alike in that. I'll make a good husband to you, but I'm not going to spout a bunch of pretty lies about love. You wouldn't respect me if I spoke of such. Instead I'll talk about what's important."

"Love's not important?" Another tear rolled down her cheek.

Rafe gritted his teeth to keep from saying anything, speaking any words he could that would make her stop. "Life and death are important."

"Of course."

"And to me, getting married looks like a choice between life and death for you and Audra and the babies. Can you say I'm wrong?"

"I . . . I . . . I know life would be easier with help. But —"

"Good." Rafe cut her off before she could talk more nonsense. "I want honesty between us."

"Honesty? Then maybe you should know that I have a dream I want to follow. It doesn't include being a rancher's wife."

Scowling, Rafe asked, "What could be better than being a rancher's wife?"

For some reason that jiggled a small smile out of her. "Did you know there's a man writing a book listing all the dinosaurs ever found? I have his address. If I send him the information about that cavern, he might use some of my findings in his book. He might pay me and give me credit for my discoveries. They won't be named a Julia-saurus, but I could support myself and earn some respect for my work studying dinosaur bones."

"Again you're talking about dinosaurs, Jules?" He raised his arms like a surrendering outlaw. "What's the big deal about a bunch of animals that're all dead?"

"I could get more papers published. I can earn money doing that. I can support Audra and the babies."

"You won't need money if you're married to me."

"But there's more than that. The things I've found in Seth's Cavern. The fish."

"Someone's lunch." Rafe raised his eyes to heaven asking for patience.

"No, there's more than fish. There are layers in the stones. There are fish overhead, where no one ever ate a meal. It's the flood."

"What flood?"

"Noah's flood!"

Stunned, Rafe couldn't quite say the next word. He managed to get his jaw to quit gaping open. "Look, sweetheart —"

"I'm not your sweetheart!"

He leaned over her and roared, *"Yes, you are!"*

She should have backed down. Rafe knew his temper, and he knew any sensible person backed away when he started yelling. Instead, Julia jammed her fists on her hips and poked her little nose up so it almost touched his. "You can't yell at me to get me to say I'll marry you. That's just about the worse way to convince a woman to marry you that I've ever heard of."

Rafe's chest heaved. He wanted to yell again. Julia had to marry him. Why didn't she see reason? She was breathing just as hard. Her eyes flashed. Suddenly, instead of fury, he had a glimpse of the fear he knew lived inside him. As if all this fire had thawed out the worst part of himself.

She *had* to see reason. She *had* to understand. She *had* to marry him.

Whatever he had to do, to get her married to him, he'd do. And he could only think of one thing that she wanted badly enough to pay almost any price. It didn't suit him. In fact, it felt so wrong it bordered on a sin. And he knew this was the thing that would drive Ethan away. Rafe swallowed hard as he tried to figure out how to tell Ethan, or how to sneak this past him. But he had to get her in front of a preacher. His need to marry her went so deep it was like a hunger, and he was a starving man.

So he said it. The stupidest, sinfulest, wrongest thing he could imagine. "If you marry me, I . . . I . . ." He forced himself to go on. "I'll let you explore that cavern."

The fire went out in Julia's eyes, replaced by a gleam of excitement. "Really? You really believe in what I'm doing? You want to find out about the dinosaurs, too?"

"No, of course not."

Her eyes narrowed.

Before she could start nagging at him again, he said, "But it's important to you, and I want you to be happy. So, if you make me some promises so I can be sure you're safe, I'll go down there with you." He felt a chill so cold it hardened in his gut. "First, we have to find whoever stranded you down there. That's promise number one."

She looked undecided. Which Rafe thought was a big improvement over *Absolutely not.* So, to distract her from all the thinking she seemed bent on doing about what seemed simple and obvious to him, he did the one thing that seemed to make her cooperate. He kissed her.

When she got to kissing him back with her usual enthusiasm, Rafe risked lifting his head. "What do you say? Will you marry me?"

She sniffled.

Rafe braced himself for more tears.

Instead she nodded.

All his talk of logic and practical matters didn't explain the almost explosive relief he felt when she accepted his proposal. He hoisted her up into the air and spun her around with a laugh of pure happiness.

Then he kissed her because he was afraid of what she'd say next if he gave her a chance to talk.

He decided that'd be his approach to all their disagreements.

CHAPTER 14

Three days and still the circuit rider hadn't shown up. It was driving Rafe out of his mind.

Ethan had gone home yesterday to see how the Kincaid Ranch was running.

Not being able to go and see to his ranch was driving Rafe out of his mind, too.

His whole life was generally shaping up to turn him into a lunatic.

Ethan returned from the ranch in the early morning hours with two horses in a string, loaded down with supplies.

"Steele hired on a few more men." Dismounting, Ethan grinned, his usual charming self. "He wasn't happy when I told him I was taking over. I think Steele might want to come and work for you at your new ranch."

Rafe figured that had to pinch, but Ethan didn't show it. "You keep him over there. He knows how I run things."

"I thought I was running things." Ethan said it like he was joking, but Rafe remembered Ethan's resentment and knew his little brother wasn't real happy.

"Sorry, yeah, sure. I expect you to do things your way." Except Ethan didn't always do things the best way. He was too casual. Rafe couldn't just turn the reins of the ranch over to him completely. "Just ask Steele if you want to know how it was before. I might want a few men working my place after we start running cattle over there. But first I've got to figure how best to drive the cattle in. I didn't even get a chance to scout the big gap on the south."

Because he'd been running like a scared rabbit.

"But hired hands and cattle both have to wait until we've caught that varmint who's skulking around. Are the men coming today?"

"We had a chunk of the herd run off last night during the thunderstorm. A couple of men will come as soon as they can. But they had to do some rounding up. None of us got more than a couple hours of sleep."

Rafe looked closer at Ethan and realized that under the usual grin, his brother was exhausted. The lines of fatigue were there, but Ethan had shown up just as Rafe had ordered. He'd started out long before sunup to get here this early.

"Were any cattle hurt?" Rafe almost grabbed a horse and ran for his ranch. He should be there. He should just drag Julia and her family home and forget that beautiful mountain meadow. But it was a long, rough ride for Audra. She hadn't had any more labor pains, but they were all making an extreme effort to keep her sitting down.

Still, he itched to manage his ranch. Handing it over to Ethan wasn't easy.

"None we've found. But about two hundred of them ran until they were tired out. We're still combing them out of the woods and moving them home. Steele said he'd come with a few of the men as soon as he could."

Rafe didn't like it. Especially since he needed to go in that blasted cave again. "We'll wait a while to explore the mountain valley. Otherwise I'll have to go alone. We can't both go because someone needs to stay here and watch the women."

"No one" — Rafe winced at the sound of Julia's voice — "is going to *watch* the women."

He squared his shoulders and turned to face her. Her red hair was loose, curling around her shoulders, and her green eyes flashed with annoyance and intelligence and stubbornness.

Where is that parson?

"Now, Julia, honey —"

"We're coming with you." She jerked some no-nonsense riding gloves on her graceful hands. She had a satchel hanging from her wrist that Rafe suspected contained her hammer and chisel. She had on the same worn shirtwaist she'd put on to replace her green one with the bloodstain, and her same green skirt. The woman needed some more clothes, and Rafe couldn't wait to buy them for her.

"That's not a good idea." He used the same tone to calm a nervous filly. "I don't want you and Audra and the baby over there until we're sure it's safe."

"Well, if you don't want us there" — Rafe relaxed; she was going to be reasonable — "then you are doomed to be disappointed."

He sensed he was facing a lifetime of disappointment.

"Because we're going." She tossed her head and raised her chin defiantly.

She was a contrary little green-broke filly, and he still wished the parson would hurry so he could toss a lasso on her for good. A gust of wind sent her red hair to curling and dancing. Rafe clenched his fists to keep from reaching for her. When he'd kissed her, every time he'd kissed her, he hadn't spent enough time touching her hair. Her temper sent a little thrill of fear up his spine, and he knew he was gonna have his hands full teaching her about how a wife needed to obey her husband. But she was a bright little thing. She'd admit that was the way things should be.

Eventually.

He hoped.

If he was real lucky.

He looked at those pink lips and knew he was. Real lucky.

When he caught himself wishing that Ethan, who'd been waiting for him impatiently, would go away, Rafe knew he was turning into a locoweed.

"Fine." Rafe was already learning which fights to bother with. He'd pick a nice, safe cave with no tunnels and no breakable floor, and set her to chiseling. He'd explore it thoroughly for danger before he left her there with Audra resting and Maggie napping and a posted guard — Ethan.

She'd be fine. Probably.

Rafe thought of that black tunnel he was going to have to explore today. And it looked like he'd have to do it alone.

For a few seconds he wrestled with a fear

so strong, he wasn't sure he could control it.

It occurred to him that maybe it wasn't fear. Maybe it was a warning from God. Which might mean the devil really was in that cave.

Rafe had a very unmanly urge to give the whole idea up and drag the womenfolk back to the Kincaid Ranch for good.

But he wanted that mountain valley, and he couldn't move Julia and her family there until he was sure it was safe.

"Can Audra make it over there?" Ethan asked.

"Probably, if we go slow." Rafe was worried about Audra, too. "And you carry her on your lap and Julia carries the baby."

"I don't want to carry that woman on my lap." Ethan's scowl looked strange on his face. Ethan never so much as frowned.

"And I don't want to sit on your lap, Ethan Kincaid." Audra came around the corner, looking so fragile and overburdened that Rafe started forward to take Maggie.

Julia beat Rafe there, handed Maggie off to Ethan, and slid an arm around her stepmother's waist.

Rafe thought of that meadow and the vents. That man he'd barely seen with the heavily bearded face. He thought of Julia and Audra and little Maggie in some tunnel with a madman climbing up out of a pit to drag them down. The chill that raced up his spine wasn't a bit like the cool control he liked.

Maggie grabbed for Ethan and yelled, "Papa!"

Ethan almost dropped her. He thrust the little one back into Julia's arms. "I'll unload these supplies."

Ethan led the packhorses toward the cabin at a near run. Since his own was still saddled, along with the two he'd led over, that left one horse to get ready, unless Maggie started hollering that she could ride alone, too.

As Ethan walked away, Maggie waved wildly, whacking Julia in the face. The little tyke screamed, "Bye-bye, Papa!"

Papa?

It was an idea with merit. Someone needed to marry Audra. Rafe decided he'd get himself hitched to Julia first, then turn his attention to his brother. Who'd be the father of two about the same time he got married.

That oughta wipe that fool grin off Ethan's face.

That was a distracting enough thought that Rafe shook off his dread of the mountain meadow. He was smiling as he saddled his horse.

Rafe had as good as dragged her through that vent without giving her a second to study what she was sure was a large fish.

The tyrant.

She also really wanted to explore the tunnel Rafe had abandoned her in chasing that man. There were quite possibly more vents to be found. Perhaps more fish. At the top of a mountain. How did it get up here except maybe during a massive flood? The Great Flood. Noah's Flood.

She'd write a book.

It made her almost desperate for the cavern she'd gotten stuck in the day she'd met Rafe. She hadn't been back, and it made her edgy to think of all she wanted to see in that bigger cavern.

Instead they'd rushed through the vent and ridden straight to the big arched gap they could see all the way through. There were no tunnels or fossils to be found here, though she hadn't examined it closely.

Smiling, she realized she could happily live in this area for the rest of her life.

"Look at that." Rafe pointed down the slope. "No one would know you could ride up here. But it'll be easy. We can drive the cattle with no problem."

The four of them stood beneath a stone arch ten feet high and twenty feet wide. The rock overhead looked solid though it was only a few yards wide. It reminded Julia of the rainbow God had sent as a covenant with Noah.

"I can't believe someone hasn't climbed in here before to settle." Ethan shoved his hat back on his head and studied the steep mountainside. "But from down there, I'll bet this opening isn't even visible because of the ledge."

"Such a beautiful place." Audra stood beside Julia.

Ethan had Maggie sleeping in the pack on his back.

"Audra, let's find a spot where you can sit down and rest while Maggie takes her nap." Julia rested a hand on Audra's shoulder.

"We're going to make this work." Rafe nodded, no doubt planning every minute of their lives for the next fifty years. Julia felt a bit savage as she wondered when he'd inform her of how things were going to be.

"But first we need to find whoever is skulking around this place."

The man clearly had a list of their activities all laid out. She thought scornfully that if she chose, she could live quite nicely without ever having to think again.

Rafe turned from the beautiful view in front of him to look across the meadow. Julia turned with him. The whole thing was oval-shaped, with edges reaching up all around nearly one hundred feet to the jagged top of the caldera.

This big opening was on the south. The vent they'd come in through was on the east side within a couple of miles of her cabin. Julia wondered where else they'd find caves in here. Rafe wanted to live here. Her heart began pounding to think of all she could find. A caldera — she could research that for a long time.

She had some ideas about volcanoes and earthquakes and the Great Flood. The Bible said water had come from rain, but it had also erupted from the deep. Who was to say this was formed by a volcano. Maybe flood-water had exploded upward with the force of lava.

It would be easy to spend her life writing it all down. Definitely a book of her own, instead of contributing to magazines and books written by others. Or maybe someone would serialize it. A lot of magazines and newspapers carried stories that way.

She'd agreed to marry Rafe. Or at least she hadn't put a stop to the idea. Her heart sank as she thought of tying herself to another man who didn't love her. It had taken her years to shield her heart against her father. Now she needed to make this choice so there would be a safe place for Audra and the children.

Rafe . . . Well, Rafe wanted her. But mainly he wanted to run her life. He was protective by nature, and he'd decided she was his responsibility. Whether he would ever love her, Julia didn't dare to hope. Julia pictured the years ahead in a loveless marriage. She'd write. She'd explore. She'd care for Audra and Maggie and the new baby.

If she didn't marry Rafe, she'd have to leave this mountain, which dashed her dreams of writing a book. She'd have to get to a town somewhere, find a job, earn enough money to care for her little family. It wouldn't be easy. In fact, it might well be impossible.

She needed help and Rafe was willing to give it. Her chin lifted. It was practical. Julia knew a dream was dying. The dream of one day finding a man who would love her. But she wasn't a woman for foolishness.

Audra needed what Rafe could give her, and Julia loved Audra and the babies enough to do what needed doing. At least she wouldn't be as lonely as she'd been growing up.

She looked around the valley that was very possibly going to be her home, and her eyes were drawn to that dark crack in the east side where Rafe had been so scared. It might be another cavern like the one she'd been exploring when Rafe found her.

"I want to go look down there." It was truly a wondrous place they planned to live.

"This is a terrible place." Rafe turned to look where she pointed, and his jaw stiffened. "How can I ever make it safe?"

Julia shook her head at Mr. Dark Cloud. "Let's go. You're determined to explore all of it. Hunt down the man we saw, right? We might as well start there."

How many caves might there be? How many fossils. Yes, they'd seen a man. And someone had been in that cavern with her and frightened her badly and tampered with her rope so she couldn't escape. But they'd hunt that man down. Run him off or have him arrested. Then this treasure trove would be hers, all hers. Well, and Rafe's, but he'd be busy with cattle. Just like her father, he'd be gone more than home, even if they were both in this valley together. All she lacked was a way to get to town and mail her papers back East. Rafe could run that errand for her.

She struck off toward that low cave. She had so much to explore, she almost couldn't get it done in a lifetime.

But only almost.

She had a feeling being married to a bossy man who didn't love her was going to make for a very long life — she'd find time for everything.

Her pulse picked up, as she got to the clump of aspens. There had been some fossils right inside. Glancing behind her, she saw Rafe glaring at her, almost daring her to charge in without him.

Giving him her sweetest smile, she did her best to conceal her impatience, though she caught herself standing with her arms crossed and her toe tapping on the stony ground. Would Rafe notice her impatience?

If it had just been Rafe, she might have scolded, even gone in. But what could she say when he had Audra leaning on his arm?

"Just calm down." Rafe didn't seem to have a problem scolding. And yes, he noticed her attitude. That didn't exactly make him a genius.

"I'm perfectly calm." Well, she wasn't going in without him, which wasn't the same as calm, but it was the best he was going to get.

"You and Audra stay out here." Rafe let go of Audra, took a step toward the crevice, and pulled his gun from its holster. There was a loud metallic *crack* as he cocked the pistol. A shiver of fear touched Julia for the first time. His eyes fixed on the dark opening.

She grabbed at Rafe's arm as he approached the cave. "Do you really think you need that gun? I don't want you to be in danger."

The intense expression on his face relaxed as he turned to look at her. "Worried about me, sweetheart?"

Julia huffed but held on. "Of course I'm worried about you. If you think you need to be ready to shoot, then there's something to worry about."

Rafe shrugged. "We saw a man in here. A man who ran when he spotted us. Not only that, but a cave can hide a bear or a mountain lion or a rattlesnake. It makes sense to be braced for trouble."

Ethan came up, still carrying Maggie. He'd staked the horses to grass and stripped their saddles, all with a sleeping baby on his back and that vapid smile on his face. "Got shootin' trouble, big brother?"

"Stay with the women." Rafe turned back to the cave.

Julia hung on to Rafe. With one impatient look at her grasping hand, Rafe yanked himself free and headed for the cave.

Julia took one step after him.

"Oh no you don't." Ethan's hand landed on her shoulder.

Rafe looked back, saw Ethan had a hold of her, and smirked before he headed on.

Julia tugged against Ethan's grip. He held on. "Just give him a minute."

Then, still holding her shoulder and toting a baby, he turned to Audra. "Why don't we get you settled on the grass by those trees?"

"I don't need to sit down all the time." Audra plunked her fists on her greatly expanded waist.

"Well, could you take the baby?" Ethan's smile faded.

Julia wondered why the man who never stopped grinning was suddenly gruff with poor little Audra.

"I'm tired of carrying her and I thought you could help."

Audra pinked up with temper and a bit of embarrassment. "Of course I'll take my baby."

"Well, sit down first. We're gonna be here awhile and you don't want to try and sit once you've got her. I'll just have to take her again while you settle in."

Somehow Ethan made it sound like Audra standing made more work for him and it'd be a kindness to him if she'd sit.

Audra sat on the plush grass in the shade of the aspens. Ethan arched one brow at Julia. "Can I let go of you without you running into that cave?"

Which reminded Julia of how much she wanted to run into that cave. "Of course."

Ethan's eyes narrowed, but he released Julia to gently swing Maggie around and ease her out of the carrier. Then he knelt in front of Audra.

"How are you feeling?" Ethan's words were spoken so quietly they might have been to not bother the sleeping baby, but Maggie hadn't stirred and he'd been speaking in his regular voice before. Now, it sounded . . . intimate.

"I'm fine." Audra sounded exasperated as she reached for Maggie.

"I know you're fine." Ethan kept murmuring as he crouched beside her. "Why do you have to fuss at me so? I'm just trying to make things a little easier for you."

"How would you like everyone treating you like you were incompetent? A burden. How would you like it if no one would even let you make your own decisions?"

Ethan smiled and went from crouching to kneeling. "You mean like a bossy big brother?"

Audra reached for Maggie, and as their arms touched, bound together supporting the little toddler, Audra looked up. Her irritable expression faded and she smiled. "Yes, I guess it's just like that."

Julia wondered if a bossy stepdaughter qualified.

"I know *just* how I'd feel."

"You'd hate it. You'd try and stand on your own."

Nodding, Ethan said, "I'd light out and wander the world. I'd try to prove to everyone, especially myself, that I could run my own life. But that doesn't mean it's wrong for me to encourage a woman who's most of the way toward having a baby and who seems to be threatening to rush that baby into the world, to take it a little easy on herself. It doesn't mean I think you're a weakling."

"Really?" Audra whispered the words.

"Yeah, really." Their eyes met. Their arms stayed entwined.

Julia felt like she was intruding.

Ethan was a kind man.

"Julia, get in here."

Unlike his brother.

"Hurry up." Rafe's voice echoed in all its tyranny from the cave. Then his head popped out. "It goes back a long way. We need lanterns. Ethan, you fetch the lanterns from the supplies and bring me a lasso. Audra, stay put and try to take it easy on yourself, and tend the baby. Ethan, once you get those lanterns, bring 'em in to me and Julia. The tunnel splits a few yards in. Stay to the higher path. Then you get back out here and look out for Audra. She needs to get some rest, and someone has to stand guard. Hurry up with those lanterns. We can't go deeper without light."

Ethan and Audra exchanged a look that spoke volumes as he eased his hands free of holding Maggie. Then he rose. "I'll get those lanterns right quick, boss." He gave Rafe a short, hard salute, and that smile was back. A smile that almost concealed the angry glint in Ethan's eyes.

He headed for the horses.

They'd brought a lot of lanterns. Julia had already noticed the Kincaid men liked a lot of light. They'd all learned that lesson the hard way.

She eagerly climbed behind the aspen trees, where she and Rafe stepped back into the cave. Her eyes went to that fossil she'd seen last time, but Rafe caught her wrist and dragged her past it. Rafe's broad shoulders almost brushed the sides of the cave, his head skimming just under the roof.

"There's light up here." Rafe kept moving. Julia knew they should have left all light behind by now, yet she could still see.

"There's a hole overhead. See that tunnel, the one that goes down?" Rafe pointed.

"Yes."

"I went that way last time because I heard running. But in this direction, there's a good-sized hole overhead. It acts like a window in the cave roof." Rafe turned another corner, and Julia saw him stand straighter. The tunnel was lighter and wider. He stopped. Julia came up and stood beside him. Once there, she saw a beam of light shining down on the stone floor. And on the floor were the remains of a fire.

She gasped. "Someone's living in here."

"A buffalo robe and a bedroll."

"No saddle." Julia realized what else was missing. "No horse. He'd have kept it in the meadow. How did he get so far from town?"

"There's more. At the cave entrance I saw fresh footprints overtop of the ones we left."

Julia looked back toward the tunnel. "So he's still here."

"Yep. Which means you can't come in here. And, Jules, I've thought it through.

This just isn't safe to have this cave here. We need to . . ."

"Oh, Rafe, look." Julia turned to study the wall. "On the wall here."

". . . close it off."

"It might be another fossil. These caves are a wonder. I could explore for —"

"To be safe, I think I should get some dynamite."

"What!" Julia turned from the rock. "Are you out of your mind?"

"Nope, pretty sure I'm not. I'm wondering about you though."

Julia abandoned her latest find. She battled with the idea of just yelling at Rafe until he saw reason. But considering his complete lack of respect for fossils, she doubted she'd live long enough, even if she died an old, old woman. She would try to use honey instead of vinegar. Though she'd never had much use for that approach — nor success with it.

"Rafe, that would be a sacrilege."

"Now, Jules, I heard what you said about Noah's Ark before, but —"

"Don't you see?" She stepped close and rested a hand flat on his chest. "I could write a book about this. We might have, right here in this cavern, scientific proof of the Bible. Of a sort never found before." As she spoke, she gained enthusiasm for her project. "I could bring people to a better understanding of God. I could lead lost souls to the Lord with my work. It's not just about my interest in fossils. It's about God allowing me to see a . . . a miracle."

Rafe looked around the dingy cave. "God isn't here, Jules."

"Of course He is. He's everywhere." She clutched the front of his brown broadcloth shirt, her thoughts rabbiting around, trying to think how she could stop him from the travesty of sealing this cavern.

"No, I don't mean that. Of course He's everywhere." Rafe rested his strong, deeply tanned hand on hers, where she held him. "There are people in the Bible who witnessed a miracle and still didn't believe. There were people who *received* a miracle and didn't believe. You think if you write a book about Noah's Ark, that you found evidence of water in the high-up mountains, people will read it and be forced to admit there is a God and they should worship Him?"

"That's exactly what I think."

"It doesn't work that way." Rafe's arms came around her.

She felt his strength. She knew he was a good man. But he just didn't understand.

"I can change the world with the knowledge to be found in this cave. I can help open people's minds to God. I can —"

"This is not about God."

She stared straight forward into his chest and felt a stubbornness welling up in her. "Yes it *is*."

"No." Rafe caught her chin and lifted until she had to look him in the eye. "It's about you being alone."

"What does that mean?" Julia tugged at his grip, but she realized his hand on her face was warm. She liked it. More quietly she said, "I'm not alone."

"You've always been alone."

"I've got Audra and the baby."

"Now maybe, but you've spent your life trying to fill empty hours. And you've found something that is meaningful to you."

"There's nothing wrong with that."

"This is about you wanting to be —" Rafe swallowed hard — "wanting to be *worthy* of your father's love."

Julia felt like she was being forced toward something she wanted to avoid.

"I know because I spent my whole life doing the same thing."

Their eyes met, and Julia realized she was being held in the arms of a man who might understand her better than she understood herself.

Rafe went on. "All my life I tried to get my father and mother to love me. Now, even with them both gone for years, I think I'm still trying. I'm still trying to be good enough, smart enough, hardworking enough to make them love me."

"And you think I'm doing the same thing," Julia asked, "by searching for . . . for . . ."

"For God in a cave?"

Shaking her head, Julia said, "That's not what I'm doing."

"Searching for proof written in stone that there's really a God, when you already know in your heart He exists?"

"But it's not proof for me. It's proof for the world."

"The world's got all the proof it needs. All that's left is for them to accept it or reject it."

Julia let her eyes fall shut. Silence stretched between them. At last she said, "You think I've wasted my life."

"No." He pressed a kiss on her forehead. "I think you've found a way to fill the empty hours. But you don't have to do that anymore. A ranch wife has all the work she can handle. And there are people around who care about you and depend on you. And love you."

She waited for him to include himself.

She waited in vain.

He was asking her to give up her life's work and was offering nothing in return. At least her father had given her freedom . . . even if it was freedom rooted in neglect.

Without his pledge of love, she couldn't abandon her fossils and geology. "I'll make you a deal, Rafe."

"A deal? About fossil hunting?"

"Yes, I want you to see what I've seen. I want you to go with me just once to look at the fossils I found in Seth's Cavern. I want you to listen to my theories and see the fish and other evidence of water at the top of a mountain."

"Julia, honey, I —"

"Rafe, I've got the lanterns."

Julia thought her husband-to-be looked relieved.

"Bring 'em on in, Eth."

Ethan emerged with three lanterns, one of them lit, and a lasso over his shoulder. His teeth were clenched and he was breathing hard as he delivered the gear needed to explore the tunnel.

Julia took a lantern, happy to turn her attention to something she was better at than inspiring love.

CHAPTER 15

"Ethan, you go back and keep an eye on Audra." Rafe judged from Ethan's expression and the speed when he headed out that he was only too happy to go. Rafe looped the lasso over his neck and under one arm and led Julia back to that steep downward tunnel.

He needed to explore all these caverns.

He needed to catch whomever was lurking around here.

He needed to get a cabin up.

He *really* needed to get the wedding over and done.

Then he had to make sure Ethan was handling things right at the Kincaid Ranch.

And to drive a herd into this meadow.

But first — He'd given this some thought. A lot of thought. Haunting, nightmarish thought. He wondered if that sloping tunnel would lead to the place Rafe suspected.

He'd stopped at that pit the last time. This

time he'd go on if he could. Rafe started slowly, carefully descending, mindful of stone floors as thin as an eggshell.

"I've got no idea how far back this goes, but do you feel the breeze?" he asked. "And I'm smelling fresh air. I think this leads to a way out."

Julia nodded. "Which means someone living down here will be hard to trap if he knows the cavern and has a dependable back door."

Rafe smiled at Julia. She was a smart woman and she was his. He considered taking a break from all his planning to kiss her. But he turned back to the job at hand. "Let's go."

With the way that floor had broken under Seth all those years ago vividly in his mind, Rafe inched forward. The tunnel sloped downward so quickly the footing wasn't great. "If it gets any steeper, we may need to tie a rope off. We've got to be able to climb back up."

"It must be okay — there are still footprints."

Then Rafe found something else. Torches. Unlit, rigged in the walls in a way that reminded Rafe of the way he'd done it when he was a kid.

"Let's light these." Rafe lifted the glass

chimney of his lantern with a scratch of metal on glass and lit the first torch.

"Look." Julia pointed at the flow of smoke gliding back the direction they'd come. A breeze was coming up from the depths.

"There's definitely cross ventilation. That means this leads outside somewhere." His voice echoed with every word.

The tunnel kept going down. Rafe lit any torches he found. The light helped, but still the roof seemed like a weight hanging over his head. Julia's quiet steps echoed behind him, her little boots scraping on the floor, and he wondered if he shouldn't go back. Get her out of here. What was he doing leading her down here? She was in danger. He should have —

"Do you hear dripping?"

He looked back at Julia. Then he listened. "Water?" The cavern seemed to press against him. He fought to stay calm.

"Could we have possibly . . . ?" Julia came up beside him and lifted her lantern to a spot in the low ceiling that glistened. She reached up to touch it and pulled her hand away wet.

She sniffed it. "It's just water."

"What else could it be?" Rafe had a sudden image of blood dripping down. He remembered how Julia had been bleeding when he'd pulled her out of the cavern. He remembered how he'd bled from the cut on his head so many years ago. Touching his scar, he forced the memory away. "Of course it's water."

"I wondered if it could be water heavy with calcium or limestone, dripping down, the same thing that forms stalactites and stalagmites. But there's nothing on the floor to show it's building up."

"Well, it could be a spring." The water formed a tiny trickling rivulet on the side of the tunnel, and ran downward out of sight in the dark. "But considering how far we've walked, mostly east, I wonder if we could be walking under that stream that runs between your cabin and Kincaid property."

"You really think we might be under it?" She looked up and Rafe saw fear. He hoped his fear didn't show.

"And if we're under it, we're not far from the cavern where I found you."

She straightened and turned to look ahead. "This might be a back door into it. I've never been able to find one."

Her fear had vanished. Rafe sure wished he could scare her good enough to keep her out of this place. Instead —

"Do you know what this means?"

Rafe knew.

"I can walk from a cabin built in that caldera straight into the cavern. Exploring will be simpler than ever." She smiled, and the excitement flashing in her eyes caught the flickering lantern light and made her look just the littlest bit like a raving lunatic.

And he was planning to marry her. He couldn't wait, which probably meant he was a raving lunatic, too.

"Let's go." She strode off, leaving him behind.

The little fanatic headed down the slope fast.

Like any good soon-to-be husband, Rafe had made his woman very happy.

He would have stopped and bashed his head against the rock wall if he wasn't afraid she'd get ahead of him and maybe fall through the floor in some spot that was eggshell thin. Or better yet, find a place where a stream came gushing down from overhead to sweep her into the bowels of the earth.

"Look at this." Julia pointed to a break in the tunnel wall. "There might be dozens of trails in here. Who knows how long it will take to explore all of them."

Rafe raised his lantern and managed to light up a few feet of this side tunnel, but he couldn't tell if it ended or just went beyond the reach of the light.

Rafe hurried to catch up to her, and together they went on downward.

He breathed a sigh of relief when the man went on and eased his gun back in his holster.

She'd come.

Moving in the darkness like a shadow, he slid his hand to his holster and knew he wasn't going to let her slip through his fingers again. Maybe watching the man die would help loosen her tongue.

Rubbing his scars, he felt how wet his palms were and wiped them on his pants. He shifted his eyes between the light of the man's lantern and the dark of this passageway. It wasn't fear. His hands didn't sweat because of fear. Down here he feared nothing.

Excitement — that's what it was.

A tiny laugh escaped his lips, and he immediately stifled it. As soon as the man and woman went around the corner, he went back and doused the torches. He wanted pitch-darkness. He didn't like them getting ahead of him, but it was necessary. When he made his move, they'd be left in utter darkness and that would put him in control.

He returned to the crevice where he'd almost been found and followed its winding trail to get ahead of them.

Maybe it was time to be done with his friend, too. He no longer served a purpose.

Now. Finally. It was time.

"It's time to go back. Ethan might be worrying." That sounded good. Make it about Ethan, or better yet . . . "And who knows if Audra might be getting nervous. We don't want her fretting when she's so delicate."

Julia just kept on going. Rafe ran his hand up and down the lasso Ethan had brought. He could rope her, hog-tie her, toss her over his shoulder, and be back outside in about five minutes.

She stopped so suddenly, Rafe ran into her back. Julia squeaked and stumbled. Rafe grabbed her and pulled her against himself just as he saw the hole in the floor right ahead of them. He backed away, dragging her along, wondering if the floor was going to collapse like it had under Seth. Then, as soon as that thought occurred to him, he pushed Julia behind him and dropped to his knees. Leaning forward with the lantern, he crept slowly forward until he could see down into the pit. The bottom wasn't that far away. He rested his hand on an outcropping of rock beside him where a rope had been tied and someone had been climbing down.

Or up.

He thought of how, when he was here before, he'd kicked that rock and it had bounced and bounced as it fell. He looked at the bottom of this hole and saw a corner that was pure black. That rock he kicked could have gone on down.

As he studied the pit, Rafe saw something that made him feel like he was a boy again. "There's a broken lantern down there." He knew instantly that it had to be the lantern Ethan had dropped on Seth all those years ago. Well, it didn't *have* to be. But it was. Rafe was sure. He saw charred remnants of the hemp rope he'd used to hang the lantern around his neck.

"Where?" Julia asked from behind.

He leaned down far enough to see the edge of the hole and nearly shuddered with relief to see solid rock under them.

"The floor isn't going to break off. It's safe." As safe as this place ever got. "Come and look. Get down here."

He wanted her beside him. He needed her here, to see what he'd done, what he'd survived. Julia knelt, and he held the lantern as far forward as he could reach, casting light in the pit. "See that metal down there?"

"Yes, it's the base of a lantern just like this one."

"It's mine." Rafe looked away from the pit. Julia turned to him. They were only inches apart.

"Yours? It's all rusted. It's been down there for years."

"Thirteen. Thirteen years. This has to be the tunnel Seth was running down when the floor cracked and he fell through." Rafe looked to the other side of the pit. "Only we were coming from that direction. Seth had run ahead. Ethan and I were figuring he was planning to jump out and scare us. Then we heard him scream. A rumble of falling rocks. Another shout. Seth never asked for help. Never showed fear.

"I took off and ran toward the voice, Ethan at my heels."

The tunnel took him back to the worst time of his life.

Rafe running down the tunnel, Seth's shouts getting louder. Bats, outlaws, ghosts, Satan — Rafe's mind went wild as he ran toward his yelling little brother. Ethan was right beside Rafe with the lantern.

Another loud crack, the sound of tumbling stones. A wild scream froze Rafe in his tracks. Ethan plowed into him. Rafe turned to Ethan and saw the horror in his brother's eyes from that last terrible scream.

Rafe almost ran away. It was an evil impulse. But he wanted out.

Seth was being eaten by monsters.

The cave was a monster coming for him next.

They'd slid down into the mouth of a creature who would feast on their bones. To run, to leave Seth was weak and ugly, but for a moment Rafe almost did it. He almost abandoned his little brother to run for the sunlight.

How many times had Pa told him he had to protect his little brothers? Then Pa would ride off for days, weeks. But instead of protecting them, he'd brought them down here, and now he wanted to run. Save himself. He fought to do the right thing, and it felt as if sleet coursed through his veins.

Just a couple of steps behind Rafe, Ethan pointed at a black entrance to a side tunnel. "He's down there."

Ethan rushed into the opening.

"Be careful," Seth yelled. "There's a hole!" Seth was talking, warning them. He wasn't being eaten alive. He wasn't already dead. They ran toward him.

Wherever their little brother was, he was keeping his head. After those few shouts of terror, he'd gained control of himself and shouted directions and caution.

It was a good thing he did.

Seth's warning saved Ethan. With a short cry of fear, Ethan skidded to a stop right on the brink of a gaping hole in the cavern floor.

"Seth!" Ethan dropped to his knees.

Rafe went cold clear through but was glad of it because his mind seemed to work better with his gut turned to ice.

"Back up." Seth's voice came from the darkness below where Ethan knelt. "The ground won't hold."

Rafe knew there were holes in this place that seemed to be bottomless. How would they get Seth out of there?

"Won't hold what?" Ethan reached out his lantern. The light trembled as Rafe came up beside Ethan without looking at his face. He couldn't stand to see how Ethan was. Of the three of them, Ethan was the one who didn't like this place. He always came along and never acted scared. In fact, he delighted in pretending all his spooky ideas were for fun, but Rafe could tell Ethan really was spooked.

Rafe leaned forward. Ethan lowered the lantern past the edge of the pit, and Rafe saw that he and Ethan were kneeling on stone as thin as an eggshell.

The ground won't hold.

"Back up, Ethan," Rafe ordered as he quickly scuttled backward. Then he shouted, "We'll get you out, Seth."

Ethan started back just as the stone under his hand cracked and his whole arm fell through the floor.

Ethan landed hard on his face and belly. An ugly crack sounded when his chest hit. Ethan yelled in fear and scooted away from the fracturing hole, flat on his stomach.

"Hurry, Ethan!"

Ethan shoved himself backward and the stone broke again and again, as if the collapsing ground followed him, wanted him. Was hungry for him. Then it all shattered and he plunged forward. Rafe grabbed him by the waist of his pants before he went into the abyss.

The lantern fell and shattered. Flames shot up from below as the kerosene spread and ignited. Ethan dangled, head down.

"Fire!" Seth screamed in pain. "Rafe, help me!"

The ground quit breaking off. Terrified for Seth, Rafe yanked hard and heard Ethan's pants rip.

Seth's screams grew louder. Flames shot up until Rafe thought he was staring right into the entrance to Hades.

Ethan cleared the ledge with a backward lunge. Rafe flew back along with Ethan. A jagged piece of rock raked Rafe's forehead. Stars exploded behind his eyes. Seth screamed again and Rafe threw himself forward.

Flames coated the rocks below. Seth was lit up, leaping. "I'm burning. I'm on fire. Rafe! Ethan!" One arm and the whole back of Seth's shirt blazed, splashed with kerosene.

"Get your shirt off, Seth!" Rafe roared to be heard over the distance and the yelling and the crackling fire. "Get it off!"

Seth caught the front of his shirt with both arms, one on fire, and jerked his shirt open, throwing it aside. Throwing the fire off himself. Seth slapped at his hair, still on fire, and shrieked with pain.

"You're all right. We'll get you out."

"My arm is burned, Rafe!" The rocks were still flaming between Rafe and Seth. There was no way down or up. Rafe's cool control slipped. He fought down his panic. How would they get Seth out of there?

"Just be careful of the fire. We're here. We'll get you."

"My arm hurts. I don't think I can use it to climb up, even if there is a way." Seth's voice cracked, and a muffled sob came from down in that awful, burning lake of fire.

The fire on the kerosene-soaked rocks was dying. Which made Rafe think of something else. He gave one look at Ethan, who even in the darkness, looked pale as milk. Ethan was sitting, relaxed, leaning against the wall of the tunnel as if he didn't have a single worry in the world.

"Ethan, go get one of the torches." A moment of dizziness almost stopped Rafe, but he fought it off.

"What?" Ethan sounded unsteady, dazed, his eyes locked on the flames.

Rafe lifted his hand and touched hot liquid coating his face. Blood. There was no time to attend to that. "Ethan!"

Ethan barely managed to turn his eyes from the glowing depths. Ethan wasn't close enough to the hole to see Seth. But he could see the light cast by the flames. Rafe knew, even if Ethan didn't, that when those flames died, they'd be trapped in the pitch-darkness.

He lunged toward Ethan and grabbed his arm hard enough to leave bruises. "I'm going for a torch."

"What?" Ethan lifted his head too slowly and looked Rafe in the eye, but he didn't seem to understand.

"We're going to be down here in the dark

in a couple of minutes. I'm going for a torch while the fire from down there can still give me a little light. Talk to Seth. Make sure he knows we haven't left him."

Another of those muffled sobs sounded from below. Seth was the toughest guy Rafe knew and had been since Rafe's earliest memories. He must be in agony to cry.

The light diminished. Even now, Rafe would be fumbling along in the darkness for a long time walking back to the last torch they'd left.

"Talk to him!"

Ethan shuddered so hard he almost shook off Rafe's hand.

From fury and fear and a simple need to hurt somebody, Rafe clenched his fist and slammed it into Ethan's face.

"Hey!" The blow seemed to bring Ethan out of whatever shock he'd been in.

Seth's cries grew louder as the fire dimmed. "Talk to him. Talk to Seth. I'll be right back."

"No, don't leave us!" Ethan clawed at Rafe. That was when Rafe figured out his brother wasn't thinking right at all. He probably *had* hit his head. And Rafe had just hit him again. Stupid, cruel thing to do.

"I'll be right back. Talk to Seth." Taking a split second to wonder if the floor of this place had any more stretches made of rock that broke like glass, Rafe jumped to his feet.

He ran away from the light and suddenly he was running wild. Running away.

Rafe shook his head and was back with Julia.

"Seth was so badly burned. For weeks we weren't sure if he'd live. After he'd cheated death, he was never the same. The pain made him . . . made him crazy. He had terrible nightmares. Ma and Pa couldn't stand it. Ma was always a quiet woman, but after the accident she spent most of the time crying and sitting in her chair. Pa couldn't stand the nightmares and got so he didn't come home much. Ethan got so he wouldn't take anything seriously. He knew, more than anyone else, how close I came to abandoning him and Seth in that pit, and he's never fully trusted me again. Never cared about me or anyone again.

"If I'm tested like that again, I can't promise to do the right thing." He didn't look her in the eye. He couldn't. "I wouldn't blame you if you were afraid to join your life to mine."

They knelt face-to-face on that tunnel floor, and he waited for her to stand up and walk away in disgust. Leave him. Any decent woman would.

Her arms came around him and she gathered him in.

He shouldn't let her. He wasn't up to the job of protecting her and her family. He should let her find a man who was strong enough, controlled enough to put her ahead of everyone else, for sure ahead of himself.

Her arms tightened and Rafe couldn't push her away.

He set the lantern aside and dragged her into his arms.

He smiled to think of coming at them from the deep heart of the cavern.

Then he thought of where they must be standing, right on the brink of that hole in the floor. It was the one place he hated. The ledge was so narrow on the side of it and he'd have to cross it.

He found one of the many torches his friend had made and struck a match. He'd reveal himself and see if they let him get close. If they did run, he'd shoot out their lanterns and they'd run into pure darkness.

Fervently he hoped they wouldn't recognize him as a danger until it was too late.

He quickly set his torch aside and took off his holster, then tucked his gun into the small of his back. Laughing quietly, he reclaimed the torch, then made his way forward, wiping his palms on his tattered pants.

Tired of the waiting.

By the time Rafe quit kissing her, he was almost completely in control again — except for the part of himself that kept finding excuses to kiss Julia. At least he was distracted from all the twisting shame inside him.

They held each other, kneeling together.

"And . . . and you were here?" Julia asked. "You knew this exit to the cavern was here all along?"

"No, we were on the other side." Rafe's eyes followed the hole to the far side just as a man holding a torch stepped into view.

Julia screamed and tightened her hold. "That's him! The man I saw duck into this cave the other day. And it's got to be the man who stranded me down here."

The man tensed for a moment as if prepared to run, but he . . . didn't.

Instead he straightened and lifted his torch.

Rafe stared, slowly rising to his feet, pulling Julia up with him. The man looked bone thin. He had a full beard and hair so shaggy, long and wild, a grizzly would have offered him a comb. The clothing hanging from his skeletal frame was in rags, the sleeves torn into strips. Holes showed his legs to the point of indecency. Rafe rubbed his eyes and looked again. And saw the same impossible thing.

"We need to get him." Julia yanked on Rafe's arm. "We'll take him to town and turn him over to the sheriff."

"We're not going to have him arrested, sweetheart."

"Oh, yes we are."

"Oh, no we're not." Rafe couldn't look away.

"But he's dangerous. I could have died."

"Not only aren't we going to have him arrested," Rafe said, looking down at her but only for a moment, afraid he was seeing a vision that would vanish if he looked away from the man, "we're going to have to let him live with us."

"What?" Julia's voice was so high-pitched, Rafe thought his eardrums might have sustained some damage.

"Rafe?" The man's voice sounded ragged, like he hadn't used it in a long, long time. "Rafe, is that you?"

Nodding, Rafe tried to reply, but his voice failed. He cleared his throat and found himself so close to tears that he was terrified he'd shame himself. Clenching a fist, he bore down on his feelings and breathed in and out slowly until his throat stood a chance of working.

Finally he could answer. "Yeah, it's me. It's me — Rafe."

"What are you doing down here? You never come down here."

"Today I'm glad I came."

"Me too. Can you help me find my way home?"

That question made Rafe realize he was dealing with a man with only a slim grasp on reality. "I'd be glad to help you find your way home."

Julia sank claws into Rafe's forearm. "What are you saying?"

"Thanks. I keep getting lost." The man's voice sounded hollow and forlorn as it echoed off the tunnel walls. "I'm so tired of being lost."

"Well, you're not lost anymore. Welcome home, Seth."

Seth scampered along the edge of the pit as if he'd done it a thousand times. Rafe's stomach twisted to think the floor would crumble, and he opened his mouth to order Seth to stop. But Seth was already across, and he threw himself into Rafe's arms.

Julia shrieked and stumbled and fell on her backside. Rafe needed to pick her up, but he couldn't let go of Seth. Not when he had just taken hold of him after so many years.

Seth smelled like a thousand gallons of stale sweat soaked in unwashed clothes that'd been stored in a dung heap. Rafe had a fight on his hands to force himself to hang on to his filthy little brother. Then he realized anew the miracle of Seth coming home and it wasn't so hard at all.

Rafe was holding on to skin and bones. Seth didn't feel weak, though. He had a grip like an Apache warrior minus the tomahawk. Rafe immediately began making a mental list.

He needed to fatten Seth up.

Dunk him in the creek with a big bar of soap.

Cut his hair and get him shaved.

Get him some new clothes.

Hopefully while Rafe was doing all that, Seth would calm down enough to make a little sense.

Then Rafe thought of something else. "Ethan is outside the tunnel. Come out and say hello to him."

"Ethan? Ethan's here?" Seth lifted his head. Rafe felt like he was face-to-face with a bear. Seth was so furry and such a mess, it was a wonder Rafe had recognized him. Seth swung his shaggy head to look at Julia, still on the ground. Rafe hadn't gotten around to helping her up yet.

Julia squeaked, and Rafe turned to see her sliding away, up the tunnel, on her backside. She was terrified of Seth, and who could blame her? Seth had to be the one who'd scared her so badly that day and left her stranded in the cavern.

Rafe remembered Seth's wild blue eyes. The color was hard to make out in the torch-lit cave, but the wild was there for sure. "Yeah, he's back to stay. I've bought this . . ." Then Rafe realized about five things that changed his list considerably.

To keep Seth around, Rafe was going to have to take him home to the Kincaid Ranch.

And Seth needed Rafe there to take care of him.

Which meant Rafe wasn't going to be able to live in this caldron.

Judging from the horror in Julia's eyes, he wasn't going to be able to claim her and hold her close day and night.

Giving up living with Ethan had come hard, but Ethan was thinking clearly and he'd live nearby and could ride over and visit anytime. But Rafe saw clear as day that Seth needed help. He needed both of his brothers to take care of him, but especially Rafe. And it wouldn't be the work of a few days to help him. It might well be the work of a lifetime.

Which meant, considering Seth might well be dangerous, Rafe wasn't going to be able to take on responsibility for anyone else until Seth got his senses back — which might never happen.

He had to choose between his brother and Julia. And either choice broke his heart. This was exactly why a man wasn't supposed to let his heart warm to anyone.

Rafe decided to drag Seth out to see Ethan and see if daylight made his thoughts any clearer.

As they walked out, Rafe realized it was pitch-dark the whole way. "When did you put the torches out, Seth?"

Seth was busy scratching his belly and didn't answer.

CHAPTER 16

Ethan saw movement at the cave mouth, took one second to look and went for his gun.

"Stop." Rafe appeared behind a walking grizzly. With pants on. The grizzly not Rafe. Well, Rafe had pants on, too.

"It's Seth." Rafe's hand appeared in front of . . . Seth?

His brother Seth?

Ethan dropped his gun back in his holster, and with his eyes riveted on the bear that was eating his little brother, he approached until he could see the eyes. The reckless, wild blue eyes — just like Pa's.

"Seth?" Ethan hesitated because they weren't a hugging family. Then he remembered how Rafe had grabbed him when he'd first come home and how good it felt. He launched himself at Seth, and Seth grabbed on just as tight. When the smell hit him, Ethan's arms went slack.

Then he met Rafe's eyes over Seth's shoulder and saw so much love and concern and determination that Ethan stayed hanging on. Finally he thumped Seth hard on the back and withdrew enough to look him in the eye. "Seth, it's you. I've missed you, boy."

Seth smiled. Green teeth shone through that wild man beard and hair. The boy needed a bath, a shave, a haircut, and a whole lot of other stuff.

"Ethan." Seth's eyes met his, then wavered and looked past Ethan to the canyon. "Where's the house?"

"We're going to build one." Ethan eased around so he stood looking at the valley with Seth. He slid an arm around shockingly bony shoulders. "Rafe is going to —"

"He means *our* house, the Kincaid house, Ethan. Seth is lost. We're going to help him get home."

Ethan turned to look over his shoulder at Rafe. Rafe came up beside them, Rafe on Seth's left, Ethan on Seth's right. The three of them. Brothers. Together again after far too long.

Then Ethan looked at Audra. Her mouth was hanging open as she looked in horror at the amazingly messy man Rafe and Ethan surrounded.

Ethan waited until she looked at him, and he gave a tiny shrug, hoping she'd hold off on screaming until she understood a little of what was going on.

Ethan wouldn't mind understanding, either. But he could clear up some of it. "Audra, I'd like you to meet my brother Seth."

That didn't seem to help much. She still couldn't close her mouth.

"He's been gone from home a long time." Ethan looked at Seth again. Seth's shirt was torn, the collar completely ripped away and the shirt hung nearly in ribbons. Ethan saw through the shirt, and the tattered woolen undershirt beneath it to the ugly scars.

The scars. Ethan's fault. Every one of those scars was Ethan's fault.

Seth's back was a mass of gnarled skin. Most of one arm. The side of his neck. Seth's hair had caught fire, and twisted lumps of skin showed through if Seth's hair was ever cut short.

Ethan remembered it all. He remembered burning his little brother. He remembered being frozen and useless after he'd dropped his lantern on Seth. Ethan hated the cavern almost as much as he hated himself. He'd never gone back again after that day he'd burned Seth so badly.

Today he'd entered this cave, only a few dozen yards deep and with at least dim light the whole time. And he'd hated every minute of it.

And Seth . . . here he was. His eyes as wild as a rabid wolverine. His smell far worse. Lost only a few miles from home. And living in a cave. The same cave that nearly killed him.

All Ethan could think was *I should have never come home.*

"Seth, would you like something to eat?" Rafe's question pulled Ethan out of his dark thoughts.

Food, of course. Ethan had held Seth in his arms. He was a walking skeleton. Rafe was the smart one. The one who did the thinking and the doing. He would be practical and take charge while Ethan stood around feeling sorry for himself.

"Sure." Seth turned quickly — too quickly. "I'm real hungry."

Ethan let him go and went back to being the useless brother.

Rafe drew Seth toward the bag of supplies and eased him down onto the ground. Way too close to Audra and Maggie. Audra gave Ethan a helpless look, and Ethan had to fight the urge to drag Seth away, downwind.

Rafe dropped to his knees and pulled beef

jerky out of his bag.

Audra eased away from Seth, trying to be sneaky but putting inches, then feet between her and the smell.

"Ethan, start a fire." Rafe's voice cracked like a bullwhip. He was in full control now. Full command. "We brought supplies for a meal; let's get it started. Julia, get coffee on. Use the water in the canteens. Seth, let's go refill the canteens and get you washed up a little before we eat. Take this with you." Rafe handed him the jerky.

Seth wiped his hands on his pants as if his palms were soaking wet, then sat up straight, focused on the jerky. The little brother who'd always gotten a lot of orders. Most of which he defied. This time, probably part confusion, part hunger, he grabbed the food.

Julia came up to stand beside Ethan, her arms crossed. The two of them, side by side, standing over nervous Audra, confused Seth, and tyrannical Rafe. She hadn't been around Rafe long enough to know that when he used his bullwhip voice, a person needed to just obey and obey quick. Ethan turned to warn her.

"Hold it right there, Rafe Kincaid."

Too late.

Seth set to gnawing and watching Julia at

the same time, fear in his eyes.

Ethan felt the need to protect his little brother, but then he sort of understood how Julia felt.

"What?" Rafe barely spared her a glance over his shoulder before he went back to getting the supplies in order. "We need to get Seth fed. He's hungry."

The tough meat was quickly vanishing down Seth's gullet, and Rafe had more ready, along with a couple of biscuits. Seth was probably going to choke if someone didn't get him a drink of water real soon.

Rafe lifted a canteen before Ethan could even move.

"I have some concerns about this man you *claim* is your brother."

"Claim?" Rafe finally gave Julia his full attention.

Watching her defy Rafe was a pure pleasure even if she was a little mean-hearted about Seth. Ethan didn't even try to keep the smile off his face.

"He left me in that cavern." Cranky Julia wasn't jumping in to take care of Seth. That seemed unkind. The kid obviously needed help. Ethan had noticed before that she had a bossy streak. But being left in the cavern, well, honestly, that'd bring out the cranky in a woman.

Seth quit chewing and sat up straight. "I what?"

"He what?" Audra scooted farther away from Seth.

Every drop of amusement drained away, and Ethan crossed his arms and glared at Julia. "Seth wouldn't do that."

After what they'd all gone through in that cavern, no Kincaid would ever leave a person stranded down in that pit.

"I . . . I wouldn't do that." Seth looked past Julia at the cave entrance. Ethan didn't like the uncertainty he saw in Seth's eyes.

"Now, Julia." Rafe sounded like a real careful man. "You didn't see the man who scared you."

"Scared me?" Julia's voice climbed to a near screech. "You're saying now he just *scared* me? He left me down there to *die*."

"To die? This man did that?" Audra turned on Seth, and even with her round belly and her arms full with a baby, she looked fierce.

Julia was too busy cutting into Seth's hide with her razor-sharp words to answer Audra. "It's only the wildest chance that you came along and heard me screaming."

"You were screaming, Julia?" Audra's eyes filled with tears. "You said Rafe found you, but you never said y-you might have d-died."

334

Ethan hated when women cried. It surprised him, the urge to go comfort the poor, leaky little female.

"You never said you were screaming . . ." Audra's voice broke.

Ethan jerked a kerchief out of his pocket and abandoned his stance by Julia since she was saying awful things about his brother. He handed the cloth to Audra. A man couldn't hardly keep a dry kerchief with all these weepy women around.

"I'm so sorry you went through something so awful." Audra pressed the handkerchief to her lips. Maybe it meant she was going to quit talking, because she was talking herself into tears, and Ethan was sure hoping his kerchief had the power to stop that.

"I'd never leave someone in that cavern." Seth took another bite of jerky, and though he kept staring at Julia — whether distracted by the food or just sure the issue was settled — went back to chewing as if she had never suggested that he left her to die.

Or maybe he was starving.

Ethan couldn't tell which.

Audra blew her nose, mopped her eyes, then turned back to aim a furious gaze at Seth.

"Seth's been through a lot." Rafe thrust the canteen toward Seth, who was riveted on Julia. Rafe shook Seth's shoulder hard, and Seth noticed the water and grabbed it to drink deeply.

"You can't blame him for anything if he's not thinking clearly."

Seth quit chewing and looked at Rafe. "You mean . . . you think I did it? Left her down there?" He sounded genuinely curious. Like if Rafe said it, then it must be true.

"No, we don't think you did it, Seth." Ethan knew even if no one else did. Even if Rafe had some doubts. Even if Seth wasn't so sure. That was a low no Kincaid brother would ever stoop to.

"Maybe my friend did it."

"Friend?" Ethan turned to his brother and saw everyone else pivot to look at him too.

"What friend?" Rafe asked.

"There's someone else in that cave?" Julia took a step toward Seth, as if she intended to shake the truth out of him.

"Uh . . ." Seth quit chewing. "I . . . yes. I think, yes. I had a friend. I came here with a friend. He was supposed to help me get home."

"Who?" Ethan wasn't sure if Seth was making up the friend or not. He sounded anything but sure of himself.

"His name was . . . was . . . horse. Where's

336

my horse?" Seth took another bite of beef jerky.

"His name was Where's My Horse?" Ethan asked. He thought Julia might attack Seth with her bare hands.

"It was?" Seth quit chewing to look at Ethan. "Sounds like an Indian."

Julia definitely coiled her muscles to pounce. "Was there someone in there or not?"

"Probably . . . my friend is still in there." Seth said it like it was a complete lie.

"Look," Rafe said, his voice cutting through Audra's tears, Julia's anger, Seth's confusion. "This is my brother."

"You used to have a lot of made-up friends when you were a kid, Seth." Ethan remembered too many of them; they were to blame for most of the scrapes Seth got into. And for the first time, Ethan wondered if maybe Seth really had left Julia down there. He hated the idea, but who could be sure? "Is this friend real or not?"

"He must've stolen my horse." Seth looked around the valley. "Can we go home now? I miss Mom."

Who'd been dead for nearly ten years. Ethan swallowed hard and exchanged a look with Rafe.

Rafe's jaw went rigid, his eyes displaying

cold control. He turned to Julia. "I don't know who bothered you in that cavern, but —"

"I wasn't *bothered* in that cave. I was left to die." Julia's voice went up to a near shout.

"Maybe not. If Seth knew there was a way out — as he clearly did, since he came out that entrance and lived near it — he might've moved your rope with no notion he was stranding you."

"Now you're making excuses for him?" Julia jammed her fists on her hips. Her hair seemed to almost stand on end with temper, though the wind might've been involved.

"This is my brother, Jules. He needs us to help him. He needs food and a bath and a haircut and new clothes. He needs all of that *more* than you need answers right now."

"But is someone else in that cave or not, Rafe? I think we need to know *that* right now."

"No, we'll talk about things later. I didn't see any sign of anyone else in the place he was sleeping. No second bedroll. And Seth was always one for . . . making up . . ."

"You mean lying about . . ." Julia said.

". . . uh . . . friends when he was a kid." Rafe shot Seth a worried glance. The worry turned to anger. "He might be thinking more clearly once he's had a good meal, so do you *mind* fixing dinner now? If you do, say so and I'll get a stew on *without your help.*"

Rafe had a knack for giving orders, and he had a knack for slashing a person with his words if they didn't obey. He'd've made a great general in the Civil War. But this was Julia. This was the woman he'd said he was going to marry. A bossy woman, who had her own way with a well-given order.

The air practically crackled between them as Rafe rose from where he crouched beside Seth. Ethan held his breath while he waited to see how well Julia would like the scathing tone of command from a man whom she was planning to spend the rest of her life with.

"I'll make the meal."

Ethan heaved a sigh of relief. She was going to obey. He sent a short prayer of thanksgiving to heaven.

"But this is not settled, Rafe."

Ethan had breathed too soon.

"Not even close to being settled." Julia slashed with a pointy finger almost as well as Rafe did with his voice. "Your brother is a *menace.* If he left me in that cavern, stole my rope, stranded me there and never came back, then he's a danger to me, to Audra, to Maggie, and probably to you and Ethan.

He is *not* going to live in *my* house."

"Rafe, when are we going to go home?" Seth suddenly turned away from Julia and looked around the valley. "This isn't home. I need you to help me find my way home."

There wasn't going to be a wedding.

Taking care of family was Rafe's first purpose in life. Rafe had been willing to let Ethan run the ranch, though Ethan knew, even if no one else did, that Rafe would be in charge from miles away.

But leave Seth? When Seth was in such need?

No. Rafe wasn't capable of that.

Ethan saw Rafe's chance for happiness slipping away.

If things went as they probably would, Rafe would choose Seth over Julia. Which left the women alone and helpless. Ethan's eyes went to Audra, and he considered that someone needed to care for them.

It might not happen today. Or even this week. But Rafe was going to figure out very soon that Julia and Seth could not live under one roof. Which meant Julia was out. Which left Ethan with a choice to make about Audra.

Ethan did his best to not leap to his feet and run away screaming. The only reason he didn't was because no one had actually turned the care of the leaky-eyed women over to him yet.

But he saved the idea of running and screaming for later, pretty sure he'd need it.

It was all Julia could do not to run away screaming.

Rafe had a couple of marks against him when it came to being a husband.

He didn't love her. That was a huge mark.

He was far too bossy. And she liked being in charge herself — it would take a while to teach him that.

He didn't respect the work she was so passionate about. Which made her seriously question his intelligence. Any reasonable person should be able to see that fossils were important.

He came with a brother who met every situation by grinning like a mule eating saw briars.

Okay, that was more than a couple. But she'd decided she could handle all of that.

But living in the same house as a madman? A furry, stinking madman? It was too much. Worse yet, letting Audra and two babies live with him.

Who knew what the lunatic might do? She began filling the cook pot with water, emptying the canteens and tossing them toward Rafe with a little more force than necessary.

"Take these with you and refill them." Issuing orders gave her tremendous satisfaction. "And for heaven's sake, fill them before you let your brother in that stream. He's so filthy he'll foul the water."

"Hey!" Seth scowled. At least from his tone she assumed he scowled. She couldn't really see much through the pelt on his face. Well, good. Why should she be the only one scowling.

But considering he appeared to be furiously mad, it was a wonder the man had the sense to be offended.

"Rafe, take your brother and get him cleaned up. Give him your outer shirt to wear so he's somewhat decent. He needs clean pants, too, but we're fresh out." The ones he had on were so torn they barely covered enough to be called decent.

"He needs a bar of soap." Julia pulled out the soap she'd brought along to wash the cook pot and slapped it into Rafe's hands.

Julia turned to Ethan. "Go with your brothers." There was no real reason to send Ethan other than she was heartily sick of the whole Kincaid family. Including the one she intended to marry. "I'll get a fire started and the stew on."

Ethan gave her a tiny salute. He'd done that to Rafe before, mocking his big brother for issuing orders. Julia had found his insubordination amusing then. But this was different. Julia was only telling these men everything that had to be done.

And done her way.

And done *now*.

She decided she could learn to loathe this charming, grinning fool who never took anything seriously. Except of course he was serious about staying out of the cavern, the one thing she wished Ethan *wasn't* serious about. The idiot.

"Audra, I've got to gather sticks for a fire, but I won't go far." She looked at Audra, who had to be overwhelmed with her burdens and certainly stunned with Seth's behavior and scent.

"I'm fine, Julia."

"You keep an eye on him, Rafe." Julia looked at Rafe so hard, a wise man would have backed up a step. Of course, Rafe didn't budge. "I know you love your brother. But I'm not even close to loving him, and I sure as certain don't *trust* him. So it's on your head." She pointed at him and almost jabbed him in the nose. "You make sure he doesn't hurt anyone."

"Now, don't go acting all fussy, little darlin', just because —"

"We. Will. Discuss. This. Later." Julia pointed at the stream. "Go."

She spun away from Rafe and strode toward a slightly larger stand of trees about twenty yards away. She could see considerable dead wood lying on the ground. She gathered an armload of sticks and carried them back.

Julia busied herself breaking off branches with sharp snapping energy. When the men were well out of earshot, she said, "What are we going to do, Audra?"

Tears welled up unexpectedly. Julia had done more crying since she'd met Rafe Kincaid than she'd done in her whole life. Of course, she'd been stranded in a cave and her father had died — not that she'd cried over him, but it had been a trying time.

"Can you put out the blanket so I can lay Maggie down?" Audra asked.

Julia hurried to help, doing her best to keep her brimming eyes turned away from Audra. When she was done, and Maggie was settled into her nap, Audra rose.

"I had no idea you went through something so terrible in that cavern, Julia." Audra drew Julia into her arms, and for just a few seconds, Julia forgot Audra was the fragile one. They hugged and Julia got her tears

back in the cave as she had been. A little spooked. Far more eager to have Rafe along for company. She was contented for now to stay out here and cook and care for Audra and Maggie.

Then later . . . tomorrow . . . she'd nag Rafe into going into that cavern with her. He'd promised after all, when he'd been wheedling her into marrying him.

She knew she'd have her hands full dealing with the stubborn man as it was. It would be impossible if she told him she'd been spooked.

The big dummy.

If maybe, just for a second, she pictured one of these uneducated troglodytes — bossy Rafe, Seth the lunatic, and that always stupidly grinning Ethan — choking on an undercooked chunk of potato, well, it was a sin sure enough.

But a woman couldn't stop her thoughts until she had them, now could she?

She prayed for forgiveness and added an onion to the pot, hoping a savory stew would make up for her violent daydream.

"Scrub up his pants, Ethan. He'll just have to wear them wet." Rafe stripped his brother naked and saw Seth's scars, the old burns and some new ones that looked like he'd been peppered by a shotgun all across his back. Rafe almost eased up, but that wasn't how Seth wanted things. He hated pity. So Rafe tossed him in the stream.

Seth hollered, then came up sputtering. "Cold!"

Rafe looked at Ethan. The two of them laughed, tore their clothes off and jumped in.

Ethan screamed next. "It's like swimming in melted snow."

Rafe only had a second to notice Ethan had thought to bring Seth's pants with him before Ethan threw them in Rafe's face.

Rafe shouted and dove. Before Ethan could move, Rafe jerked him under.

Ethan came up coughing. Rafe met his eyes, and the two of them turned to Seth, who was grinning . . . or at least he seemed to be under that beard.

"You're getting a shave and a haircut and the bath of your life, little brother," Rafe said, advancing on Seth. Seth's eyes flashed like wild blue lightning.

The war was on. The three of them splashed and wrestled and laughed like loons for so long they started to get warm, almost, and clean, definitely. They'd wrestled like this all the time as boys. Sometimes a fist would land a bit hard or some buried resentment would come to the surface and the fight would get a little heated. But they'd worked it all out with their fighting and had gone back to being best friends afterward. Fighting with his brothers made having them together again more real.

Once they were exhausted, and half-drowned, Rafe turned to Seth. "Now we use Julia's bar of soap and give you a shave and a haircut."

Seth ran his hands through his slicked-back hair, then tugged on his beard. An uncertain look flickered across Seth's face, and he looked down as if surprised to see he had a beard. "Sure."

"It'll hurt," Ethan said. "Better to wait until we can get a basin of hot water."

Rafe nodded.

"Nope, let's get it done. I'm not much of a one to worry about a little hurt." Seth went under again, and when he came up he shook the water out of his hair, twisting his body so Rafe could see his back. His scarred-up ugly back.

Rafe looked over at Ethan and saw that Ethan was noticing the new wounds. Rafe wondered if Seth still had nightmares.

"My knife is razor sharp. I shave with it all the time. Let's get rid of that fur." Rafe turned away. He had his brothers again. His dearest wish. He knew they'd left because of him. Going into that cavern drove Ethan away. Being overprotective had driven Seth away.

So he'd change.

Except he'd promised Julia he'd go in that cave. And he had to protect Seth.

But he'd do it better. Ethan didn't have to know Rafe went into the cavern. Seth didn't need to notice he was being protected.

And what about Julia? He needed to take care of her. He didn't even like to admit how badly he wanted her for his wife. How was he going to control her when she clearly loathed Seth? Well, he'd figure it all out. He'd make it work. He had to.

He got his knife, checked the edge, and dove back in the water to get busy turning this wild man back into his little brother.

CHAPTER 17

Ethan and Rafe had left with a furiously mad, subhuman, cave-dwelling skunk man and returned with a very handsome, wounded boy barely out of his teens.

Audra's ladle stopped in midstir. She couldn't take her eyes off Seth. He was gorgeous, and he looked so sweet and vulnerable. He was close in height to his brothers, and his hair was dark and cut raggedly short. His bone-white cheeks were raw and nicked from being shaved and having no sun on them, probably for years. And his eyes were a shining blue that seemed more alive than any eyes Audra had ever seen.

She rose from where she crouched by the fire, and Rafe hurried over to balance her. She jerked her elbow out of his hand. "I can stand up myself."

Rafe rolled his eyes.

Audra winced. "I'm sorry. Thank you. I've just . . ." Her eyes cut to Seth and Ethan, both of them listening to every word. Well, fine, they could hear what she had to say. "When I was so scared about Julia being missing and Wendell was being so ugly about it, I . . . I made a promise to myself to stand on my own."

"From a campfire?" Ethan asked. The idiot.

"Who's Wendell?" Seth rubbed his clean-shaven face. Poor confused baby.

Julia had wandered off muttering, Maggie strapped on her back, to gather more sticks. So Audra had the undivided attention of all three men. When Julia was around, none of them looked at her except to relieve her of any burden that came her way. All the help annoyed her, but the not being noticed wasn't so bad.

"I'm recently widowed from Wendell Gilliland."

Seth's eyes went to her very round belly. She was tempted to whack him on the head with her ladle. "He always ran my life and he did a poor job of it. Right before he fell sick, I told him I wasn't going to live by his dictates anymore. Apparently the shock was too much and he died."

Ethan laughed. Rafe rolled his eyes but had a smile on his face. Seth looked a little scared.

"I've been trying to do things for myself. You've been nothing but kind, but I can't seem to stop being annoyed that everyone treats me like I'm fragile and stupid."

"No one said you're stupid, Audra," Ethan said, in a tone that clearly called her stupid.

"Anyway, I apologize. Rafe, I appreciate you helping me stand. Seth, you look really nice. Much better, though the soaking wet pants can't be comfortable."

Seth had on the broadcloth shirt Rafe had been wearing. Rafe was wearing only an undershirt. Audra had to avert her eyes from the pants. Seth's legs shined through in several spots. But that couldn't be helped right now.

"The stew is done. Why don't you come and get it?" She pointed at the pile of tin plates and spoons.

"No, let me serve the food to you," Rafe said, then reached for the ladle.

A short tug of war ensued, but Rafe wouldn't be denied. Audra knew she was being rude, so she let him dish her up a plate of stew. Then Rafe picked up a plate and handed it to Seth. "Eat up, kid."

They had enough tin plates now because Ethan had brought some. Julia came back with more sticks.

Rafe got up to fill a plate for Julia. She

took it and turned to sit down but then stopped and stared at Seth. Finally she shook her head and sat beside Audra. "Well, you look a lot less like a madman. We'll see how you act."

"We have to go back to the cabin now." Rafe stood in front of them, his arms crossed, his face grave. He addressed them as if they were schoolchildren. "We'll leave our exploring for another day. Seth needs to change clothes and get some rest and a few days of good food in him."

"Why don't you and Seth go on back, Rafe," Julia said sweetly. Too sweetly.

Audra braced herself for the clash of the tyrants.

"Ethan can stay here with me and Audra and Maggie. I'd like to further explore that cave."

Three voices sounded at once.

"No!" Rafe cut her words off with a slash of his hand.

"No!" Ethan shouted. Maggie jumped.

"No!" Audra set her mostly empty plate aside. She'd had a bellyful of everything today.

"I'd like to explore with you," Seth offered.

"Please don't go back in that cave." Audra dreaded the very thought.

"I have to," Julia said. She was still eating, but she was chewing now with enough energy to wear her teeth down.

Seth turned to look at the black cave opening. "It's like going home." He visibly gathered himself, and Audra's hand shot out to grab him. He wasn't nearly so disgusting now; she would have had a hard time even touching him before.

"Finish your food. Then we're going to my cabin." Audra was watching carefully, and she saw Seth turn his eyes away from that cavern to meet hers.

She saw loneliness. Fear — wild fear. And unfortunately just a whisper of madness. Could a madman regain his sanity? Audra prayed he could. He turned back to stare into that cave, and Audra followed the direction of his gaze and thought she saw . . . something. No, nothing. She wasn't sure.

A clump of aspen stood between them and the cavern. She'd seen a shadow shift — that was all it had been. Shaking her head, she turned back to Seth. Her heart turned over and she softened her grip but didn't let go.

Some of the madness faded from Seth's eyes as they stared at each other. "We're going home, right?" Seth sounded so bewildered. "I want to go home."

"Rafe and Ethan are visiting at my house. You're very close to the ranch where you grew up, though. They can take you there. But for today, let's just go back to my house. You can rest and eat. My husband is dead and his clothes won't fit you, but I'm good with a needle and you're so thin I can lengthen his pants and the sleeves of his shirts, maybe let out the shoulders a bit. I can figure something out so you can get into some fresh clothes."

"Fresh clothes?" Seth looked down and stared at his knee, clearly visible through his tattered pants. His hands were battered. His neck was stained with what must be dirt, though it had been scrubbed almost raw. His hair was much better, hacked off with a knife so it was ragged but short. Birds could've built nests in there before.

Seth poked at his skin through the knee hole and began to hum. Then a stick fell in the fire and drew his attention, and he stared at the fire as if it owned his soul.

Definitely a whisper of madness.

Audra got the distinct impression he'd forgotten the rest of them were there. She reached out and rested one hand on his shoulder, and he jumped as if she'd pulled a knife. He knocked her hand aside so hard her fingers went numb.

Then his eyes locked on hers, and she saw the confusion and regret and apology. Then Julia hit.

"You get away from her." Julia grabbed Seth by the arm and yanked at him.

Seth tore loose of Julia and began scooting backward. It took Audra a few seconds to realize it, but Seth glanced back and looked at the cave opening again.

They couldn't let him vanish back in there. They might never find him in that place. Audra was on her feet, pretty fast for a really round woman, if she did say so herself. She rushed toward the cave before anyone else figured out Seth's goal.

He jumped up, and she got there just as Seth tripped and stumbled into her. They both went down in a heap.

Seth caught her and rolled so his body took the brunt of the impact with the ground.

Before they quit skidding, three sets of hands were dragging Seth off of her. Julia was yelling threats and orders. Rafe had Seth in a headlock. Ethan very gently helped Audra to her feet.

"Are you all right?" Ethan asked.

Seth quit struggling at the question. He turned wild, scared eyes on Audra. "I'm sorry. I just wanted to go home."

For one second, Audra was afraid Julia was going to throw a fist. She didn't even yell out a warning. She had bigger problems to deal with than Julia's attitude toward Seth.

"I'm fine." She was anything but fine.

She did her very best to keep a composed expression on her face when the truth was, she needed very badly to panic. When she'd landed on top of Seth, she'd felt a gush of liquid that could only be one thing.

So how did a woman with a sturdy backbone act?

Now was *not* the time for the truth. "Yes. I'm fine. But I think we should get away from this cave, don't you? It seems to upset Seth. Let's get back to our cabin."

"Yes, we'll go right now." Julia's voice was as crisp as a ripe apple.

Rafe scowled. "We needed to hunt around some more. Lay out a house site."

"Well, you can't do that if your brother is going to run for the cave every time he gets a little upset," Audra pointed out.

"Especially when the wind blowing and the sun shining and the birds tweeting upset him." Julia kept an arm around Audra while Ethan supported her from the other side.

"Yeah, let's go. We can do this later." Ethan wasn't smiling. "Seth, Rafe, saddle the horses. I think I'd better stay with Audra."

And he was giving orders to Rafe. Another surprising event.

Rafe obeyed him, dragging Seth along. Now Ethan just needed to make Julia mind and Audra would know the world had turned upside down.

Ethan didn't even try.

Audra had her first pain before they got the horses rounded up and saddled. She did her best to hurry everyone along, but they all seemed bent on dawdling. With Seth along, they were short a horse. When Rafe offered to give Julia a ride on his horse, leaving Audra to ride alone, she was grateful because, though it had gone unnoticed, she was quite damp in certain unmentionable places.

Her stomach contracted again before they'd climbed to the vent to get out of this valley. It had taken much longer to have her second contraction last time.

She was glad she had the stone wall of the vent to lean on and the cover of darkness when the next pang hit so hard she almost collapsed. They were coming much too close together. Was she going to have pains of this intensity and this often for all those hours?

Once mounted up, they rode with ridiculous slowness back home. Of course, Audra wasn't exactly up to galloping anyway.

With the time spent bridling the horses and the snail's pace of the journey, they were over two hours getting home and the pains kept coming faster, hitting harder and staying longer.

She was going to have a baby much too early.

She didn't have any idea if a baby could live under those circumstances.

She started to cry.

So she turned her thoughts to the ride, counting off the steps, the minutes, until she could get home and lie down. There'd be no stopping this birth, not this time.

She had plenty of time, of course; babies could take a long time being born. But this laboring was much harder than the last one. With Maggie she'd had mild birth pangs for nearly a full day, and her water hadn't broken until nearly the end.

It looked for all the world like this baby was going to be much harder to deliver than the last one.

And Maggie had been about all Audra could handle.

And the baby was coming much too early.

And she didn't have any idea if a baby

could live under those circumstances.

And she started to cry.

And then turned back to counting each step.

Chapter 18

"I think I'll go take a nap."

"You need to lie down *now?*" Julia asked.

Audra nodded, gasped, then forced a long slow breath through her lips.

Julia's eyes went wide. She turned to the Kincaid men, who had crowded into their small cabin. "Get out."

"What?" Rafe studied her through narrow eyes.

"You have to get out. Now."

"Uh . . . uh . . . why?" Rafe looked from her to Seth, as if she was throwing all of them out because she didn't like his brother.

Which she didn't.

Even less now, because it was clear to Julia that Seth running into Audra had brought on this round of pains.

"Audra needs complete rest." *If we're going to stop her labor.*

But Julia didn't say that. It was too outrageously personal.

"She's been doing nothing but resting all day," Ethan, the insensitive nitwit, said with his brainless smile.

"I need rest, Ethan. A lot of rest." Audra headed for her bedroom. She didn't go toward the one she'd shared with Father. Neither Julia nor Audra had slept in there since he'd taken sick. Julia, Audra, and Maggie slept in Julia's room. The men slept under the stars.

"Well, go on in and rest." Rafe gestured toward the back of the cabin. "We'll be real quiet while we get a fire going and get supper —"

"She's having the baby!" Julia clapped a hand over her mouth.

Audra froze. "Julia, honestly." Audra leaned against the bedroom's doorframe as her cheeks turned a fiery pink. She'd almost made it before Julia opened her big mouth and blurted out the truth.

"Really?" Rafe stared at Audra's stomach so hard and in such horror, Julia wanted to backhand him.

"She just needs rest."

Ethan, the idiot, smiled as if he'd just been given a juicy steak and didn't have a care in the world. His eyes had a panicked look, though, as they flickered between Audra and her belly.

Seth said, "It's my fault."

"Yes, it most certainly is," Julia said, jamming her fists on her hips.

"No, it isn't." Audra turned away from the bedroom door and came back to pat Seth on the shoulder. "Now, don't you go blaming yourself. It's just time for the baby to come is all."

Seth turned his wild eyes on Rafe. "Let's go get the doctor."

"There's no doctor anywhere around." Rafe looked helpless, which shook Julia badly. "The closest one might be in Colorado City, and I'm not even sure about that. We'd be all day riding for him."

Julia couldn't decide if the men were desperate to help, or escape. She pushed her way between Seth and Audra as if to provide a human shield. "It is not time for the baby to come."

"I'm not that sure how, ummm . . . I mean I don't know when Wendell and I . . . I . . . I . . ." Audra turned a shade of pink that Julia had never seen on a human being before. "I mean . . . uh . . . I'm not sure when it's *due*. When the baby is due. I don't know that. Not for sure. It's probably now. Right now."

Audra squared her shoulders, and even pink she sounded strong and calm. "Yes, obviously it is due now."

Well, fine, Audra can be in charge of calm. I'll be in charge of work.

"We'll get you in bed. With rest maybe we can put this off. The pangs have stopped before."

"Not this time. The baby is definitely coming."

Julia wasn't sure how Audra could know that. In truth, though she'd helped deliver Maggie, Audra had only called out to her at the last minute, waking her from a sound sleep. Then most of it was a blur. Beyond catching Maggie, Julia had no idea exactly what went in to bringing a baby into the world. The two of them had even questioned what to do with the baby's tummy and the long cord. It had taken every ounce of nerve they'd possessed to finally cut it off. Neither of them knew a thing about birthing babies.

Julia had kind of hoped she'd be asked to do nothing but catch again. And she would be confident about the cord this time. That had clearly been the right thing to do. And she'd be glad to give it a bath again, too.

"It will be a while," Audra added. "It certainly was last time. So, yes, gentlemen. Though it isn't very hospitable, you're going to have to leave. The baby probably won't come until morning, but I'd prefer if you occupied yourselves elsewhere."

"But it's too soon, Audra." Julia slid an arm around Audra's slender shoulder and felt Audra's whole body tense up. Julia turned away from the men, to help Audra to her room.

Audra clutched her stomach. "Wait. Stand still. Let it pass."

Julia did as she was told.

"Let me help." Rafe appeared at Audra's side to slide his arm around her waist and make sure she didn't collapse. Julia shot him a grateful glance.

When Audra relaxed, she said faintly, "The pains are so much harder than last time."

"I didn't help you at the beginning before. You went through most of it alone."

"Yes, but it was very mild at first. It was hours and hours of pains. And they started out so far apart last time. I felt them most of the day before Maggie was born."

"You did?" Julia had no idea.

"Yes, but I only figured it out late that night. I knew I felt awful, but I didn't even know what was going on exactly. I'd never had a baby before, and I'd certainly never seen one born nor talked with a woman who'd had one."

"How can you be sure the baby is coming, then?" Rafe asked.

"My water broke." Audra clutched at her stomach.

Rafe vanished. A door slam turned Julia to look over her shoulder. The Kincaids had all run.

Thank heavens they were gone.

Don't leave me here alone!

Both thoughts were at war in Julia's head. But of course it was best they were gone. At least they'd taken Maggie. She wouldn't have put it past the cowards to leave Maggie just because it was an abandon-the-girls moment.

"Help me, Julia." Audra's knees gave out. "I need to lie down."

Julia kept Audra on her feet by pure force. Where was Rafe when she really needed him? Gone! Typical man. Just like her father.

She was never more grateful for her tiny stepmother. Much easier to carry. She practically bore Audra's entire weight as they staggered to the bedroom. Julia eased her down on the floor. Audra's eyes were closed so tightly it wrinkled her smooth brow. Lines of pain were etched in her face and her whole body was rigid. For one black, furious moment, Wendell Gilliland was lucky to be dead and beyond Julia's reach. If he'd been here, Julia would have given him the beating of his life. His wife shouldn't be giving birth without even a bed to lie on.

And those worthless cowardly Kincaids were lucky to be gone, too.

"Julia, I feel funny. If I didn't know better, I'd say the baby is being born right now. But that's im . . . impossib—" Audra's voice broke. "Impossible. I can't . . . I can't bear this. Hours and hours like this. I can't survive it."

Julia decided she'd better take a quick look. Audra didn't stop her. She seemed to be beyond modesty for the moment.

Julia adjusted Audra's clothing. Audra gave a loud shout that turned into a roar. Julia was just in time to catch the baby.

"No, wait!" Audra's head fell back to the floor. "No, this isn't right. It takes all day." Tears leaked from the corners of Audra's eyes.

Julia had nothing to care for a baby. She awkwardly rested the messy, wriggling baby on the same blanket Audra lay on, and the little one let out a thin, wavering cry, then another until she was wailing.

"It's another little girl. Look at her dark hair." Not the bald head Maggie had come out with.

The baby kicked and her arms flew wide

and she cried with every breath. Audra turned to look at the baby, and Julia saw a look on Audra's face she'd seen before. When Maggie had been born.

"She's so tiny. Was Maggie that little?" Audra asked.

"It doesn't seem possible." Julia really couldn't remember. "Until this moment I was thinking Maggie was *still* tiny."

Audra twisted around to better see the little one. "She looks big enough, doesn't she? She's not born too early."

"She looks perfect, strong and lively. Crying her head off. That's a good sign."

Tears trickled down Audra's face. With hands visibly trembling, she reached for the newborn. Julia helped arrange the tiny one in her mama's arms.

Julia felt a connection that had to mirror Audra's. This little one would be surrounded by love all her life.

"How can I love her so much when I didn't love her daddy at all?" Audra stared at the baby, then blinked and raised her eyes to Julia. "I'm sorry. I shouldn't have said that about your father."

"No, I know how he was. But that doesn't change how much we can love this little one, does it?"

"And she has dark hair like him. Except . . ." Audra looked closer. "I think there might be a tinge of red to her hair. It looks dark, but dark red, I think, not brown. She'll look like you, I hope."

"My mother told me once I looked like my father's mother. She was a redhead."

"Good." Audra shook her head and turned back to the baby. "Can you help me . . . help me feed her?"

Julia rolled a second blanket to prop Audra's head up a bit. Julia helped Audra arrange her clothing and balance the baby in just the right position. The strange newborn cry was something else Julia had forgotten. She hadn't realized Maggie's cry had changed until she heard the sound again. "What shall we name her?"

"I . . . I'd name her Julia." Audra looked away from the baby to Julia and smiled. "But that might be confusing."

It was an honor that warmed Julia's heart almost to the point of pain.

"It might be. Thank you, though, for thinking of it." Julia ran one hand over the baby's head as Audra turned back to help with the baby's first fumbling attempts to eat punctuated by the wailing. "You're so much better at that than last time."

Audra cradled the baby closer. "She needs a bath. And I don't want her to get cold."

With awkward desperation that made Audra laugh and cry at the same time, the baby finally latched on to eat and the room fell silent.

"I'll get a diaper and a blanket, then warm some water. We'll keep her wrapped up tight and you just cuddle her close. It's a warm day, but we want to make sure she doesn't get a chill, especially with the cool mountain evenings coming."

Julia returned with the diaper and blanket, tended the cord, and wrapped the baby tight, all while Audra held her in her arms.

Julia carefully exposed each arm and leg, bathing the baby in warm water without letting her get fully uncovered. She positioned the diaper and finished the bath without disturbing mealtime.

"Your middle name is Lily, isn't it? Julia Lily?"

"Yes, Lily was my mother's name."

"Lily, then."

"How about Lily Sarah. Sarah is your middle name, right?"

Audra looked up from the baby. They exchanged a smile. "I like that. We were certainly in charge of bringing her into the world, weren't we?"

Julia's smile widened.

Turning back to the baby, Audra said, "Hi,

Lily Sarah." The glow of love in Audra's eyes made tears burn in Julia's. At that moment, Julia knew she had to have a child. She had to feel this powerful love. She thought of Rafe and wished she could have his child. She wanted it to be a child born of love, and she saw little sign that Rafe loved her. But Wendell certainly hadn't loved Audra, and yet Audra glowed. Julia could get love into her life with a child.

Julia adored Maggie, and she already loved Lily. But it wasn't the same. Nothing could be as beautiful as the radiant love shining on Audra's face. Feeling she was intruding, Julia left the room, doubting Audra noticed. She stepped into the front room of the cabin and broke down and cried.

For all the years she'd spent alone.

For her father who never loved her.

For the man who wanted to marry her and didn't love her, either.

For the glory of a new life and a mother's love.

Not wanting Audra to hear, she went outside as quietly as possible, and found all three men standing in a row, staring at the cabin. Ethan held Maggie in his arms.

"We . . . uh . . . heard the baby cry," Rafe said.

"It's born already?" Ethan asked.

"She. She's born already. Audra had another little girl." Julia reached out and tickled Maggie's tummy.

Seth said, "We need a doctor. And I need to go home."

"We don't need a doctor," Julia snapped.

Rafe pulled her into his arms. "Are you all right?"

"Yes, it's just an emotional thing to see a baby born. I'm sorry for the tears. Everyone's all right."

"The baby isn't too early, then? I didn't hurt him?" Seth came up beside Rafe, looking so worried that Julia had one brief moment of the easing in her disgust for Seth Kincaid.

"It's a girl. And no, you didn't hurt her, much. Luckily. Miraculously. I hope. She's so tiny." A glance at Rafe warned him to keep Seth away from Audra.

Seth leaned closer to Julia. "Can I hold the baby?"

"You're as crazy as a swamp rat, aren't you?" Julia felt Rafe's hands tighten on her as if he was holding her back from punching Seth in the nose.

Wise of him.

Seth shrugged. Ethan grinned. Rafe held on tighter.

"I like Audra." Seth ran his hands over his face as if he wondered where the fur had gone. "She's pretty. And nice." He said that in a tone that clearly suggested Julia was *not* nice. "I wanta see the baby."

Julia arched one warning brow at Rafe. If he didn't control his brother, she would. "No, you can't see the baby yet. She's too . . ." Julia couldn't think of an excuse. "Uh . . . too young. She's too young. I'll let you know when she's old enough." *Never.* "Until then, leave that baby alone. She's so little, and she's s-s-so beautiful."

What she'd seen in Audra's eyes overwhelmed her, and she wept into Rafe's shirt.

Rafe didn't know much about women, except that they did tend to cry over everything.

With some hesitation — over where it'd been — he stuffed an extremely limp kerchief into Julia's hands and let her lean on him. And thought about how impossible it was to imagine Seth and Julia living in the same house. He flipped possibilities over in his mind until finally the storm of her tears passed.

When she calmed down she straightened, lifted her chin, and looked at him with shining, soggy green eyes. Eyes so deeply moving, he wondered if she might have seen a miracle.

"So the baby's going to be all right?" Rafe spoke quietly, well aware his brothers were only a step away. He'd really like to have some private time with Julia. And with two babies, a stepmother — good grief, if he married Julia, Audra would be his mother-in-law — and a locoweed brother living with them, that probably wasn't *ever* going to happen.

Private. Rafe loved the sound of that word.

Julia nodded, blew her nose, and nodded again. "She's a little thing, but full of energy. We named her Lily Sarah. I left Audra alone with her for a while, just to hold her baby in her arms privately."

Julia obviously liked the word *private,* too. Her lips looked swollen, like maybe she'd been biting them while she did something as terrifying as delivering a baby. Her cute little nose was as shiny as a new penny. Her eyes were awash in glory and love.

"So I didn't harm her, then?" Seth asked.

The green eyes shot lightning bolts. "Not for lack of trying." Julia stepped out of Rafe's arms and moved sideways so she could glare at Seth.

"Can you help me find my way home?" Seth's eyes lost focus, and he took a step closer to Julia, which proved his brother was crazy.

A noise started low in Julia's throat and got louder. Sounded a little like Rafe imagined a volcano would when the lava first started boiling, getting ready to blow.

Rafe should go, too. Seth needed him. But he couldn't leave Julia and Audra alone, which meant Ethan would have to stay. But Rafe wanted to stay. He wanted to take care of his woman.

"Ethan," Rafe said, against his better judgment, "take Seth home."

"Yes, good idea." Julia's eyes flashed as hot as lava. "He wants to go home really bad. I say take him."

"Aren't we home now?" Seth asked. "I like it here almost as much as the cave." He rubbed his face. "Didn't I have a beard?"

Julia's rumbling built toward an eruption.

"We'll go in the morning." Ethan ignored the fact that Julia was an eyelash away from attacking Seth, and Rafe had given a direct order. "We could get there faster if we forded the creek and had horses waiting there. I think I'll put up a corral over there and do that next time. Otherwise, with our horses here, we'll have to go the long way and we'll be riding all night."

Rafe hadn't been making a suggestion.

Looking down at Maggie, Ethan added, "Say, why'd she have it so fast? I thought she said it'd be morning."

That cut off the animal sounds. Julia threw her arms wide. "I don't know. It's only the second time I've seen a baby born. Maybe they're all as different from each other as night is from day. It was a lot longer than this with Maggie. I don't know what changed, but she had it so fast this time we barely got her to lay down and get her clothes —"

"Julia!" Rafe cut her off. He felt heat climbing up his neck. He cleared his throat. "I . . . ahem . . . I don't think we need more details."

Julia clamped her mouth shut as if she had to physically hold back the words. Maggie yowled.

"Oh, my goodness." Julia looked up at Rafe, her eyes wide with worry. "We don't have any milk."

"There's some in the supplies I brought from our place." Ethan tweaked Maggie's nose and smiled at her.

Maggie giggled.

"I thought a baby might drink milk. I set it in the stream to keep it cool. Seth, you want to take Maggie?" Ethan handed her over.

Rafe moved before his clueless brother brought down volcanic fury from Mount Julia. "Let me have her."

He snatched her before Seth could get a firm hold. Ethan headed for the stream to get the milk. Rafe turned to face Julia. It wasn't like he was scared of her or anything. He just wanted her to love his brother as much as he did.

"I wanta see the new baby now." Seth bounced a little, clearly eager.

Julia jabbed a finger right at Seth's nose. "You stay away from that baby."

Rafe balanced Maggie in one arm, clamped the other around Julia's shoulders, and turned her around to drag her inside. "Let's go introduce Maggie to her little sister."

"I think I will." Julia took Maggie and went back in the house, slamming the door in Rafe's face.

Which seemed a little rude. He'd sort of thought she'd let *him* in.

Rafe turned to Seth just as the door popped open again. Julia stuck her arm out with a bar of soap in her hand. "Have you got a change of clothes? I'm a little busy to do any sewing right now."

"Yeah."

Sewing?

"Then run your brother under the water again. It takes more than one bath to wash off five years of stink. And tell that grinning fool of a brother of yours . . ."

Rafe assumed she meant Ethan.

". . . to get back here with the milk. Maggie's hungry."

Maggie grinned and waved bye-bye to Rafe. She looked okay to him.

Rafe took the soap.

Julia slammed the door in his face again.

Turning to Seth, Rafe said, "Let's go find Ethan."

"I'm not taking another bath." Seth took a step back.

"Have you seen the stream?"

Seth looked suspicious. Rafe glanced at the cabin. "Let's get you some dry pants. Yours are wet, and mine'll fit good enough." Rafe dropped his voice to a whisper. "You don't need another bath, but we'll let Julia think you took one. You smell fine to me."

"I heard that, Rafe Kincaid." Julia's voice echoed out of the cabin like the voice of Doom.

Rafe flinched. He grabbed clean clothes from his bedroll. Then he jerked his head toward the back of the house — and water. "Let's go find Ethan."

Seth might have forgotten about the bar

of soap, or he might really want to see
Ethan, but he came along quietly. The poor
crazy kid.

CHAPTER 19

"It burns! Rafe! Ethan! Help!"

Rafe jerked awake, his gun already in hand. Save Seth. Someone was hurting Seth.

"I want to go home. No, no! Put it out. Stop. It burns!" A terrible scream ripped Rafe the rest of the way out of sleep and he remembered. Seth was home.

In the bright moonlight, Rafe saw Seth, tossing and turning in his sleep. Ethan was sitting up on the other side of him and had a gun drawn, too.

"Seth's having a nightmare." Rafe spoke loudly, hoping to pull Seth out of his dreams.

Rafe was on his knees. He reached for Seth, and Seth punched him in the mouth. Not ready for that, Rafe fell over backward.

"Seth! Wake up!" Ethan ducked a fist, jumped back, and turned to Rafe.

"Seth!" Rafe eased forward. "Let's each grab an arm."

The cabin door slammed open and drew Rafe's attention. Julia stood with a rifle in her hands.

"He's having a nightmare, Jules. Put the gun down." Rafe looked at Ethan. "Ready?"

Seth shouted again. "It burns. Stop. Help me, Rafe. Help!"

"Seth!" Ethan yelled. "Wake up!"

"It's like he's trapped in the dream." Rafe was sick to think that all these years later, his little brother still had nightmares about the fire. "Remember his nightmares after the accident?"

"But they stopped," Ethan said through clenched teeth. "Why was he hiding in that cave? Why are the nightmares back?"

Seth screamed again, a perfect echo of the noise he'd made that day when he was on fire.

"Let's grab hold so he can't hurt himself or us. Then we'll wake him up somehow."

Cold water hit all three of them in the face.

"Hey!" Rafe turned to see his fiery little woman standing with a basin in her hands. Empty. Now.

"What's going on?" Seth sputtered. But he'd escaped from the prison of sleep.

"Julia, why'd you do that? Now we're all soaking wet." Ethan drew an arm across his face, but his shirt was just as wet as his hair, so he kept dripping.

"I want to go home." Seth sat up and stared at Julia with wide, wild eyes.

"I want you to go home too, Seth. Believe me. You woke Maggie up with your shouting. Her crying woke Audra and the baby. Now I've got a night's work ahead getting everyone settled again." Julia jammed one fist on her hip.

"You have a nightgown on," Seth said. "You're pretty."

Looking down, Julia gasped in dismay, wheeled, and ran back into the cabin. She slammed the door so hard, Rafe watched to see if it would just come flying straight off the hinges to land on the three men.

It held, so Rafe turned back to Seth and shoved him hard enough that he landed flat on his back. "Don't talk about Julia's nightgown."

"Izzat you, Rafe?"

"Yes, it's me."

"And Ethan? Am I home?"

Rafe looked at the door of that rickety cabin. "Close, kid. You're mighty close to home."

"Can we go on home now?"

"It's night." Ethan used his blanket to mop his face and hair, then reached for his saddlebag, pulled a dry shirt out, and changed. "We'll head for home in the morning."

"Well, then why'd you wake me up?"

"You were having a nightmare." Rafe forgot his dripping hair and looked at Seth.

Seth stared into the distance and finally spoke. "They're crazy, twisted up. Some of 'em stay with me while I'm awake."

"Do you have a lot of them?" Ethan clapped him on the shoulder, then offered him a dry shirt. While Seth changed, Rafe saw the scars and exchanged a long look with Ethan. How could Seth *not* have nightmares? Rafe shook his head and dried himself off. There were more pants, too. Enough for everyone. Most of the clothes he owned were over here — not that he owned all that many.

As he buttoned his shirt, Seth said, "Just since the war. No, before that. I was having them even before Andersonville."

"You were in Andersonville?" Rafe sat down on Seth's right while Ethan sat on his left. Rafe threw more kindling on the low fire crackling in front of them. They were lucky Julia had missed it with her water. "No wonder you're so thin. I heard about the living skeletons who came out of that place."

"No food. Lots of men died." Seth

shrugged. "Yeah, I had lots of nightmares there. But they started . . . I've had them all my life."

"Not all your life." Ethan's hand rested on Seth's back. On his scars. "Just since the cave accident. They started after we took you home. For months after that, you'd yell in your sleep. Always on fire." Ethan stopped speaking, as if he didn't trust his voice not to break.

Rafe could understand that. He picked up the story. "We'd have a terrible time waking you up."

The door jerked open and Julia came out, properly dressed, with Maggie sitting up, rubbing her eyes.

"Sorry about that." Seth sidled behind Rafe. Which meant Seth had picked up on the fact that Julia was not happy with him. That didn't make Seth a mind reader.

Stopping so she faced all three brothers, she said, "You were having a nightmare, weren't you?"

Seth moved a little, so Rafe wasn't completely protecting him. Rafe sure hoped that wasn't a mistake. Though having the baby in her arms might slow Julia down a little if she decided to attack.

Then Maggie squealed and reached for Ethan. Ethan took her. She giggled and kicked her feet.

Still, Julia didn't launch herself at Seth. "I've had a nightmare or two in my life. I know it's not your fault that you woke everybody up. I'm sorry I was so rude."

Seth now moved so he was right beside Rafe. Rafe wondered if Julia wasn't luring him in like a baited trap. He braced himself to save Seth.

"You really scared me in the cavern." Julia studied Seth in the moonlight, frowning. "I know you've been through something awful, but I'm afraid you might be . . . be . . ."

"Loco?" Seth asked.

Julia shrugged. It was the first time she'd hesitated instead of just hitting Seth with both barrels. Rafe found that encouraging.

"The thing is, I understand that you need your brothers to help you. I understand you've been through war. I've heard of Andersonville and it would be hard for anyone to survive that."

"Terrible place. I was so hungry. So much death."

"I'm sorry you went through that, Seth," Julia said quietly. "I've seen pictures of the starving men."

"Terrible. Ugly. Filthy. I have nightmares about that place more than the cavern, or maybe they're all mixed together. There's always fire." Seth was sounding rational.

Rafe wondered if they oughta change the subject.

"I had to remember how to eat afterward. It was like my throat'd close up. And if I ate too much, I'd lose it from my belly. Callie helped me get my strength up." Seth slid both hands into his hair. "And I started for home."

He looked at Rafe. "What month is it?"

"It's June."

"I started for home right after Lee surrendered."

"Who's Callie?" Julia asked.

"I don't know anyone named Callie." Seth looked into the fire with narrow eyes.

"You just said 'Callie helped me get my strength up.' " Julia threw another stick on the fire, and Seth stared into the flames and didn't answer.

"Seth," Ethan said, shifting Maggie into his left arm so he could put his right along Seth's shoulder, "that was a year and two months ago. The war's been over for more than a year."

Seth turned to look at Ethan, his brow furrowed. "Are you sure?"

Ethan nodded.

"So how come it took me so long to get home?"

Ethan shook his head. "Maybe it didn't take that long. Maybe you got as far as the cave and stayed there for a while."

"And where's my horse? The one I got from the Union army when I was ready to leave?"

"And you said they gave you a rifle?" Ethan patted Maggie's tummy.

"My friend might have it." A smile quirked Seth's lips as he looked at the little girl. "I should go back and get him out, too."

"Is there really someone else in there, Seth?" Julia asked. "We didn't see any sign of another man. There was only one bedroll. There was no sign of horses anywhere in the caldera or the vents."

"Caldera?" Seth scrubbed his face with both hands. "What's that?"

"We want to know about your friend, Seth." Rafe tried to get his brother to make sense. This was the closest he'd come since they'd found him. "And how'd you know about that exit into that mountain valley where we were today?"

Seth looked from Rafe to Julia and back to the fire, as if it were calling to him. "I've always known about that back door, I reckon . . . or no, not always. I found it after the accident. But I was still a kid when I found it. I knew almost every inch of that cave before I took off to enlist in the war."

"You know your way around in that cavern?" Julia asked.

She was interested in Seth all of a sudden. Rafe wished he'd never mentioned the cave. He also wished he could gag his little brother.

"Better'n I know my own face." Seth's shoulders lifted as if he felt strong and confident on this one subject.

"I haven't gotten to the ends of it yet." Julia had a new best friend. "I found some fish fossils and I'd —"

"Can we just leave that for now?" Rafe cut her off. "I think we need to figure out about Seth's friend down there. Was it one of your imaginary friends, Seth? Why didn't your friend have a bedroll?"

"He did."

"But there was only one," Julia said.

"Yeah, that was his. I didn't have a blanket. I didn't have anything much but the food he'd give me. My horse, though. Where'd he go?"

Seth turned to look to the west, the direction of the valley and the cave entrance. Rafe clamped his hand on Seth's wrist. "Don't even think about leaving us to go back in that cave."

"I won't." Seth looked back at Rafe and

smiled. "I don't want to live in the cave anymore. I want to go home."

"Tomorrow we'll go home, Seth." Ethan hugged Seth a bit tighter. With Maggie in one arm and Seth in the other, Ethan was pretty busy.

"No." Julia snatched Maggie away from Ethan as if to punish him. "I want Seth to show me around in that cave."

"What about his friend?" Rafe didn't like Julia being in charge. She was too single-minded about that blasted cave. "That might be who scared you and left you stranded in there. It's still not safe in there. And the floors are still thin as —"

"I don't think there is a friend." Julia gave Seth a smile that looked as untrustworthy as Confederate currency. "And if Seth has been all over, then he'll take us places he knows he's walked on before."

"Which doesn't mean the floors might not crack and collapse," Rafe said.

Seth whimpered and leaned closer to Ethan. Rafe really needed to get him home. Far from the cavern. Far from the danger of him running back in and disappearing.

"We can explore the cavern tomorrow." Julia's phony smile was even perkier. "I'll make sure Audra is settled comfortably. She can tend the baby for a few hours. Ethan can watch Maggie. Rafe, Seth, and I can go explore. Seth can show me all the rooms he's found, and I'll keep a detailed map as we walk. That way I can find it again."

Seth looked more cheerful. "Will the cave take me home?"

"We're not going down there." Rafe decided it was time to put a stop to this conversation for good. "We're not risking Seth getting lost down there, and we're not leaving Ethan here to tend a new mother and two babies. And that's final."

CHAPTER 20

"Where do you suppose Seth's horse went?" Julia thought of it as Rafe led the way toward the cavern, from the caldera entrance. "If someone, some 'friend,' took his horse, then that same 'friend' might take ours."

Rafe turned to her, his brows drawn down into a straight line, a scowl on his face. "Is this really a good time for you to remind me that someone might still be hiding in there?"

Julia clamped her mouth shut before she lost her chance to explore. Instead she focused on the madman who would soon be her brother. "So, do you know how long you've been living in the cave, Seth?"

Shaking his head, Seth looked from the cave to her. "The war's been over for a year?"

Nodding, Julia said, "They signed the peace treaty in April of 1865. It's now June

398

of 1866. It's been more than a year. I heard about Andersonville. People called the men released from there walking skeletons."

Seth seemed to look through the cave entrance and into the past. "I wasn't there that long. I . . . I was taken prisoner. I was with Sherman."

Rafe came up beside Seth, frowning. "Sherman burned Atlanta, didn't he?"

"I was . . . I was a captain by the end. I was in Atlanta with Sherman. I helped with the burning. The fire everywhere. Fire." Seth shook his head as if to jar his thoughts free of fire. "After Atlanta I was . . . I always did a lot of scouting. I liked it. It reminded me of running around the ranch when we were kids, hunting, playing hide and seek. I always had a knack for sneaking."

Clapping Seth on the back, Rafe said, "That's the pure truth, little brother."

"But when I got to be an officer, they wouldn't let me do that anymore. But our scout died and Sherman needed me, so he let me go back to it. I'd go behind enemy lines. Find their camps. Count troops." Seth shrugged. "I got caught. Shot, maybe. They threw me into Andersonville."

Rafe's hand tightened on Seth as if to help bear the weight of ugly memories.

"When I got out, I was sick awhile. I

thought I headed home as soon as I got out of the hospital. So why'd it take me a year?" Seth frowned. "I met my friend along the way."

Rafe had been watching Seth intently. When he mentioned his friend, Rafe's eyes shifted to Julia. She lifted one shoulder. Then Rafe turned to the cave.

"Is your friend in there?"

"I don't know. We both had horses. Mine must've run off. Maybe he went after it. Maybe . . . maybe he got lost, too." Seth rubbed the back of his neck. He managed to move his collar enough that Julia could see scars disappearing up into his scalp and down below his collar. "Can you help me find my way home, Rafe?"

"If you want to go home, I'll take you right now." Rafe gave Julia an apologetic look.

She prepared to argue with him, knowing she'd lose. They probably should put this off. Seth wasn't up to it now. Maybe not ever.

"No, I wanta explore. I've always loved to explore in that cavern. It's beautiful." Seth's eyes lit up. Wild and blue and, Julia was sorely afraid, just the littlest bit insane.

"You aren't going to run off, are you?" Rafe hesitated.

"Nope, I'm not running off ever again. I want to stay with you so you can help me find my way home."

"And you can show us all the prettiest things you've seen in the cave." Julia hooked one of her arms through his. Rafe must have given him another bath, because Seth smelled just fine now. His skin was chalky white and peeling, like layers of old skin that would have to be scrubbed off over time. His clothes — she recognized a blue shirt Ethan had worn — hung on his gaunt frame. But he looked much better with a shaved face and shorter hair. "Have you got the rope, Rafe? We want to be really cautious in there. You'll let us tie ourselves together, won't you, Seth? We don't want to get separated."

"Sure, whatever you want."

Julia saw a lot of the tension leave Rafe when Seth agreed. Tying himself to Seth would give Rafe a much bigger chance of keeping track of him.

"It's not dangerous, though."

Julia thought of Seth's scars. "It can be dangerous, so let's be real careful."

"I've hunted around, and I know where the cave floor is thin. I know where it's safe and where it's not."

"We can't stay too long," Rafe said. "Ethan

looked a little overwhelmed with Audra and two babies."

Scared to death was more like it. Julia didn't say that out loud. No sense giving Rafe a bigger reason to hurry.

Rafe pulled out his matches and lit three lanterns so they each had their own. He made short work of fastening the rope to each of them. Seth at the lead. Julia noticed Rafe doubled up the rope as if Seth might cut the rope and escape — though to Julia's knowledge, Seth had no knife. She sure hoped not. Seth and sharp objects didn't seem like a real good combination.

"I'm giving us a few feet of rope, so if someone falls we'll have a better chance of bracing ourselves and not be pulled down. Seth can lead." Rafe talked as he tripled the knot. "I'll go next."

Julia suspected Rafe wanted to be a buffer between Seth and her.

"Then Julia can bring up the rear." Rafe made quick work of tying them together. Then he slipped his arm around her waist and kept her beside him.

Seth headed into the cave with no hesitation, so eager to get in he could barely hold back from running. Julia was so eager to follow that she only noticed she'd left Rafe behind when the rope, tied around her stomach, jerked. She and Seth both turned back. Rafe rolled his eyes and caught up with them.

Instead of going into the downslope tunnel, Seth went straight and they found the little room where a bedroll still lay beside the cold ashes of a campfire.

"Did you sleep here?" Rafe didn't see any other exit from this room, so he wasn't sure why Seth had brought them here.

"Yep. But this is my friend's bedroll. He seemed to hate the light after he'd been in here awhile. He was kinda crazy."

Rafe and Julia exchanged a glance.

Seth bent over and picked up a little packet of some kind off the floor. "I got this after Andersonville. I wondered where it went."

"What is it?" Rafe asked.

Seth showed them a little stack of papers folded thick and wrapped in a patch of leather. "It's a bunch of pages out of a Bible. I like having it close." He stuck it in a pocket of his shirt.

"I thought we'd go down that lower tunnel, Seth." Julia was chewing on her upper lip, trying to control her impatience. "I don't see a way to go on into the cavern from here."

"I remembered sleeping in here and

wanted to see it." Seth led back the way they'd come and headed down the lower tunnel. They were quiet, Seth lighting torches along the way, until they got to the hole he had skirted alongside of when they'd found him.

"Seth, wait!" Rafe ordered.

Turning back, his eyes glinting in the lantern light, Seth said, "Why? It's a long walk to the best caves."

"I just want us to be really careful on that ledge." Rafe went ahead of Seth and dropped to his knees. He held out the lantern. "I want to make sure this part of the floor isn't thin."

"It's fine, Rafe. I've walked across it plenty of times."

Rafe didn't answer as he leaned down and tried to see the underside of the ledge. Chafing at the delay, Julia crossed her arms and tapped her foot, her mouth clamped shut so she wouldn't start nagging the man to hurry.

"It looks fine. But, Seth, I want us to string out. I've left about six feet of rope between each of us. I want you to go out slowly until you reach the end of the rope."

Julia thought about the end of her rope and how close she was to reaching it. Her toe tapped faster.

"Then I'll start across and . . . *Julia* will

404

you *stop* that?" Rafe snapped as he rose to glare at her. His voice echoed over and over. It came back from beneath them and from the tunnel in both directions, as if ten men were yelling at her.

She froze. Her tapping toe included. Annoyed that she'd obeyed him but sorry she hadn't been a bit more subtle about her impatience, she shrugged. "I'm sorry. I'm just eager to explore."

Shaking his head, Rafe said, "Go, Seth."

It was a ledge about a foot wide, narrower in some spots, wider in others. On her right was a solid wall of stone. On her left, empty space that fell to jagged rocks. There was a drop of at least twenty feet where Seth had plunged through the floor and Ethan had nearly fallen, where a dropped lantern had burned Seth terribly. No wonder Ethan and Rafe hated this place. The wonder was that Seth didn't.

Julia was careful. She'd never noticed this ledge in her earlier explorations. The hole had seemed like a dead end, and she'd turned back. The ledge was wide enough; it didn't seem dangerous so long as it didn't break under her feet. Seth was nearly halfway across when Rafe set out. Julia waited, obeying him. Seth got across and turned back. Rafe reached the midway point, and Julia set out. They crossed the ledge without trouble.

"Now, I want to show you something really beautiful." Seth gave her that untamed smile. Julia nodded and they set out, single file but closer together. They came to a torch and Seth lit it.

"Seth, why did you put out our torches yesterday?" Rafe asked.

Julia had wondered about that, too. Rafe had lit them all as they'd walked in. Then, on the way out, they'd been extinguished.

"And is there a way around that hole?" The tunnel was wide enough that Julia came up to walk beside Rafe. She walked, running her fingers along the tunnel wall, enjoying the feel of rough stone gently scratching her hand. "There has to be for you to have put out torches, then gotten ahead of us, across the broken place in the floor."

"This tunnel leads to a T just ahead." Seth's voice echoed in the confined space. He spoke more quietly, as if to stop the haunting voice that echoed every word. "To the left is that entrance where we used to come down, Rafe. To the right is a beautiful room."

"I've seen it." Julia knew the room exactly. "And I've seen side tunnels almost as beautiful, though not as big. But I haven't begun to explore the ends of it." The air was dank and cool, no matter how hot the day. Julia had never noticed the temperature change down here.

"See the markings?" Julia pointed at black lines on the tunnel on Rafe's side, clearly visible if a person looked, yet very much part of the darkness if you weren't aware of them.

"Yes." Rafe touched one.

"I marked the tunnels so I wouldn't get lost. I bring a piece of charcoal along and my arrows always point back to the entrance." Julia pulled out a blackened chunk of wood she'd fished out of the fireplace.

"Then you've been down this way?" Rafe's voice echoed. Seth looked back as he moved along.

"Yes. But I stopped when I came to the hole. I didn't realize there was enough room to walk along the side of it. To think I was so close to that caldera."

They reached the T, and Seth lit a torch located there and turned right. Julia's heart sped up to think of the first magnificent room. She'd sat in there many times, soaking in the beauty. Towering, glistening stalactites and stalagmites, the constant drip of limestone-laced water that was building on each formation it had created.

They came to the room. Seth lit a torch, then another and another until the room was visible at all but its farthest reaches.

Julia listened to the dripping water.

"I'd forgotten how beautiful it was." Rafe spoke reverently, almost prayerfully.

Light danced off the glistening wet rock formations.

"This isn't the room I want to show you." Seth sounded eager to be off.

Julia wanted to stay. She wanted to bask in the beauty of this place, but if she could show Rafe what she'd found, she knew he'd agree to let her explore.

"Can we go through that tunnel, Seth?" Julia pointed to one of several tunnels that opened off this big room.

"I like that one, but the stuff I really love is that way." Seth pointed to a smaller opening.

Julia had seen it before, but she'd never gone in. She knew better than to dismiss a tunnel opening because of its size, but she hadn't gotten to that one.

Curbing the urgent need to show Rafe her fish fossils and force him to admit they weren't just some abandoned bone from a lunch pail, she decided that if Seth thought there were things worth seeing this way, then she'd follow.

"What formed all these?" Rafe ducked low to fit through the tight tunnel. "A volcano? Is that what you think?"

From close behind him, she marked the tunnel as she talked. "Many would say a volcano, but I'm not so sure."

"What then?" Rafe's voice echoed in the tunnel, and their footsteps sounded hollow and bounced back. For a second, Julia thought she heard more footsteps than just theirs. She wanted to tell Rafe and Seth to stop so she could listen, but she shook off the notion. She'd never let cave exploring spook her. She wouldn't start now.

Then she thought of just how frightened she'd been the day she got stranded down here. Fear tightened her throat.

"God flooded the earth in Noah's time."

"I know. It rained for forty days and forty nights. How would that create these huge caves and tunnels?" Rafe straightened, and a few steps later, Julia stepped out into a cave about three times larger than her cabin, which wasn't all that large.

"It didn't just rain."

Rafe stopped and turned to her, which jerked Seth to a stop.

"Let's keep going." Seth pulled on the rope.

"It didn't?" Rafe knitted his brow.

Julia decided it was a good time to rest awhile. She drew an arrow on the wall right next to the cave tunnel they'd just come through. She didn't know if there were multiple openings in this cave, but to be safe she marked it. "No, we think of the rain, but God sent fountains of water up from the ground, too."

Rafe frowned. "I don't remember that."

"Genesis says on the day the Great Flood started, 'were all the fountains of the great deep broken up, and the windows of the heaven were opened.' The windows of the heaven, that could be rain, although I wonder about that. A very strange rain, I'd think. The rain came for forty days and forty nights. But the part about the fountains of the great deep — I think of the way a volcano erupts out of the deep, and I wonder if water didn't sort of erupt in the same way."

"And formed these tunnels and caves?" Rafe looked at the cave they were in at the moment. The three lanterns did a good job of lighting it all the way to its edges.

"That would explain the fish, Rafe."

"You have fish?" Seth came up beside them. "Because I'm hungry."

Rafe's eyes fell shut as if he was slightly pained.

Julia was surprised by her willingness to help, even if just for Rafe's sake. She didn't like the untamed look in Seth's eyes, but with Rafe right here in case Seth showed signs of being dangerous, and the heavy rope in case Seth took it into his head to run, things seemed well under control. "It feels like it's mealtime, doesn't it? I don't have fish, but I have sandwiches from last night's venison and a can of peaches."

"More peaches?" Seth reached for the bag Julia carried over her shoulder. She took a step back, then regretted the telltale movement.

Seth wiped his hands on his pants as if he was nervous. "I love peaches. My mom used to give me peaches."

She jerked her head toward a level spot in the floor, against the cavern wall. "Let's eat."

"So you think water maybe came . . ." Rafe hesitated. "Uh . . . blasting up from deep in the earth somehow?"

Julia unwrapped sandwiches thick with venison and handed them to Seth and Rafe. "It would be one explanation for these tunnels. And if the rain came down and the water came up and the earth was covered, then it stands to reason that fish, normally found in rivers and oceans, usually the lowest ground around, would be up here. They

411

simply swam here. Then, when the waters receded, they were stuck. How else do you explain the fish?"

"An Apache —"

"It's not *lunch,* Rafe. Who would come all the way down here to eat lunch?"

Rafe held up his sandwich and smirked at her.

"They've found fossils in an Arizona Territory desert that are a type of shark."

"What's a shark?" Seth spoke around a mouthful of food.

"It's a large ocean fish. It only lives in salt water. And I think this fish I've found might be one, too. I've seen drawings of sharks, and the teeth look similar. What Apache rode his horse to the ocean, rounded himself up a shark and brought it across the mountains, then climbed down here to eat it?"

Rafe swallowed, so Julia knew she was in for more of his ridiculous opinions.

"Maybe they were using the bones. They could've carried them a long way if they kept them as tools. Indians use all parts of what they catch. With the buffalo they —"

"But they don't leave it intact! This skeleton I saw wasn't cut up. No, there had to be salt water, ocean water, up here."

Rafe shook his head and chewed.

"I've seen bones in these walls." Seth

412

relaxed, stretching out, crossing his legs. He was really at home down here.

"Really?" Julia was starting to like Seth. "Where?"

"There are some in the room I'm taking you to. Up high. Strange to see them up there. My friend looked at them for a long time, and we talked about how they got up there."

A chill raced up and down her backbone. "About this friend, Seth. Tell me about him. Did he come here with you or did you find him here?"

Seth eased back as if he was preparing to spin a yarn.

Rafe moved in the exact opposite manner of Seth. He tensed up. Sat straight. His jaw chomped up and down as if he were at war with his food. Julia braced herself to be told to not bother Seth, but instead Rafe kept quiet.

"He came with me." Seth quit chewing and rubbed a palm against his pant leg.

"From Andersonville?" Julia tried to eat and question Seth at the same time since he seemed willing to talk at least somewhat rationally for once.

"No . . ." Seth's brow furrowed like it was painful to think. "We met in town."

"In Rawhide?" Rafe asked.

Julia realized that Rafe knew as little about Seth as she and was no doubt eight thousand times as curious.

"Yep. I rode in on my horse." Seth sat up straight. "What happened to my horse, huh?"

"We'll find him," Rafe soothed. "We haven't had much time to look yet. So, what's your friend's name?"

Seth looked around the cave as if he hoped someone had written the name on the wall. "He was tracking someone. Tracker. I told him I was from out this way and we rode out together. But he didn't go home. I told him I wanted to go home, but he wanted to go a different way. Follow some trail. Then I recognized this mountain and knew there was an entrance to the cave, and I showed it to him."

"When was that?" With a shiver, Julia wondered how long Seth had been hanging around. Maybe he'd been watching her explore for days.

Seth ate the last of his sandwich and seemed to be searching around inside his muddled head for an answer. When he swallowed, he said, "I don't know. Once we were down here. There's no . . . no day or night. Time doesn't mean much. And every time I talked about going home, I ended up being

414

so tired I just wanted to rest. This is a good place to rest." He eased back again, and his eyes drifted shut.

"Just like you were always good in the dark. You knew this cave better than any of us, Seth. And even after your accident, you were never scared."

"I came down because . . . well . . . because it was peaceful. The cavern eased all the wild thoughts in my head. I felt whole down here. I felt like . . . like . . ." Seth's eyes flickered open, and he absently rubbed his hands up and down on his legs, drying his palms, or maybe it was just a nervous habit.

"Whole? What does that mean?" Rafe sounded bewildered. "You made Ethan crazy worrying about you. I had to come after you and I didn't want to. But I was so afraid you'd fall and need help."

Seth closed his eyes and was silent for so long, Julia wondered if he would answer. She felt sorry for the poor man. She did. And she knew Rafe loved his brother.

Seth finally whispered, "I left my soul behind when I fell. I needed to find it."

Goose bumps rose on Julia's arms.

Seth crossed his arms and eased back until he was nearly lying down. Julia watched, waiting for Seth to speak again or Rafe to say something.

Suddenly a slow, steady noise rose from Seth. It took Julia a minute to figure out what it was.

Snoring.

She looked away, no idea what to make of Rafe's brother. Wounded, scared, lost, dangerous. Her gaze met Rafe's.

"He's asleep." Rafe shook his head. Then he looked at Julia, frowning, and slid closer to her, the rope only giving him a few feet of distance from Seth. "I don't know what to do for him."

"Neither do I."

"I think . . ." Rafe said, swallowing hard. "I have to stay with him, Jules."

"And I think he's not safe to have around Audra and the children."

"We're not . . ." Rafe closed his eyes, and Julia wished it didn't have to be said. More than that, she wished she didn't have to say it, but Rafe didn't seem capable of it.

So it had to come from her. "We're not going to be able to be together. At least not until you've seen to Seth and made sure he's okay. You have to help him because that's the man you are. You can't fail your brother."

"Not again. I can't fail him again."

"And I can't let my family live in a house

with him if he's dangerous."

With a sudden move, Rafe grabbed her arm and dragged her to meet his lips. His grip was gentle iron, but she wasn't trying to escape. Instead, she leaned closer and held on tight. He lifted her and sat her on his lap. The kiss deepened, and she knew it wasn't the kiss of a promise and a future. It was good-bye. Long moments later, he said, "I don't want to give you up. How can I give you up?"

"But how can we be together?"

They both turned to look at Seth.

"Just give me time. We'll figure something out. I'll take Seth home and —"

"And," Julia cut him off, "I want to stay and explore. Except I can't with Audra and two little children. So we'll search down here today . . . and maybe a few more times. Then I'll take my family and go. Maybe I'll have enough research to write my papers. Maybe even a book. But whether I have it or not, my family's safety has to come first. We'll go somewhere civilized, where I can find work and the children can go to school and there's a doctor nearby and a store to buy food."

"No," Rafe said, then shut her mouth with his lips, and Julia couldn't bear to push him away. She wanted him so badly that she had

417

already given up on asking for his love. Now she would need to give up on her cavern and even give up on a life with him. It was everything that mattered most to her, except God and her family. She had to do what was right by her family, and God would give her the strength.

Rafe wouldn't have been the man she loved if he'd been able to turn his back on Seth. He finally pulled away, when her lips felt swollen and her heart was so softened toward him it could be torn apart with no effort at all.

"I have to take care of him."

"I know."

"He needs to go home."

"I agree. And I can't come."

Rafe's gaze burned through her like lava. Finally he eased her off his lap. "But you can go somewhere safe. Somewhere I can find you."

"When, Rafe? A month? A year? How long do I sit somewhere while you battle for your brother's sanity? No, you have to commit to him and forget me."

"I can't."

"If you work with him all the while knowing I'm waiting somewhere, it will make you treat him differently. You'll either resent me or him or both. And I'll wait for my life to have meaning until you come to me. That's a sad, empty life for me. And I want Seth to be well. I have compassion for him. We can't ever hope to find happiness built at the cost of your brother's sanity. You have to help Seth, don't you?"

She made it a question because somehow, if he never said it out loud, she *could* wait. She could pretend not to, but wherever she went, she could make sure Rafe could find her. And she could go on with her lonely life, only less so now caring for Audra and the children. And find new places to explore, and through it all she'd wait and hope and pray that Rafe would come.

A heartbreaking way to live.

"No! It burns!" Seth suddenly cried out. "Stop. Help. Rafe, help me!"

He thrashed in his sleep, slapping at his arm as if it were on fire. Kicking and rolling side to side. "Rafe, help me. Ethan, save me!"

"Yes, for now at least, I have to take care of my brother." He held her gaze as Seth's nightmare drove home the point. The brutally sharp point.

She'd forced Rafe to say those words. And now she had to live with them. Even if they cut so deep she wanted to die.

Rafe turned away from her and shook

Seth. "Wake up."

Julia waited as Rafe struggled to pull Seth out of his nightmare. It wasn't easy, but it was a reminder of all that stood between them.

At last Seth awoke fully, and Rafe spoke quietly to him while Julia packed up their food from lunch. They needed to go back to the surface. What good was this fascinating cavern when she was crying inside.

"Let's go." Seth stood, apparently over any lingering effects of his dream.

"You want to keep exploring?" Julia had thought Seth would wake up scared and want daylight.

"I think we need to stop with the exploring for the day." Rafe looked more shaken than Seth.

"No. I want to show you a special room. It's beautiful." Seth turned his wild blue eyes on Julia, and they seemed to burn in the lantern light.

Julia looked at him and wondered, *If we headed for the surface now, will Seth even come? Or will we have to restrain him and drag him up to the surface?*

"All right." Julia felt as if the weight of the world were on her shoulders. She didn't have the will to make a decision, so she let Seth make it. "Let's go."

Julia started forward. She passed Rafe, and the rope jerked her to a stop at the same moment it stopped Seth. They both turned to face him.

He looked like a mountain under pressure. She wondered if it was the end of their plans to marry or his dislike of the cave.

"Can't you feel it?" Rafe asked, so quietly that Julia came a step closer to hear him, Seth with her.

"Feel what?" Seth asked.

"This place. It's like I can feel the weight of the mountain on top of me."

Julia felt it, too, but hers was for a different reason. She looked at Seth.

"It feels fine to me." Seth turned away, but Julia thought he did so too quickly. Like he didn't want to see his big brother show any weakness. "Let's go. I want you to see this."

Julia waited. If Rafe really wanted out, she'd go.

Rafe drew in a deep breath and, without meeting Julia's eyes, went after Seth. She followed, wondering what all this was costing the man she loved. She knew what it was costing her.

Seth kept moving. Rafe kept moving. It was easy for Julia to keep moving, marking as she went. Seth bent low to enter the next tunnel. Rafe was an inch or two taller than Seth and much broader in the shoulders. He had to bend even further. Julia stood upright, but there wasn't much headroom. The only light in this narrow cave was their lanterns. No torches, but why bother? There was nothing here except passage to the place Seth was so excited about. They stepped into a larger cave. Julia looked around.

"It's farther on," Seth said. "There are a string of caves before we get to the one I want you to see."

Julia marked the cave wall with an arrow pointing into the tunnel they'd just walked through. Her black arrows would be useless if something happened to the lanterns. They'd be trapped so far below the ground . . .

Suddenly, just like Rafe, she could feel the cave overhead pressing. How far had they gone down? Had the cave floor sloped? And they were surrounded by mountains. They could be climbing up as well as down, but it didn't seem like it. It seemed like they were headed into the belly of the earth. Into the very gateway to hell.

They were being drawn in so deep, they would never get out. He would pick a spot and rob them of light. This would end. Soon.

Fighting down the laughter, he corrected himself. It wouldn't end, it would just begin. Before he was done, Rafe would be dead. His friend would be dead, too. He was tired of sharing this cavern with anyone.

Except the red-haired woman — she had secrets she could tell him about the money.

He bided his time as they went deeper and deeper. Gullible fools. They were coming along as if he were a master and they were mules moving beneath his whip.

He rubbed his hands on his pants, the excitement making him sweat. Soon it would be time to make his move, and he knew exactly where that would be. He knew the tunnel he wanted them near. So he could grab the woman and vanish. He'd leave the others alive for now. But only to enjoy their terror.

When that got old, he'd finish them and find his treasure.

In the dark.

Julia watched Seth wipe his hands on his pant legs as if he was nervous. He seemed so comfortable down here. And it was chilly and they were setting a slow pace. Why would he sweat?

It only added to her tension. Disgusted with herself, Julia fought off the fear. She'd climbed around in dozens of caves. And they had never bothered her. Much.

Of course, that had been before the day she'd been trapped down here. And she'd never been in one so deep, with such a labyrinth of tunnels.

Rafe's breathing sped up. She could almost feel the tension vibrating off of him. He didn't like it down here. But he had such iron control that he faced his fear and moved deeper into the cavern.

She wondered if he'd reach his limit. Then she wondered if they'd reach hers. How long it would be before they needed to leave?

Seth passed through a small cave and then entered another tunnel, smaller than any they'd passed through before. She saw him again wipe first one hand, then the other on his pants. It had to be nerves. Why would so bold a man as Seth be nervous?

She turned her thoughts from Seth. He was close enough to being a lunatic that maybe he was both fearless and terrified at the same time. A broken mind living in two halves inside one head. It only made her more determined to carefully mark her path. As she reached for the wall with her chunk of charcoal, she noticed her hand trembling. Thanks to Rafe putting the idea in her head, the weight of the mountain pressed on her.

Then they got to a much larger cavern full of massive stalactites and stalagmites. Their bright lanterns were feeble in a room so large, and they cast deep shadows everywhere. Seth lit torches wedged into cracks in the wall.

"Isn't this pretty?" Seth said. "But it's not what I want you to see." He headed for another tunnel.

"Wait!" Julia needed a few minutes to get her nerves calmed down and to give Rafe a chance to get used to the depths. "This room is spectacular. I want to see more of it."

As the flames from Seth's torches grew, she did see more of it. There were openings on all sides. Small, large, some might just be shadowed crevasses, while others might lead downward forever.

"No, we're almost there." Seth headed straight for the smallest opening yet, pulling Rafe and an increasingly reluctant Julia along with him. Their footsteps echoed in the room until it almost sounded like someone was following them.

Seth dropped to his knees. "We'll need to crawl through this one."

"What was *that?*" Rafe stopped, pulling

the rope taut so Seth couldn't move.

Julia came up to Rafe. "I didn't hear anything." Or had she? She wasn't wild about entering that tiny hole.

"Wait a minute." Julia saw Seth reach for the rope around his waist, clearly determined to go on with or without them. "Seth, don't!"

Still on his knees, he turned to face them. "But this is the best part. This is what you wanted to see, Julia. I'm going in."

"I don't like this." Julia surprised herself by saying it. She wanted to see what Seth had seen. She wanted to find the wonders deep in the earth. She might not get another chance.

Then a footstep echoed.

None of them had moved.

"Hey," Seth said, looking past Julia. He lit up with his wild smile. "Great. Now you can meet my friend."

The sharp *crack* of a gun cocking sounded just as an arm wrapped around Julia's neck.

"Get back!" A voice rough as gravel scraped her ear.

Rafe whirled around and froze.

A gun waved right by Julia's ear; she could just see the muzzle. "Get back or I'll kill her."

The gun pressed to Julia's temple so hard

she'd be bruised — if she lived long enough. The arm around her neck was so tight she had to fight to breathe. She grabbed at the arm, but it was solid as iron.

Rafe raised his hands slowly and backed up a single step.

"What're you doing?" Seth stepped forward, and the man lifted the gun from Julia's head and aimed down. The gun roared, deafening in the cave, ricocheting with a series of whining, echoing cracks. The man jerked her back, and when he pulled her far enough, she realized the gunshot had severed the rope that had tied her to Rafe.

"I come for what's mine." The man pulled her backward.

"What are you doing?" Seth shouted. "Don't hurt her."

"I won't hurt no one if I get what I want." Julia didn't believe him for a second.

"Tell us who you are and what you want." Rafe's voice was so steady, Julia felt the cold of it stab into her heart. His tone penetrated her terror. He didn't look at her or act like he cared if she lived or died.

"They call me Tracker." He sounded half mad, and he smelled of rancid filth. "And I reckon I did a mighty good job of tracking you down."

"What do you mean 'what's mine'?" Rafe

asked, his voice strong but collected, detached, as if he were horse trading. Julia's heart sank. She knew how she'd feel if someone had a gun to Rafe's head. It would be nothing like this.

Rafe didn't love her.

He could never have been this controlled if he did.

"She's got money hidden at her place. Her pa stole it from my boss, and I come for it."

Julia had to find a way to survive. In the face of Rafe's cool reaction, Julia knew she had to think about Audra and the children.

"My father? Wendell Gilliland?"

"Wendell is the last name of the man my boss is hunting. In town they called him Gill. I've been on his trail since he left Texas. The boss give me the job of tracking him down to get his money back."

She wondered if he knew Father was dead. "Why come for me?"

"Your pa is beyond asking, isn't he?"

Julia's jaw tightened, not sure what to say next.

"Yes, I know your pa is dead. I been watchin' you mighty close."

She shuddered at the rough tone of his voice. "But why?"

"In Rawhide, I caught up to your pa. I laid low and bided my time, but there was no chance to grab him and force him to hand over the money. It took me a while to figure out he was sneaking out of town on weekends to come see you. I finally figured it out early one Monday morning when I saw him slipping back into town. So I set out to see where he'd been. I couldn't follow his trail the whole way the first week or the second or the third. And I couldn't spot your pa leaving town. He was a wily man, and he went out of town a different way each time. But finally his back trail led me to your place. I headed for town to catch him out alone but missed him."

"So are you really Seth's friend?" Julia hated the thought that maybe Seth was in cahoots with this man. Maybe they'd planned all of this together.

"If he's my friend, he oughta put down the gun." Seth nearly bounced with energy, but Julia thought he showed a lot of restraint not to come running at them. A lot of sanity.

"I met up with Seth headed this way for home. When I realized how well he knew the area, I convinced him to ride along with me. I threw in with him figurin' he'd know everyone who lived around these parts. But Wendell's tracks didn't go toward Seth's home. And Seth's the next thing to loco."

"Hey!" Seth clenched his fists. But again he stayed in place. Or maybe he just didn't care that much that she had a madman threatening her.

"Now, Seth," Rafe said, "you gotta admit you've been acting a little crazy, even for you." He crossed his arms as if he didn't have a care in the world.

Julia caught a little smile on Rafe's lips, as if he was having fun teasing his brother.

"He led me into the tunnel in that mountain valley and showed me how close it was to Wendell's cabin."

"I didn't know you were looking for Julia." Seth's eyes flashed wildly in the torchlight. "You said you liked caves."

"Why didn't you just go on home from the cavern, Seth?" Rafe leaned his left shoulder on a man-sized stalagmite.

"I . . . I meant to." Seth rubbed both hands through his hair.

"I figured out real quick he knew his way around down here and I wanted him to show me the tunnels." Tracker's voice was calm as he enjoyed boasting. "It's a mighty good hiding place, easy to slip up close and watch for Wendell. So, when Seth woke up the first night screaming, I gave him some laudanum."

"You drugged me?" Seth lifted his head,

430

his fidgeting stopped.

"The first time I did it just to shut you up."

Julia had heard Seth's nightmares. Terrible to listen to.

"I forced you to drink it while you were awake enough to take the medicine but asleep enough to forget I done it. You woke up so confused the next morning, it was easy to keep you here and get you to show me this place."

"I . . . I don't remember taking anything." Seth turned to Rafe. "But I've been feeling so wrong, so lost."

Rafe crossed one leg over the other, nodding. "Makes sense. You'd be an easy one to fool, Seth."

Julia wanted to despair of Rafe's tone. He didn't seem to care about her or his brother.

"Once we were down here, Seth seemed to forget all about how to get home. He'd say he wanted to go, but he never did, not as long as I kept dosing him with the laudanum."

Tracker leaned forward, and Julia saw him for the first time. His face was horribly scarred. He smiled and the scars drew his face into a nightmarish mask. He wore an eye patch on his left eye, the one closest to her as he leaned over her right shoulder, us-

431

ing her as a shield. Julia noticed his grip on her neck had loosened as he mocked Seth.

"You seemed happy down here exploring, and I was learning my way around." Tracker's laugh echoed through the cave.

Rafe's eyes suddenly met hers. They hardened, then his gaze slid downward to the cave floor, and back up. The expression was gone almost instantly but it changed everything.

Julia realized he wasn't *detached,* he was controlled. Two very different things.

Rafe was keeping his head. He was asking her to be ready. For what, she didn't know, but he was planning something.

"Seth always knew this cave best," Rafe said. He reached up to rub the back of his neck. He looked for all the world like a man stretching, getting ready to yawn. But his right hand, his gun hand, settled at his side only inches from his revolver.

And Julia needed to distract Tracker so Rafe could make his move. "What happened to your eye?" she asked, then turned just a bit so she could see him. She was on his blind side, so she was hoping he'd feel the need to turn his head to see her.

"I spent a few years with no sight as a child after an explosion. A second accident, years later, restored the sight in my right eye. I was right at home in the dark and started liking it down here."

How much could he see? Enough, but maybe not everything. She leaned forward just a bit, until she was no longer pressed hard against his foul body.

Busy gloating, he didn't seem to notice. "We got here after your pa had gone back to town. By that time I'd figured out he wouldn't be back until Saturday night. So we had some time to explore."

Julia bent just another fraction of an inch away. She only needed one tiny chance, and then she'd slip to the ground. She needed to mess up his aim. Rafe would never beat Tracker to the draw if Tracker's gun was already out and cocked.

"I have no idea where my father put his money," Julia said. "I doubt he even has it anymore. He bought supplies to travel out here, and he bought a house and a business in town. I'm sure the money is all gone."

"Nope."

"How can you be so sure?" Julia took a quick look at Rafe, who was calm as ever. He didn't even seem to be paying much attention, and Tracker had definitely decided he was in charge of the situation. "My father liked to gamble. He could have lost it."

Tracker scowled, then shook his head. "He

stole a whole lotta money. Not much chance he could ever spend or gamble it all, even if he'd had it for a lifetime."

"Well, then why didn't he buy us a nicer house?" Julia decided arguing with him was the best way to draw his attention away from Rafe. She watched out of the corner of her eye to see if Rafe would signal her again and realized the rope around Rafe's waist had gone slack; he'd untied himself from Seth.

"Your pa was pure mean, that's why. Besides, I'm sure he didn't want to draw any attention to himself by being a big spender."

"But what do you expect Julia to do?" Seth asked.

Julia wished he'd be quiet. Now Tracker was watching the men.

"If her pa died, then the hiding place for the money died with him." Seth sounded so reasonable. "So what's the point in threatening her?"

"If she doesn't know where the money is, at least she knows her pa." Tracker turned to her. She was grateful he was again focused on her, until she saw the cruelty in his eyes. "You might have some idea of where he'd hide it."

"If I did, I'd tell you. Did you search his

business in town?"

"Yep, little rattrap of a building. Nowhere to hide much of nuthin'. He didn't have anything in there but a deck of cards or two and some whiskey. No money I could find. I had to be careful, though, so your pa or anyone in town wouldn't notice I'd been there. I didn't want him to hightail it."

"But our cabin is so small," Julia said. "There's nowhere it could be hidden. I can't help you. I give you permission to search for the money as long as you like. Let me go, and we'll walk out of here. If my father stole money from someone, then I'll gladly return it. But I have no idea where to begin searching."

"I think you might know more than you realize. I think if you stay down here long enough to know I'm dead serious and willing to hurt you, you'll try hard to come up with a hiding place your pa might use." He looked toward Rafe and Seth.

"She knows her pa as well as anyone. And I think, if I let her go, she's gonna want that money just like anyone else does and she'll decide not to share it. So I'm gonna take her away." He gestured toward a tunnel opening with the gun.

Rafe drew his Colt. Julia dropped. Tracker's grip slipped, but he dove for the floor.

Rafe's bullet missed. Seth ran straight at Tracker, putting his body between the gunman and Rafe, just as Tracker fired. The bullet slammed into Seth, but the forward momentum kept Seth flying forward. He struck Tracker but dropped to the floor like a dead man. Tracker staggered back. His gun fired into the ceiling again and again. A massive stalactite cracked overhead just as Rafe rushed into the fight and grabbed Tracker's hand, trying to wrench the pistol free.

Julia scrambled to her feet. "Rafe, look out!" A heavy stone plummeted from the ceiling, striking Rafe on the shoulder and knocking him down. Tracker was on his feet, still shooting and laughing like a madman. He grabbed Julia as more stones cascaded down.

Dust exploded from all directions. Screaming over the thundering gun, Julia saw Rafe slump to the ground unconscious. Seth sprawled facedown on the floor as more stones bounced off both of them, burying them.

Flames whooshed up from one of the lanterns, racing in a path straight for Rafe and Seth, who lay under falling stone.

"No!" Julia twisted wildly to escape Tracker's grasp.

Tracker laughed wildly and continued shooting into the ceiling.

She screamed as he dragged her into a tunnel. An unmarked one, pitch-dark. The man had no light. Her lantern was gone.

The cave ceiling continued to collapse. Stone crashed down.

Tracker laughed. Hot breath blasted her face. His clawing hands sunk into her belly, latching on to the rope she had around her waist.

Crying out, Julia grabbed the edge of the tunnel, but Tracker tore her hands loose just as the entrance to the tunnel vanished under stone.

Seth and Rafe were buried. Her only way out was cut off by tons of stone.

The mountain had fallen on Rafe.

And Julia was buried alive, trapped in total darkness with a madman.

CHAPTER 21

Rafe raised his head to see Julia dragged into a tunnel. Stone poured down, cutting him off from her and leaving her trapped with a madman.

"No! Julia!" Rafe shouted in horror. Grimly he shoved himself to his hands and knees.

I'll dig my way to you if it takes me the rest of my life.

Something slugged his back. Twisting, ready to fight, he saw a floor-to-ceiling column of stone yaw in his direction. Stones rained down from the ceiling as the column pulled loose overhead. Flames from a shattered lantern crawled along the floor toward him.

He leapt to his feet, staggered from the blows of battering rock. The column tilted straight toward him. With a rumble, jagged cracks streaked away from the shuddering stone tower where it attached to the cave ceiling.

A tug on his arm turned him to face Seth, bleeding from his chest but on his feet, alert.

Sane.

"Now! Move!" Seth jerked Rafe backward as stones avalanched. It was Rafe's own nightmare come to life. The mountain collapsing on him, crushing him.

Seth dragged him. For Seth the nightmare would be the fire. Burning.

The column rushed toward him. Rafe saw where Seth was headed, the only way out of this disintegrating space.

They ducked into a tunnel just as that stone column slammed onto the cave floor, trapping them. Choking grit billowed in. White-hot flames blasted in with the dust and blew through the tunnel.

Seth screamed and fell backward. Rafe threw his arms in front of his eyes. The flames crackled and raged, then with no kerosene to feed them, vanished.

"We've got to save Julia." Rafe remembered when Seth had nearly died so many years ago. He remembered the panic. Running. Abandoning his brothers.

He remembered it, and for the first time remembered that, yes, he'd been terrified, but he'd gotten control of himself. He'd done the right thing. He'd do it now, too.

"This way." Rafe's arm was caught, and Seth dragged him downhill, away from Julia.

"No, we have to go back." The darkness was total. Rafe could see nothing.

"There is no *back*, Rafe. We can't get out that way." Seth quit yanking on him, and with a scratching noise, a light popped on.

A match. Light down here in the deep. And Seth walked only a few yards forward to a torch.

Just like light could be down here, so could God. The thought steadied Rafe, and he turned to face that cave. He *would* dig his way through.

"We can't go back. The whole cave was coming down. We can't get through there."

"We have to. We have to get to the tunnel she went down and save her. Even if we have to move an entire mountain's worth of stone, I'm not giving up."

In the growing light of the torch, Rafe saw his little brother smile and was prompted toward violence. He'd decided too soon that Seth was sane.

"No, we're not giving up." Despite the stupid smile, Seth looked more rational than Rafe had seen him since he'd come home. "Tracker may think he knows his way

440

around down here, but he hasn't begun to learn this cavern as well as me."

"What do you mean?" Rafe clenched his fist, in no mood for Seth's games.

"I mean, down this far these tunnels twist all around like a maze, curve up and down, and cross each other."

"Cross each other?" Rafe wasn't sure what that meant.

"Yep. We may be cut off from Julia the way we came, but there are other ways to get where Tracker is going." The wild look was back in Seth's blue eyes. "Faster ways."

Rafe had just a second to wonder if Seth was loco. Was he going to lead Rafe to Julia or lead him forever down?

Right now, his choices were real limited. And he'd prayed for God's help. And Seth, the man who knew these caverns better than anyone else in the world, was what God provided. He could either pick up a whole mountain, one stone at a time, or . . . "Lead the way, little brother. Let's go get her back."

Seth's eyes flashed, and he turned and rushed in the exact opposite direction from where Rafe had last seen Julia. If Rafe followed and Seth didn't know what he was doing, then Rafe might never see Julia again.

Rafe charged after his brother into the

belly of the earth.

Julia thought of Rafe, buried under the crushing weight of the mountain and wanted to die, too. But it wasn't in her to give up. The lunatic had a firm grip on the rope still tied around her waist.

Slow him down. Think. I need time to think.

She dropped to the floor, and he dragged her along for a few feet.

"Get up, pretty lady. Or I'll drag you by that long red hair."

"I fell." Julia didn't have to try very hard to get her voice to break. "You're going too fast."

She swept her hands along the ground, wishing she could find a nice heavy rock she could use on the man's skull. Finding nothing, she had another idea. Not as good, though honestly, nothing would sound as good as bashing his head in. But it was something, until a rock came to hand. She thought he'd dropped his gun in the melee, but even if he opened fire, she was going to make her break, and soon.

She stood as slowly as she thought she could without earning his fist. She had enough time, in the pitch black, to get herself ready to fight back the only way she could think of.

He caught hold of the rope.

"Please, I'll fall again if you move so fast. What's the point? Rafe and Seth are . . ." Her voice broke again. No need to fake it.

"I buried 'em good, didn't I?" His laugh was mad. Ugly. Cruel. All things that described this man perfectly.

"So, th-then . . ." She fought to control her voice, not sure if it mattered. Maybe if she cried and begged it would help, but it was so distasteful to be so out of control. "What's the hurry? If you want me to stay on my feet, slow down."

He did.

Julia kept the pace slow and stayed at full attention. She was being led along like a trained dog, which reminded her of a wild dog she'd tried to tame once.

He'd bit her.

Her right hand was busy running along the wall of the tunnel. But with her left hand, she felt around at the rope, doing her best to jostle her body so he wouldn't notice a few extra tugs. They stopped.

"We'll rest here." His voice echoed in a way that told her they'd stepped out of the tunnel into a room. "You're right. There's no hurry."

"I . . . I need to sit." She let her legs give out; her knees were shaking violently. Her collapsing tore his hand free of the rope.

The echo of her voice told her they were in a good-sized cave, but she couldn't see a thing. She heard her captor panting and gasping.

Suddenly it occurred to her that if she couldn't see him, he couldn't see her.

She felt at the stones around her, behind her, and realized she was within reaching distance of a stalagmite. And she also sat hard on a rather sharp stone. She tugged it out from underneath her and considered how easily Tracker moved in this cave and how used to blindness he was. That meant he could hear her breathing. Hear every footstep. When she made her break, whatever else she did, she had to be silent. He'd never find her.

"I think it's time we talked about your pa and where he might've hidden my money." Tracker grasped a handful of hair at the nape of her neck, and his hot fetid breath blew against her face. "And you're right. We've got all the time in the world."

His hand tightened and he laughed, and the laughter echoed as if a thousand madmen had her in their clutches.

Just when she needed to be calm, her breathing even and shallow, she felt a terrified need to gasp for air.

Just when she needed to be utterly silent, she wanted to scream.

He'd followed Seth for so long now he wanted to scream. The next instant, that need was gone.

"Look at that." Rafe pointed to the cave wall. At a thin black line. Julia had marked her trail.

"What is it? I've never marked anything down here."

"It's Julia." Rafe smiled to think of how smart their children were going to be. "She's left us a trail."

"And I know exactly where Tracker would take her down here. He's got a room he's real fond of, and this mark is taking us in the right direction." Seth was leading and he sped up.

Rafe was one pace behind. They moved fast now that they knew the way forward and the way back.

Yep, he was marrying a right smart woman. Now all he had to do was find her, convince her that he hadn't meant all that nonsense about giving her up for Seth, and get her married up and moved in a cabin he planned to build just as soon as he ridded this cavern of one troublemaking "friend."

And then they'd see about those smart

babies.

Julia wondered if she should ask for forgiveness for what she was about to do.

Maybe later.

She smashed Tracker over the head with the rock.

He fell backward, and rather than run — which she'd planned to do — she dove after him, swinging the jagged stone, hitting him wherever she could reach. The jolt in her arm told her that she landed some really good blows.

In her panic it took her a moment to realize he wasn't fighting back.

He lay unmoving, unconscious. Maybe dead.

Forgiveness definitely, because for right now she didn't even believe she'd committed a sin — and that must be the greatest sin of all.

"Julia!" The sound turned her, and she saw light. And Rafe.

And the love that shone in his eyes.

She cried out and jumped up just as he got to her side. She threw herself into his arms.

His arms held her so tight she couldn't breathe. He whispered, "Julia, thank God you're — *ow!*"

"Thank God I'm *ow?*" Julia pulled back. "What's the matter?"

"Did you just hit me with a . . ."

Julia lifted her arm, which had wrapped around Rafe's neck.

". . . rock?" Rafe rubbed the back of his head.

She still had the stone. Now coated with Tracker's blood. "Sorry. It was for him." She gestured with the stone over her shoulder.

Rafe looked past her to see Tracker in a heap on the cave floor. "Nice work."

"I couldn't see him when I attacked. I sort of whacked at him everywhere hoping to hit something that'd put him down and keep him down so I could run."

"Looks like you did it right."

Tracker's face was coated in blood.

Julia said, "He was an ugly man to begin with, and the blood does him no favors."

"It's just another reason why I love you." Rafe pulled her close again, maybe a bit more gingerly this time.

"You love me?" Julia's heart, so thoroughly broken earlier, healed in that instant.

"I do. And I'm not giving you up for anything."

"Not even for —"

Seth appeared beside them, grinning like

a locoweed. "You got him good, Julia." Then he saw Tracker, and his grin widened. "I always wanted a sister, and I got me a tough one."

Her body began to shake as all she'd gone through hit her as hard as any stone.

Rafe cradled her, supporting her through the reaction. "Not even for my brother."

"I thought you were dead." Julia kissed him. "I thought he'd brought a mountain down on your head. Rafe Kincaid, I love you and I'm not giving you up for anything or anyone."

The kiss ended when Seth cleared his throat loudly.

Rafe turned to look at Tracker, and that turned Julia around, too.

She said, "I really hope he's not dead."

"Me, too." Rafe held her closer. "I wouldn't want you to have to carry that on your conscience for the rest of your life."

"No . . . Well, yes, that's a good reason, too . . . I guess."

"You guess?" Rafe arched one brow at her.

"I want him alive so he can be locked up for the rest of his miserable life in the most gruesome prison this territory has to offer. That's why I hope he's not dead." Julia shrugged sheepishly. Faintly she added, "I guess that's not a very good reason, is it?"

Tracker groaned, clearly not dead. Julia decided she could live with her conscience with no problem. Then she remembered something else. "I saw you get shot, Seth. You're bleeding."

Seth looked down at his chest. Then he pulled his shirt aside. An ugly gash about three inches long, halfway between his neck and shoulder, was bleeding freely.

"That looks like a bullet furrow." Rafe let one arm loose from around Julia, but she noticed he still held her with the other. He tugged a kerchief out of his back pocket and handed it to Seth. "You were heading straight for him. How come it cut up?"

Seth fumbled in the breast pocket of his shirt and pulled out the thick packet of papers with a leather wrapper around them. "This must have deflected the bullet."

"It's a worse scratch than my father died from. We need to get you out of here and treat that wound." Julia smiled. "Hey, you know what I just realized?"

Seth looked up from his life-saving Scripture. Rafe turned to her. They both said, "What?"

"I've always wanted a brother, too."

Seth smiled. Rafe's arm tightened around Julia's waist.

The smelly oaf on the cave floor groaned again.

"Let's get him up and get out of here."

"Can we get out?" Julia froze as she remembered the collapsing tunnel that had been their way in. "Is there another way? How'd you get down here? How'd you survive the cave-in?"

"I'll tell you everything while we're walking out." Rafe smiled and looked at Seth. "There is a way out, isn't there?"

"I can get us out." Seth pulled the rope off his waist and used it to tie Tracker's hands behind his back. He shook the man until he was alert enough to stand. The flickering lantern light made his bloody head glisten and dance as if his face were on fire.

Seth pushed Tracker ahead of him, and Rafe and Julia followed behind, walking side by side when possible. As they climbed, Julia realized what she was walking out of. "God found us even down here in this pit."

"Sure He did," Rafe said. But his light tone didn't match his serious face. He still didn't like being deep underground.

"I've spent so many years searching for truth, science, learning. But once I found those fossils down here, I really thought I'd found God."

Rafe looked down at her and took her hand. "Had you lost Him?"

She shook her head. "No. No, I hadn't. I've been a believer for a long time. My mother was a woman of faith, and she raised me with God in my life. But I have always wanted to do something wonderful. Something special." She gave a tiny shrug. "Maybe something special enough to earn my father's love. What could possibly be more special than proving there is a God. Evidence carved in stone as surely as the Ten Commandments."

"God's truth is in your heart, Julia. No fossil trapped in stone will make a difference."

"You're right. I know that."

Seth called over his shoulder, "Does that mean you don't want to see all the fish fossils I've found down here? We should go right now. We're not that far."

"Well, it might be nice to —"

"Not today." Rafe started growling. "For right now, we're going home."

"Where is home, Rafe?" Seth walked slower and turned from Tracker to Rafe and Julia. "Why is my friend bleeding?"

"I whacked him in the head with a rock." Julia saw Seth flinch and give her a frightened look. Maybe she should have softened

451

that answer a little.

"I'm lost." Seth sounded weak, confused.

"You can't get lost yet, Seth. You've got to get us out of here." Rafe slapped Seth on the shoulder. He didn't even sound worried.

Which Julia found exceedingly worrisome.

"And your friend hurt Julia. That's why he's bleeding. We're taking him to the sheriff."

"Oh. Okay. Let's go." Seth's beetled brow smoothed out and he picked up speed.

Julia exchanged a glance with Rafe. He shrugged, smiled at her, stole a kiss, and followed his brother.

Rafe was pretty sure his brother wasn't seriously crazy.

He could tell Julia wasn't so sure.

When they got to the cabin, Ethan was waiting with a slender young man with wire-rimmed glasses and a parson's collar.

The circuit rider had arrived.

"Who's he?" Ethan looked at Tracker, horrified.

"I've almost never seen Ethan without a stupid grin on his face," Julia said to Tracker. "You look really terrible."

Tracker had blood dried on most of his face. Add in the eye patch and the awful scars, and yep, Rafe decided, Julia had it exactly right.

"He's my friend," Seth said, smiling like a dolt.

"No, Seth. He is *not* your friend. He shot you, remember? Then he kidnapped Julia."

"What? He shot you?" Ethan looked at the blood on Seth's shirt, right over his heart. "We need to get you to a doctor."

Seth shrugged. "It's just a scratch."

"A scratch killed my husband." Audra emerged from the cabin, empty-handed.

"Where are the children?" Julia asked.

"Asleep. Both at the same time." Audra smiled. "This isn't going to be so hard."

"You shot me?" Seth yelped at Tracker.

A loud cry sounded from inside the house.

Everyone, even Tracker and the circuit rider, glared at Seth and said, "Shhhh!"

Audra rushed in and came back out with a sleepy, grumpy-looking Maggie in her arms.

Maggie reached for Ethan, who took her.

"Julia and I are getting married," Rafe announced.

Julia smiled. "Right now, if you please."

"Don't you want to clean up first, Julia?" Audra asked.

"No, I want to remember exactly how this day went. Considering a mountain fell on us today, I think getting married in this filthy condition — with Seth bleeding, this awful man tied up, Rafe coated with dirt — is perfect. It's just exactly how our wedding should be, don't you think?"

"I'd actually kind of like a bath," Rafe said.

"Forget it. Say the vows, Parson. Before he tries to escape again."

Rafe smiled, then laughed. At the moment the last cold remnants inside him warmed fully. He realized then that what had been frozen inside him wasn't terror. It wasn't the fear that he was weak, a coward, a failure.

It was love.

He'd frozen away everything that was beautiful. He'd cared for his brothers, but he hadn't risked truly loving them for fear of how terrible it would be to lose them. He'd never been as kind to his mother as he should have been because his love was locked away. He'd worked beside his father and shown him respect but never love.

It was all there now. Full and alive and warm, all the way to his heart and soul.

He turned his eyes from one member of his family to the other. Ethan, who never risked feeling anything deeply. Seth, who risked his life searching for his soul. Audra, frail and beautiful.

Then he turned to Julia. She was a mess. Her hair was standing out in every direction. She was coated in grit and dust. Her face needed to be washed, as did her dress. The little woman even had another man's blood on her hands.

He decided then and there they'd say their vows now, and then he'd take her to the icy stream in the caldera where they could bathe together and wash their clothes and be alone in the late afternoon sunlight and through the night.

Julia must have seen something in his eyes, because her smile warmed and her green eyes glowed with happiness.

"Yes, say the vows, Parson. I'm not going anywhere."

Julia grabbed his arms and they turned to face the parson, who looked extremely skeptical. But the vows were said in good order.

"Ethan, you and Seth are going to have to help me build a cabin in that caldera."

Julia gasped and gave him a vivid smile.

"I really need to get back to the Kincaid Ranch and run things, Rafe," Ethan said. "Steele has been in charge of the place so long, he's likely to claim it as his own."

"You can ride over there with Seth tomorrow; then the next day bring some of the men back to help us build."

"I get to go home?" Seth asked.

Ethan nodded. "Sure, little brother. I'll take you home."

"Good," Rafe said, then turned to the circuit rider. "Parson, see our prisoner into Rawhide and get him locked up tight. He shot Seth and kidnapped my wife. We'll see his hands are well bound. You'll be fine."

The circuit rider pulled his coat back to reveal a holster containing a well-polished revolver. "I can ride hard and get him to town before full dark. I don't think he'll give me much trouble."

"Ethan, throw Tracker over one of our horses. We'll be coming into town for supplies in a few days, Parson. Put the horse up at the livery and tell the hostler I'll pay the bill when I get to town.

"Seth and Ethan, help get the parson on his way. Audra, take Maggie, and go on back in and get her down to sleep, and then you rest."

"I don't need to rest, Rafe." Audra took Maggie, though. Seth, Ethan, and the parson walked away, Tracker being pushed along with a bit of unnecessary roughness.

"I'm not telling you to rest because I think you're fragile."

"Oh, yes you are." She looked at him

suspiciously.

"No, you're going to need the rest because Julia won't be around to help you for the rest of the day."

"She won't?"

"I won't?" Julia asked.

"Or night."

"Oh," Audra and Julia said at the same moment.

"And Audra?"

"Yes?"

"Tell my brothers to stay away from the caldera."

With a nod, Audra turned and hurried into the house. Rafe thought he heard her snickering.

"Julia, honey." Rafe slid his arm around her back and pulled her toward their still-saddled horses. "Remember earlier when I said you might want a bath?"

Julia arched a brow. "I don't see any sense pretending I'm lily white and clean at this point."

"Can I have a few minutes of your time?"

"For what?"

"Our children are going to be really smart." Rafe smiled at the little innocent as he rested his hand on her lower back and urged her forward.

"What makes you think of such a thing

right now, Rafe?" She came along so willingly.

"Not one reason in the world, little darlin'."

"Where are we going?"

Rafe didn't really care to explain, so he turned her into his arms and kissed her.

When he pulled away, her eyes blinked open as if her lids were almost too heavy to hold up. "You really shouldn't kiss me like that, Rafe. I swear when you do it, I can't seem to think clearly."

"Why don't you just relax and let me do the thinking for the both of us for a while?"

As the evening passed and their married life began, Rafe discovered that in the arms of the woman he loved, it was safe, once in a while, to be completely out of control.

ABOUT THE AUTHOR

Mary Connealy is a Carol Award winner and a RITA Award finalist. An author, journalist, and teacher, she lives on a ranch in eastern Nebraska with her husband, Ivan, and has four grown daughters — Josie, married to Matt; Wendy; Shelly, married to Aaron; and Katy — and two spectacular grandchildren, Elle and Isaac. Readers can learn more about Mary and her upcoming books at:

maryconnealy.com
mconnealy.blogspot.com
seekerville.blogspot.com
petticoatsandpistols.com